First Edition

Daryl Green

Chapter 1 June 1960

They were always a self-contained unit, Gina and Maggie, with Caroline on the outside. In the mornings she could hear them giggling like two silly schoolgirls. Well, Gina was a schoolgirl but Maggie, eight years older, should have known better. They'd be making a souffle omelette, or something equally ridiculous, for breakfast and she'd hear the hilarity from upstairs. Always the last to come down, as she didn't start until nine thirty, Caroline liked to spend the extra time leaving her things tidy on her side of the bedroom. If she put them away, she knew where to find them. A place for everything and everything in its place. Maggie, of course, always left her stuff strewn over her half of the room. Caroline couldn't bear it. She couldn't wait to leave home. In eleven days time she'd be Mrs Graham Davenport, which had quite a nice ring to it. It was a very important sounding name.

She came into the kitchen and there was silence.

'Good morning Caroline.' Maggie turned round from the breakfast plates she was rinsing. Gina, ignoring her, was concentrating on wedging books into her already bulging satchel.

'Righto, I'm off. My train leaves in four minutes and it's a five minute walk to the station.'

Gina shot out of the back door, a slice of toast in her hand.

'She always leaves it until the last minute. Why can't she get up five minutes earlier? Come to that, why can't you get up five minutes earlier and tidy your half of our room?'

Maggie decided to ignore her dig. They frequently had this conversation.

'Any sign of Mum? I take it Auntie Ruby has gone off to work at the crack of dawn.'

Maggie dried her hands on the roller towel and started combing her hair in the mirror next to the sink.

'I wish you wouldn't do that. You'll get hairs on that clean crockery. No, no sign of Mum. You know she never gets up until she's sure we've all left.'

'Everyone else's mother gets up and makes sure her children have a decent breakfast before they leave the house,' Maggie said rubbing her lips together to even out her lipstick. 'I suppose we're hardly children though, apart from Gina, and to be honest, I think she likes to keep out of her way.'

'Well, for once I'd agree with her. I think I'll have an egg, that's if you've left any.'

'Just think, Caroline, you'll soon have your own kitchen and you'll know exactly what's in your larder. Will you miss us?'

There was a pause. Caroline had no idea if Maggie was joking. She didn't really get jokes. She didn't know whether she would miss them or not. Probably not, she thought. It was a gang of two in this house.

'I'm looking forward to having my own place. I'm looking forward to the wedding.'

The remaining egg was dancing up and down in the pan and Maggie could see the white swirling to the top.

'You've cracked your egg. I need to go now or I'll be running for my bus. Are you in tonight or going round to Graham's?'

Caroline looked at the egg in distaste and slotted two slices of bread into the toaster.

'I think I'll just have marmalade. I'm in. I've still got a lot to do with the wedding organisation.'

'Well, if you want any help...'

'That's very kind, but it's all in hand, thank you.'

'OK. Just ask if you change your mind. That's what sisters are for. Bye.'

Caroline knew she sounded like a Victorian schoolmarm. She wished she could slip into the easy banter her two sisters shared, but it just wasn't in her nature. They weren't cruel, or even unfriendly, towards her. There was something missing. A lot missing. It was like she didn't speak their language. There were only two years between her and Maggie. You'd think they would be the ones who would have things in common. It was one of life's mysteries. Perhaps if she asked for their help it would be an opportunity to bond with them. Maggie was right, that's what sisters were for. She would give it some thought. She washed her plate and made a pot of tea. She just had time to take a cup up to her mother before she left for work.

'Mum, are you awake? I've brought you some tea.' After a brief knock she opened the bedroom door.

'Is that you Caroline? I was just about to get up. I had a terrible night. Didn't sleep a wink. Cramps in my leg and your dad snoring. Put it down there. I'll drink it and then perhaps have another forty winks.'

Theresa eased herself into a sitting position and took took a thirsty gulp of tea.

'You off now? Before you go, fetch my cigarettes, will you?'

'Mum, you know what the doctor said. You shouldn't be smoking, with your heart.'

'Doctors don't know everything. Do I have to get them myself? Can't you do one little thing for your poor mother?'

'I've brought you some tea. I haven't got time to do anything else. I'll be late. You know I don't like to be rushed. I like to get to the hospital ten minutes early to get myself organised.'

'Pick up a couple of pounds of lamb's liver on the way home, will you, for tomorrow? And runner beans. Make sure they're not stringy. I had to take them back last time. I'm not spending good money on food to throw half of it away.'

'Why don't you go and buy them yourself then? You can decide whether they're stringy or not. I'd rather not have the responsibility of getting the wrong thing.'

'I don't want to go out today if I can help it, not with my legs. Anyway, I'm busy.'

Caroline knew that busy meant bingo with her cronies.

'Mum the exercise would do you good and you'd get a bit of fresh air. Look I've got to go.'

'Ever since you got that medical secretary's job you seem to think you know everything. It doesn't make you a doctor you know. All right. I'll get my own cigarettes and struggle out to get my own shopping if it's too much trouble.'

Caroline could feel her stomach knotting. Conversations with her mother generally left her feeling like that. Eleven more days, then freedom.

Chapter 2

They were sitting round the kitchen table when Caroline trudged in from work. It had been a stressful day, long waiting times and endless moaning from the patients. She hadn't even had time to catch up with Graham at the hospital. She was always the last home.

'Oh there you are. Just dishing up.' Ruby was serving sausages and chips. As Caroline sat down, she caught an under-the-breath comment from Maggie.

'Why does she think shoving the chips on greaseproof paper will absorb the grease?'

Then Gina's muffled reply, 'Because greaseproof means the chips don't get greasy. Everyone knows that.' They both tried to stifle a giggle.

'You two stop being so rude. You know it's bad manners to whisper and giggle behind your hands. Where are your manners?' asked Theresa, resting her elbows on the table and speaking with her mouth full of hot chips. 'So how are the wedding arrangements going?'

Caroline looked at her granite-faced father and instantly swallowed the comment she had been dying to make, that any other mother would be pleased to be helping her plan her big day. The slightest criticism of their mother and Dad was down on them like a ton of bricks. Toying distastefully with a greasy chip, she said,

'I need to finalise things this evening, if you don't mind. Can we talk about my wedding arrangements after tea?'

'Love to, but I've got masses of homework,' said Gina, forming her face into a sad look of regret.

'I know nothing about weddings so I'll be watching the darts on the TV. Let you ladies get on with it.'

'Dad, You said you'd sort the flowers. We talked about it the other day.'

'Righto, just tell me exactly what you want doing and I'll do it. I don't need a meeting.'

Caroline's heart sank. Was no one interested in the most important day of her life? She wanted to weep.

'I'll do whatever you want,' put in Auntie Ruby, 'it's not every day someone in the family gets married.'

'I suppose so,' sighed Theresa, taking the last sausage from the pan on the stove. 'I've done apple pie for pudding.'

Theresa's pies were a legend., but not for the right reasons. She could never get the pastry right. It was always overcooked and tended to shrink away from the side of the pie dish.

'I'll pass,' said Caroline. 'I want to fit into my wedding dress. By the way I need to pick it up from Bentalls on Saturday.'

'Ooh! Bentalls!' said Gina, 'Posh.'

'Well why not? I only plan to get married once and I've been saving my wages for a year to buy the dress of my dreams. I'm copying the look of Princess Grace of Monaco. It's lace at the top and has a tight fitting waist. I can't afford to put on an ounce.'

The wedding dress had been very expensive. Her friend, Barbara, whose family had money, had been with her when she had ordered it. Barbara had been delighted to help her choose and was more than happy to loudly air her opinion about every dress that Caroline tried on.

'Ooh that one makes you look fat', 'That's too old fashioned,' 'Too tight to walk in'. When she came out of the changing room wearing the Princess Grace dress, Barbara clapped her hands, crying, 'That's the one!'

Caroline had had to go without lunch and resist buying many new clothes or makeup for a whole year.

'Lovely idea,' said Maggie, 'and no one's saying you shouldn't have the dress you want. I wish our bridesmaid dresses were coming from Bentalls instead of me and Gina having to wear hand me downs.'

'Don't be so ungrateful, Maggie. Its not your day. Auntie Ruby's put a lot of work into altering those dresses and they're good quality. Gladys Palmer's daughter's bridesmaids wore them, and her father is the Mayor.'

And they'll be decades out of fashion, thought Caroline sadly, pushing her plate aside, which still had a mound of greasy chips congealing on it. Gladys Palmer's daughter had got three children now. Still, at least her sisters wouldn't outshine her.

'Have you finally decided what you're wearing, Mum?'

She'd manage to look ghastly in a Dior, she's

so fat these days.

'Yes, I'm wearing the navy crimplene two piece I got from the Littlewoods catalogue on the never never. It's a new material which doesn't crease. Ever so smart. It's a bit tight across the hips so I'll have to lose a few pounds.'

She decisively pushed away Caroline's chips that she had been planning to finish up.

'Anyone want these? I don't like to see food going to waste. Right, who's for apple pie and custard?'

Maggie helped Ruby with the washing up and clearing away while Theresa made the inevitable pot of tea and lit a cigarette. Caroline came downstairs with a notepad and pen.

The living room was soon a swirling sea of smoke. Caroline coughed and ostentatiously opened a window.

'Ready to start? I've made a checklist.'

'Of course you have,' muttered Maggie, sotto voce.

'Dad, you're doing the bouquet and button holes. I'd love yellow roses but I'd be happy with whatever you can get. As long as they're roses.'

'Yes, I can do that,' he replied, reluctantly tearing himself away from the screen. 'I'll do some "heavy pruning". I'll probably mention that I'm using some flowers, up at The Manor. I don't think they'll mind if it's for my daughter's wedding and it'll save us a pretty penny. I'll see if I can get you some gypsophila. Looks nice with roses.'

'What's that when its at home ?' asked Theresa. 'Sounds like something catching.'

'It's also called Baby's Breath, delicate white flowers.' Alf loved to air his horticultural knowledge.

'Oh, thanks. Dad. I've seen bouquets like that in magazines. We'll need five buttonholes. You put cut up paper doilies at the base of the button hole. It looks really pretty. Oh and the cake needs picking up from Brown's the day before. Gina passes that on the way home from school. She could get that.'

'I wouldn't risk it. She'll either forget it, sit on it, or leave it on the train. I'll get it.'

'Thanks, Maggie,' I'll tick that off.'

'Have you decided on the food?' asked Theresa, lighting a cigarette from the stub of the one before. Caroline coughed again, trying not glare at her. She needed to keep Theresa sweet. She consulted her checklist.

'I thought ham sandwiches, tinned salmon and cucumber sandwiches, cheese straws, pork pie, sausage rolls and pineapple and cheese on sticks.'

'Shall I make you some fairy cakes? I'm good at those,' suggested Maggie. 'And I'll do the sausage rolls. We don't want to bother Mum with those,' she added slyly, looking pointedly at the apple pie that was virtually untouched on the draining board.

'Yes, lovely, thanks.'

'I can't afford champagne,' said Alf, switching the television off with a sigh, 'but we could run to some beer and cider and perhaps some Asti Spumanti or Babycham for the toast.'

'Graham and I are are going to have real champagne, not fizzy wine or Babycham. His mum and dad are buying a few bottles.'

'The bride's family are suppose to pay for the wedding,' snapped Alf. 'It makes me look bad if I can't afford to pay for it.'

'Well no one will know except them and us, Dad. I'd rather have people drink champagne than fizzy wine at my wedding. Sorry but it is our day,'

'That's as maybe but I don't like it. Maybe they'd like to supply the flowers as well, a proper bought bouquet and button holes.'

'If Graham's people want to fork out on champagne, then let them. The guests will think we've bought it so what's the difference? And you know you'd like to do the flowers, Alf. Don't be so awkward. You're good with them.' Theresa stubbed her cigarette out in the overflowing ashtray where it continued to smoulder.

Caroline got up and finished stubbing it out in an exaggerated gesture.

'Where's all this food and drink going to go? It'll never fit on the kitchen table,' asked Auntie Ruby, starting to clear away the cups and saucers.

'There's an old table in the shed. I'll clean it up and we'll put a big tablecloth over the two pushed together.' said Alf, warming to his idea.

'What big tablecloth?' asked Caroline, looking worried.

'I've seen people use a nice, big, white sheet. You can't tell it's not a proper tablecloth when all the food's on it,' said Auntie Ruby.

'A sheet? I can't have a sheet on the table at my wedding. What would people say? Oh this is going to be a complete shambles.' Caroline was near to tears. 'Oh I wish we had more money. It's bad enough having to have the reception in this cramped cottage and now a sheet on a clapped out old table from the shed. I don't think I can bear it.' Tears were welling in her eyes.

'I could make you a nice white tablecloth,' said Auntie Ruby, attempting to mollify her.

Caroline's face brightened.

'But I'd make it out of a sheet to get the width, so what's the difference?'

Caroline's face collapsed again.

'So how many guests are we expecting at this wedding feast?' asked Maggie.

'Twenty four. It's the lowest I can go without offending anyone.' Caroline's voice was thick with misery.

'Have you invited Gloomy Guts, Grandma Langham?' asked Theresa.

'Had to invite her really, but she'll be on her own as I haven't got space for the uncles and aunts. Is that alright, Dad?'

'Fine by me. None of us have much time for each other. Have we finished now so I can get back to the darts?'

'You get back to your darts, Dad,' Caroline said with a sigh. 'Maggie will you come upstairs and try on the bridesmaid dresses with Gina? Are they in your bedroom, Auntie Ruby?'

'Yes, they're hanging on the outside of my wardrobe. I hope you like them. I thought them really rather pretty.'

Since there were only three bedrooms, Alf had converted the loft into a small bedroom for Ruby after Gina was born. Caroline climbed the narrow stairs and retrieved the dresses. The room was neat as a new pin.

Gina was not up to her eyes in homework. She was listening to Radio Luxemburg and sorting through her clothes. She started guiltily when the door opened.

'Time to try on our lovely bridesmaid dresses, Gina. God what a mess in here. It's even worse than my room.'

'Your half of the room,' corrected Caroline.

'My whole room in eleven days time,' recorrected Maggie.

'Just think, you can spread your mess right across the whole room.'

'I know!' replied Maggie cheerfully.

'When you two have finished, shall we get on with trying the dresses?' asked Gina impatiently.

'Why? Do you need to get on with your homework?' asked Maggie with a smirk.

'You guessed. Look I'll pile this lot up to one side. There's more room in here as I don't have to share with a sister.'

'I'm looking forward to that myself,' replied Maggie, taking her dress from Caroline and handing the other to Gina. They put them on. They all fell silent then spoke simultaneously.

'Well at least they fit.'

'They're ghastly. What the hell has she done with them?'

'It's probably too late to get anything else now.' This was Caroline. She slumped on to Gina's bed. 'But you can't wear those.'

They were frothy confections of pink satin,

net and appliqued rosebuds. When they had first tried them on they had been plain.

'I'm afraid we're going to have to,' said Maggie resignedly, 'after all the work Auntie Ruby's done on them. She kept them a secret as she thought they'd be a lovely surprise.'

'They're certainly a surprise,' said Gina, twirling this way and that in front of the dressing table mirror. 'I look like a Victorian china doll.'

'Just when I thought things couldn't get any worse,' whined Caroline, finally giving way to the tears that had been threatening all evening.

Chapter 3

Maggie was still fast asleep when Caroline woke, just after six. She had wanted to sleep longer so that she would be fresh for her big day but the knots of excitement in her stomach had woken her. She looked round the room at the shabby wallpaper, the cracks in the ceiling, the utility furniture. This was the last time she would sleep here as Caroline Langley. She got out of bed and lifted the faded floral curtain.

Her excitement evaporated. It was raining steadily. How could it do that to her today? You'd think that a wedding in September would have a good chance of a fine day. Her fresh perm would drop and her beautiful dress, hanging on the outside of the wardrobe, would go wet and droopy.

She stroked the folds of the dress. It was elegant, understated, tasteful.

'It's lovely. You'll look lovely.' A voice from the other bed. Maggie sat up. 'Bit early. Couldn't you sleep?'

Caroline turned to look at her sister, her face bleak.

'I did till now. It's raining.' She slumped on her bed.

'Oh bad luck. It might clear up.'

'I hope so or the day will be ruined.'

'You'll still be married at the end of the day, lucky you. A bit of rain won't ruin everything.'

When Caroline went downstairs to make a

cup of tea, Auntie Ruby was already scurrying around. She had put a folded tablecloth on the top of the rather handsome bureau that took up an enormous amount of space in the living room. The wedding cake looked lost in the middle of it.

'Morning Auntie Ruby. How long have you been up?'

'Not long. The rain woke me so I thought I might as well get up and get on. Staying in bed won't get the baby bathed. Busy day ahead. Shame about the rain but I'm sure it won't spoil your day.'

'That cake looks smaller than I thought. I hope there's enough to go round. Nice though.' Caroline adjusted the figures of the bride and groom.

'You get what you pay for. But anything would look small on top of that monstrosity. I don't know why your mother hangs on to it. It belongs up at The Manor, not here in a gardener's cottage. I'd chop it up and have one of those nice modern sideboards if I had my way. I thought we could put the drinks there. Might as well make use of it.'

'Good idea. I'm making a pot of tea. Do you want one?'

'No time for that. Temples fuchit. I need to get on. Now what did I do with those serviettes?'

Caroline smiled for the first time since she woke up. She would miss Auntie Ruby and her funny sayings.

'I'm off to have a bath. I've got some lovely Goya gardenia bath salts to soak in.'

'You'd better put a shower cap on then. You don't want that lovely new perm to drop out. Ah! Found them. If I hadn't put them in a safe place they'd be somewhere else and I'd never find them.'

Caroline left her happily singing, 'Get me to the church on time,'

The morning passed in a flurry of activity with everyone getting in each other's way and Theresa shouting orders from the sofa. Somehow out of the chaos, sandwiches were made and cakes and sausage rolls were arranged on plates. Ruby was right about the sheet. When everything was laid out, it looked perfectly alright as a table cloth. Damp tea towels were laid over the food and finally everything and everyone was ready. Caroline came down the stairs in her dress and all the activity stopped, the family a tableau.

'You look smashing, Caroline.' Gina gazed up at her, open-mouthed.

'Yes, you're a credit to us,' put in Theresa. 'You'll have to be careful with the hem of that dress. It'll be muddy underfoot.'

Caroline pulled the veil down over her face. 'Do I walk down the aisle with this down or up?'

'I'd wear it up if I were you or Graham won't know who he's marrying.'

'It would be awful if someone married the wrong woman because he couldn't see her face,' added Gina.

'Would the marriage be legally binding?' Maggie looked at Caroline's worried face and relented.

'Oh Caroline, we're joking!'

'Behave yourselves, you two. It's your sister's big day. You wear the veil down as you walk up the aisle and throw it back when you meet Graham at the altar. You look really lovely. You have a look of me on my wedding day to your father. What do you think, Alf?'

'She looks a picture. Here, what do you think of your bouquet?' He thrust it into her hands.

Caroline lifted it to her face. 'You managed to find yellow roses and, oh, they smell wonderful. So that's Baby's Breath. It's perfect, thanks, Dad. She took a step forward to kiss him on the cheek, but he had turned away.

'Well we'd best get cracking. I'll take the rest of you to the church and come back for you in twenty minutes, Caroline.' And he was gone.

The house was eerily quiet. Caroline looked at her face in the hall mirror. A pretty woman wearing too much makeup, stared back at her. Oh well, it was her wedding day. From now on she could do what she liked. She had been upset at Alf's coldness. When her friend, Barbara, had got married, her dad had hugged her and said heartfelt things about how proud he was of his precious daughter. What a cold fish he was. She looked round the room. They'd done the best they could, especially Auntie Ruby. It would have been lovely to have had a reception in a posh hotel, with waitresses in black and white uniforms, and her and Graham sitting at a top table, with a band and dancing afterwards. She and Graham would be twirling round the dance floor in each other's arms and he'd be saying,

'You look beautiful, Mrs Davenport, I can't believe you're mine.'

'Ready to go, Caroline?'

Dad was standing at the door, jangling his

keys, a stranger in his stiff new suit and tie, his unruly curls slicked down with Brylcream.

'The traffic's building up with the Saturday morning shoppers. Don't forget to lift up the hem of that dress as we cross the garden.'

The large Catholic church soon swallowed up the small number of guests, who only occupied the three front rows. Caroline had wanted more but they'd had to make it family only. As it was, it was going to be a squash back at the cottage, especially if it rained and they couldn't spill out into the garden.

'Look at Graham's sister, Maureen. She can barely fit between the pews. Let's hope her baby doesn't choose now to come into the world,' whispered Maggie.

'At least they could get it christened at the same time while they're here,' replied Gina. This was rewarded by a glare from across the aisle by Granny Langham, rigid in violet seersucker. A few strangers lurked at the back, passers by coming in for a breather, and women who could never resist having a peak at the bride, whoever she was. As Caroline walked up the aisle on Alf's arm, everyone turned round to watch her slow, regal journey towards Graham, the dress swishing as she walked. His face broke into a nervous smile when he saw her, his love and admiration shining out of him.

Maggie nudged Gina as Caroline threw her veil back from her face.

'At least now he knows he's marrying the right bride,' which sent Gina into an uncontrollable fit of giggles. Luckily, Grandma Langham, was too busy sniffing into her lace handkerchief to notice them this time. There was something about the suppressive atmosphere of churches that made them hysterical. The nuptual mass lasted forever.

Finally, they poured out into the sunshine. The rain had stopped, coating the leaves with iridescent drops, and the air was fresh and clean after the mustiness and heady smell of incense inside the old church. Groups formed and reformed for the photographer in the damp gardens. Graham looked as though he had come up with eight draws on the football pools while Caroline held her head high, savouring every moment of being the centre of attention.

Maggie realised that Gina had disappeared and finally located her behind a gravestone which appeared to be on fire.

'Ha! Caught you.'

Gina jumped, throwing the cigarette into the grass, where it smouldered accusingly.

'Oh, God Maggie, you made me jump.'

'Why are you smoking? You're only thirteen and it looks even more ridiculous with you in that rosebud dress,'

'I look ridiculous in it anyway. Ali and I started having sneaky ones after school. Actually, in school sometimes, behind the statue of Our Lady. It's cool.'

'Well it won't be if you get found out. And you can't afford it. Come on, Dad's started ferrying people back home.'

Soon the small cottage was bursting with people and chatter. Auntie Ruby had made a lovely job of the table. The plates, some of which had seen better days, were covered with doilies and piled high with food. There were flowers in all manner of receptacles, which Alf had 'pruned and tidied' from the gardens of The Manor. He made a short, stilted, speech about welcoming Graham into the family and wishing them a long and happy life together. Graham replied, thanking them for entrusting him with their beautiful daughter and Caroline just sat looking very pleased with herself. Auntie Ruby scurried about with plates of food, Maggie drank too much scrumpy and said the goldfish were laughing at her and had to be helped up the stairs to bed. Granny Langham averred that alcohol never passed her lips, but she also had to go and have a little lie down after she was seen walking rather unsteadily into the garden. Theresa sat in her favourite armchair, where she gave audience to anyone who would listen, only stirring to refill her plate. At one point she was heard referring to Ruby as 'my housekeeper' as though she were the Lady of the Manor. Granny Mary made herself useful clearing plates and washing up while grandad George looked as though he would rather be anywhere else but here. Alf slipped out to his greenhouse and George followed him, no doubt to discuss his allotment. Gina disappeared to her bedroom when she thought she wouldn't be missed.

'So what do you do for a living, Graham?' inquired a cousin of Caroline's. Before he had a chance to open his mouth, Caroline cut in with,

'Oh, he arranges patient transport at the hospital where I work, That's how we met, isn't it, darling?'

Graham looked slightly confused before obediently snapping his mouth shut.

At five-thirty everyone reassembled to wave off the bride and groom, who were driving down to Netley, near Southampton, for a week's honeymoon. Auntie Ruby had packed them some left over sandwiches, slices of wedding cake and a thermos of tea for the journey. Caroline had changed into her going away outfit of a cornflower blue cotton sheath dress with a matching duster coat. A tiny hat, sprigged with cornflowers, hugged her tight perm. She got into Graham's Austin A35 by sitting first and elegantly swinging her legs into the car, as she had seen Princess Grace do on the TV.

When the food had been eaten, apart from a few curling sandwiches, and every last drop of alcohol had been drunk, the guests finally drifted away.

'Leave that clearing up Ruby, it'll do tomorrow.' Theresa settled down in front of 'Take Your Pick' with Hughie Green.

'Oh I might as well get it shipshape now,' Ruby replied. 'It's so much better when it's Bristol fashion.'

'Suit yourself,' said Theresa,' I'm exhausted. I'm so ashamed of Maggie and Gina, one nearly passing out with drink and the other disappearing to her room for a fag. I saw her hanging out of the window puffing away. She thinks I don't know. Well one daughter taken care of, two to go. And that holier than thou mother in law of mine, she certainly showed her true colours. Teetotal my foot. Where's Alf? Have you seen him?'

'He's taken himself off for a walk. You know he doesn't like being around a lot of people, he's not a

talker, your Alf.'
'That's an understatement. Talking to his plants is the most sociable he gets.'

Chapter 4

Graham patted Caroline's knee and smiled at her as they drove away. Caroline turned round to give a static wave out of the window with her gloved hand as she had seen the queen do on television, The wedding party was gathered outside the front door of the cottage to wave them off but they were already turning to go back into the cottage.

'The wedding and everything went well, didn't it? You looked lovely.'

'Thanks, It went well enough, I suppose, considering my family. Maggie and Gran getting drunk was a bit of a surprise. As far as I knew neither of them touched a drop. Maggie doesn't seem interested and Gran always went on about the evils of alcohol. She blamed it for most of the bad things that went on in the world. What a hypocrite.

'At least there wasn't any fighting like at Jack's wedding. I've never seen him act so violent. My brother generally wouldn't say boo to a goose but there he was laying into Don, his best man.

'Best men don't usually make a pass at their brother's new wife at their wedding,' said Caroline icily.

'Oh it was something and nothing. It was meant to be a joke. He only said something like what a smasher she was and if she ever got fed up with Jack then Don would be happy to step in. It was all innocent.'

'Well I thought it was all a bit common.'

'Oh your family are alright. A right bunch of characters. Your dad doesn't say much, does he? You never really know what he's thinking. But if he was a POW it probably affected him. So tell me about this place we're going to. I know it's Netley and you used to go there for holidays. Your mum's friend is very generous to let us have it for nothing.'

'She's called Eileen. Mum used to work with her during the war. My mum found her a husband after her first one died and she moved to Netley. He's a dry old stick if you ask me. She's fat, caked in make-up and never stops talking. Apparently she's a catalogue model for outsize clothes. They're chalk and cheese, but Eileen seems eternally grateful to Mum, for some reason, so when we were kids we got a week's holiday in their house every year when they went away. It's near the sea so, living in London, we used to love it.'

'A week on our own by the sea sounds perfect. It's hard work getting married. I'm glad it's over. Your Auntie Ruby's a grafter.'

'Just as well, as my mum uses her supposed illness to do as little as possible. The more Auntie Ruby does the less she has to.'

'It's not much to write home about but it's free, I suppose,' said Caroline, swinging her legs out of the car. The little terrace house certainly wasn't much to look at. It seemed a lot smaller than when they used to go there on holiday when she was a child. He followed her down the side passage, past an overflowing dustbin.

'I can see the sea between those houses

across the road,' said Graham, trying to lift her spirits. 'Shall we dump our stuff and have a walk on the beach?'

'I'm tired,' she said, 'It's been a long day. The beach is pebbly, no sand.'

'A beach is a beach. We can look at the sea and paddle. I've brought my trunks. I expect I'll go in for a swim.'

Caroline retrieved the front door key from under a large pebble just outside the Anderson shelter in the narrow back garden.

The house smelt slightly damp, overlaid with a lingering odour of fried bacon. Caroline opened the kitchen window.

Graham wanted to get down to business immediately.

'Have some patience,' said Caroline, 'we've got our whole lives ahead of us.'

She wasn't looking forward to the sex, especially after having had a little pep talk from Theresa, who told her it would hurt at first but she would just have to put up with it. Theresa, herself, hadn't been keen, apparently. Good Catholics didn't have sex before marriage and Caroline had managed to keep Graham at arm's length for the year of their courtship. She would plead exhaustion after the excitement of their big day, but she knew she was only putting off the inevitable.

The little terraced house was very basic. The kitchen had apparently been an afterthought, an offshot with a corrugated plastic roof; the bathroom and toilet were on the ground floor and the two bedrooms were accessed by steep stairs. Apart from that there was a tiny front living room overstuffed with furniture. Caroline looked disappointed. It wasn't how she remembered it. But Graham was delighted.

'Well this is nice and cosy. We'll be snug as a bug here. That corrugated roof makes the kitchen nice and bright.'

'We'll have to come downstairs to the toilet,' sighed Caroline.

'Yes but think how handy that'll be during the day. I'll take these suitcases upstairs and perhaps you could put the kettle on, there's a good wife.' He put the two suitcases down and gave her a hug.

'There's not much in the larder, not even anything for breakfast. We'll have to go shopping tomorrow,' said Caroline.

'And there's no telly,' he replied. trying to hide his disappointment. 'We'll have to find other ways of amusing ourselves.' He gave her a hopeful look.

Caroline made the tea while Graham took the suitcases upstairs. When he returned, Caroline had plumped up the brocade cushions and had arranged herself elegantly in one of the armchairs, her legs crossed as she had seen models do. She was sipping her tea and flicking through a magazine she had found in a rack. Graham had been hoping they would snuggle up together on the sofa, their limbs wrapped round each other. He sat back and studied her. She looked composed and beautiful. He felt inadequate somehow. He had always wondered what she saw in him. He cleared his throat.

'You know, at the reception, when your cousin, Linda, asked me what I did for a living, can you remember what you said?'

Caroline shifted uncomfortably. 'No, not really.'

'You said I worked in "patient transport" as though you were ashamed of my job. Why couldn't you have just said, "He's a porter"?'

Caroline couldn't think of a reply. He was right, She wasn't exactly proud of his job. She would just have to make sure that he moved on to something better.

'I'm glad you brought that up,' she said. 'Of course I'm not ashamed of you, it's just that it must be a bit boring for you just wheeling patients about.'

'Well, having left school at fifteen with no qualifications I don't know what else I can do. I admit it's not well paid but I like it. I get to meet people, I'm on the move all day and I'm part of a team.'

'That's all very well.' She suspected she sounded like her mother. 'What happens if we have children and I can't work? Your wage wouldn't support a family. There must be other things, better paid. Perhaps you could go to night school and get some qualifications, or learn a trade.' She sighed.'Let's not talk about it now, it's beginning to spoil things.'

Caroline's face was pink.This wasn't a conversation to be having on their wedding night. She knew they should have it a long time ago. She wished he hadn't brought it up, but he was right, she didn't like telling people what he did. It was bad enough her father being a gardener. The gloss of the day had worn off and she wondered if she had made a mistake, marrying him. She had been so eager to leave that awful, cramped cottage and be the mistress of her own home. She mentally shook herself. She was tired; of course she loved Graham. She looked across at him and smiled. He was kind and thoughtful. He was never moody, like she was; he was always the same, always seeing the glass half full. She had seen how popular he was at work, having a cheery word for everyone and remembering patients' names on repeat visits. When she talked to him, he always gave her his full attention as though everything she said was important.

Graham now looked as though the cream had been taken away from the cat. He loved Caroline so much and wondered if he could make her happy. What she had said to Linda had eaten away at him for most of the day. Was she really ashamed of him?

She didn't know how to retrieve the feeling of euphoria she had felt earlier when she had been the centre of attention Why did he have to bring it up?

'Oh Graham, I'm sorry,' she said, uncrossing her legs and moving to the sofa.

'You must think me awful. It's just my nerves. It's been a wonderful day but I'm exhausted. You must be as well. Of course there's nothing wrong with being a porter. Shall we go to bed?'

It had been the right thing to say. He jumped up with alacrity and took her hand.

'Yes let's go to bed. Things will be better in the morning.'

When he tentatively took her in his arms, she didn't plead tiredness, as she had planned. She felt she had to be generous to make up for their earlier discomfort. It had been no way to start their life together. He was always ready to do what she wanted.

He was dressing more smartly now, with her guidance, and that was a start. She moved towards him. He was clumsy as he tried to remove her nightdress. Without a word she slid it off and put her arms round him. He began caressing her and she started to relax but suddenly stiffened as she realised he was inside her. She gave a gasp of pain. She thought he would stop but he must have thought it was a gasp of passion and that she was actually enjoying it. She opened her eyes and studied the faded floral curtains, biting her lip. He quickened his pace and yelled that he loved her and rolled off. She was relieved it was all over. She was also relieved that he had put on a French letter. They couldn't afford a child for a very long time.

'That was wonderful,' he groaned. 'Was it for you?'

She didn't answer. It had been thankfully quick. She hoped it would get better, otherwise she was in for a life of misery.

Chapter 5

The Netley house had been perfectly alright for a week. The had walked on the beach and rediscovered the places she had visited as a child. Graham had taken a chilly dip in the sea but hadn't been able to persuade Caroline to join him. It had been sunny for most of the week so they hadn't been stuck in the tiny house. Hamble had been as pretty as she remembered, with its fishermen and bobbing boats. They went to the cinema in Southampton and had watched the sun set over the horizon. Caroline's attempts at cooking simple meals hadn't been totally successful but Graham stoically ate every morsel and even complimented her on her efforts. She resolved to go to cookery classes when they got back to Wimbledon.

Graham had wanted sex every night and didn't hide his disappointment when she said it was too much. She endured it twice more that week and it hadn't been as bad as on their wedding night. She thought it could be better than it was but didn't know how to broach the subject. It was too intimate and embarrassing to talk about. She wished she could talk to someone about it but she couldn't think of a single person she could share it with, particularly her mother. She had a few friends but they never discussed things like that. In the meantime she decided to grin and bear it and hope things would improve by themselves.

By the end of the week she couldn't wait to

return to their new home and start their real life together. They were renting a self-contained flat in the attic of a handsome Victorian house in Wimbledon, owned by an old couple called Mr and Mrs Turnbull. There was a faded grandeur about it, she thought. It had its own back staircase and comprised a bedroom, a living room, a bathroom and a tiny galley kitchen. The living room was sparsely furnished with a chintz settee, which clashed with the patterned carpet and the wallpaper, an oak sideboard, a small table and two chairs. She and Graham had painstakingly totted up their joint earnings and potential expenditure and had decided this was all they could afford at present if they were to save to buy one of those lovely maisonettes on the new estate in Clayton Park. The Turnbulls were more than happy for them to redecorate the flat and Graham had already started on the kitchen.

Weary after their journey from Netley, the stairs to the attic seemed steeper and longer than they had been during the previous month, which they had spent gathering a few bits and pieces to build their first home together.

'Phew,' said Graham, dumping the suitcases in the living room, 'this'll keep us fit.'

Caroline looked around their new home. She had her own space at last.

'No parents breathing down our necks, telling us what and what not to do,' she told him. 'No Maggie throwing her stuff round the bedroom, no Gina playing loud music and getting out of the washing up "because she's studying" no mum eating all the best food because the doctor said she had to for her health, no dad washing his filthy hands in the kitchen sink. Oh! it's going to be lovely when you've finished the decorating.'

'And only ten minutes drive to work and the shops on our doorstep. We'll be in heaven here darling. Look out of the window, you can actually see the hospital. Won't it be funny going off together in the morning?'

'It will. We could walk to work from here, save money on petrol. I'll have to get used to the traffic noise. You couldn't hear a thing at home in the cottage, except birds first thing. I'm dying for a cup of tea, aren't you?'

Caroline went into the tiny kitchen, with its fresh blue and white painted cupboards, and sighed with pleasure. She felt like one of those ladies on the cover of Good Housekeeping, neat in a white apron and fresh lipstick. She imagined cooking delicious budget meals in her gleaming, wedding present saucepans. Mrs Turnbull had put a bottle of milk and some butter and cheese in the fridge and a fresh loaf in the bread bin. Tomorrow, after work, she and Graham would go to Sainsbury's and buy the groceries for the meals she had planned for the rest of the week. She laid their new contemporary cups and saucers on the tray, with the matching milk jug and sugar bowl, and put it on the table.

'We need one of those low coffee tables,' she told Graham. 'They're so handy for entertaining. We could invite Mr and Mrs Turnbull up for afternoon tea at the weekend as a thank you for the food.'

She had read in magazines about having visitors for afternoon tea or inviting friends and neighbours round in the evening for a drink and dainty sandwiches. Her parents had never done any entertaining. She couldn't imagine her father making polite small talk or Theresa relinquishing her precious sofa which she stretched out on every evening and most of the day. She and Graham were going to be different.

The months passed and they fell into a routine. They couldn't afford to go out much but when it was fine they walked on Wimbledon Common or window shopped. Caroline invited one or two people from work for afternoon tea at the weekend but this soon fizzled out when Caroline decided that she didn't want people to know that they lived in a poky attic flat. Also it seemed like a lot of effort for little reward. Graham could be sociable and quite entertaining but she found it difficult to let her hair down and spent her time worrying about what to say and what people thought of her. They visited their parents on alternate Sundays; they read and listened to the radio. Graham said he would love to own a television but they couldn't afford to buy one. She didn't know how to relax and be herself. Some of the evenings were long and dull; neither of them had a hobby apart from reading and listening to the radio. They were both relieved when they had saved enough money to rent a small television set with a magnifier strapped across the nine inch screen, as by then they had run out of things to say to each other.

Chapter 6 January 1961

'Have you seen Maggie? Auntie Ruby has gone to her health and beauty class so you and Maggie can wash the dishes and clear up.'

Theresa had settled herself down for the evening with The Daily Mirror and a Cadbury's fruit and nut. Alf was immersed in his crossword, drawing thoughtfully on a cigarette. Gina had been just about to escape to her bedroom. She had a mound of homework every night so she had fallen into a routine of an hour's study with an interval of ten minutes listening to Radio Luxembourg before working for the next hour.

'Maybe she's gone out.'

'She would have said. No I've noticed she disappears most evenings after tea. She's up to something in her bedroom but I haven't got the energy to go up and find out. Nip up, will you, and see what she's up to.'

Gina tentatively knocked on Maggie's bedroom door.

'Friend or foe?'

'It's your favourite sister. Can I come in?'

'I suppose so.'

Gina pushed open the door. The whole room was now as messy as Maggie's half had been before Caroline moved out.

'I'd apologise for the mess but yours is probably just as bad.'

Maggie was sitting at the dressing table mirror putting curlers in her hair. He face was shiny with face cream.

'You've just caught me. I was about to go to bed.'

Gina looked at her watch with an exaggerated sweep of her wrist.

'Maggie, it's eight thirty. Are you ill? Is your watch wrong? Have you lost your mind?'

'None of those things. I just fancied an early night.'

'We've got to wash up, Mum says. Auntie Ruby has gone to her class.'

'Well, I'm not coming down in this state. Could you do it tonight and I promise I'll do it next time?'

'I suppose so.' Gina looked perplexed. 'Are you sure there's nothing wrong?'

'Sure. Close the door on your way out. Night night.'

Maggie went through her sparse wardrobe and selected a new red ballerina-length skirt and a white blouse. She polished her shoes and arranged her makeup, and the jewellery she was going to wear, on the dressing table before climbing into bed where she daydreamed until she eventually fell asleep.

Her alarm jangled half an earlier than was necessary and she combed out her hair and fixed it with hairspray, then carefully applied her makeup. She appraised herself from every angle in the triple mirror. She couldn't face breakfast so she slipped out of the house without anyone noticing and made her way to the bus stop.

She trembled as she stood outside the door to the solicitor's office, where she had worked as a typist for the last three years. It was a fairly dull job, or it had been until a month ago. She checked her hair and lipstick in the mirror of her compact and walked in. She was early and the office was empty, apart from Mr Harris, the senior partner, who appeared to live at his desk.

'Good morning, Miss Langham, couldn't you sleep?'

Maggie laughed. 'You can talk, sir! It's a lovely morning. Cold and bright. There's even a bit of snow in the air. I thought I'd make an early start. She fed a sheet of paper into her typewriter.

'Can I make you a cup of tea?'

'That would be most welcome.' He disappeared behind the piles of papers on his desk.

The whole office was cluttered, lined from floor to ceiling with brown, musty books which had the look of a library that was never used. A rickety ladder stood drunkenly in the corner. Maggie went into the tiny kitchen at the back and put the kettle on, her eyes on the door. Her heart leaped as it opened.

'Good morning, William, I'm just making a pot of tea.' She made her voice sound casual.

'You're a star, Maggie Langham. It's brass monkeys out there. I could do with warming up.' He hung his coat on the stand, dropped his briefcase by his desk and came into the kitchen area, rubbing his hands.

'You look chipper today, considering it's Monday.'

Maggie, embarrassed, couldn't think of a

reply. She didn't know whether his earlier comment had been a double entendre or not. Normally chatty, her brain invariably became paralysed when he talked to her. He must think her a complete idiot. Trembling, she poured three cups of tea and carried one in to Mr Harris, who grunted when she put it on his desk. The cup rattled in the saucer as she set the other on William's desk.

Chapter 8 July 1961

'So any plans for the weekend, Maggie?' William was stuffing papers into his briefcase as she put the cover on her typewriter. She didn't know how to reply. If she told him she had no plans he might think her either unsociable or deeply unpopular. If she said she had, he might think she was attached and then she had blown her chances of him ever asking her out, that is if he was at all interested in her. He was always friendly and chatty with her, but he might be the same with everyone. She had access to the staff personal files and his clearly stated that he was single but that didn't mean that he had no girlfriend.

'Not much really. I don't tend to make plans. I'll just see how I feel. What about you?'

What had made her ask him that? If he had a girlfriend then she really didn't want to know. It would probably break her heart. She had invested so much time daydreaming about him, had had so many early nights, trying to make the mornings arrive more quickly. She wanted to stop the words before they left his mouth.

'This bulging briefcase might give you a clue,' was all he said.

She replayed that sentence many times on the way to the bus stop, but it told her nothing. She felt she wasn't getting anywhere. The weekend stretched before, empty, boring and completely pointless.

Theresa's nagging started the moment she walked in the door, the state of her bedroom, she never wanted to spend time with the rest of the family, she treated the house like a hotel, it was about time she pulled her weight. Maggie, normally equable, snapped.

'I've had a busy day at work. I'm tired. Will you stop your bloody nagging? I don't suppose you've lifted a finger all day.'

'How dare you talk to me like that and me with my bad heart! If I died of a heart attack it would be your fault and you'd have it on your conscience for the rest of your life. You wait until your father gets in, you won't know what hit you.'

Maggie froze to the spot. Her dad had a violent temper when he was riled and he always took her mother's side, whether she was in the right or not. She wished more than anything that she could take the words back. She thought of walking out of the house in the hope that things would die down but she knew she would have to face the music at some point. Without a word, she went upstairs and vomited into the toilet. Gina gingerly opened the bathroom door, looking concerned.

'Maggie, are you alright? I could hear raised voices. What's happened?' She looked at Maggie's ashen face. 'You're not pregnant are you?'

'No of course not,' Maggie rasped, wiping her mouth with the back of her hand.

Alf's voice boomed up the stairs. 'Maggie! Come down now!'

Trembling, she went downstairs. Her father was standing in the kitchen, tall, erect, clenching his fists, open and closed, open and closed. He had been violent before, but had never looked like this.

'I hear you have been disrespectful to your mother, something I will not tolerate.' His voice was cold, quiet, measured. She had never felt so frightened in her life. His fist rammed into her head, then her face. Maggie looked aghast, screamed, trying to shield herself from his blows.

Theresa shouted, 'Alf! Stop! That's too much!'

Auntie Ruby stepped forward and tried to still his arm but he violently shook her off. He was in an uncontrollable frenzy; images of German soldiers, brutally attacking him in the prison camp, had robbed him of all reason. He was an animal, lashing out at them, not at his vulnerable daughter, who was now staggering back and falling to the floor, covering her face, screaming. Blood was trickling between her fingers.

Gina came in, saw what was happening and also screamed, her hand over her mouth. Auntie Ruby ran out of the room saying she was calling an ambulance. Alf finally ran out of steam and walked out of the door, leaving behind a scene of blood and hysteria. Theresa was clutching her heart and Auntie Ruby was running between her and Maggie, who lay limp and sobbing on the floor, with Gina cradling her in her arms. After what seemed an eternity, they could hear the distant jangle of the ambulance. Ruby opened the door.

'There's been an accident. This young woman has been attacked.'

The two ambulance men knelt beside

Maggie and quickly assessed her. They said they thought that her nose had been broken and whoever had done it wanted locking up. They managed to staunch her nose bleed and then they carried her out to the ambulance, on a stretcher, her face covered in bandages. They received no satisfactory reply from anyone as to how this had happened, other than a white-faced Ruby saying it had been a man who had now disappeared.

Theresa had sunk into a chair, her hand to her head, saying she felt faint, but she recovered enough to go with her in the ambulance. Gina wondered what her mother would say when there were further questions. Would Maggie be OK? Would her dad go to prison? She thought he deserved it for hurting her beloved Maggie, but what would they live on if that happened? At that moment she hated him and her mother. She wished she had been old enough to leave home like Caroline. As the ambulance drove Maggie away, Auntie Ruby was washing blood from the lino, her mouth set in a thin line.

Gina slowly climbed the stairs to her room, her heart pounding and her body leaden. She switched on the radiogram and lay on her bed, shaking uncontrollably. She didn't know how her family could possibly recover from this. She completely understood why Maggie had sworn at her mother. She, herself, had often felt like it. Her mother couldn't let anything go when she had a bee in her bonnet about something. Nag nag nag. She didn't know when to stop. Present bad behaviour would evoke past bad behaviour so it became a litany of the shortcomings of either her or Maggie. She knew her father had a temper but she hadn't known he could do something so violent to his own daughter. She cried for her poor sister and she cried for a life that could never be the same again.

Chapter 9 July 1961

David Harris occasionally came into the reception area where Caroline worked, and he always ate in the canteen, even though doctors generally ate in the doctors' mess. If they passed one another in one of the hospital corridors, she would turn round to find him also turning round to look at her.

One Saturday she was doing the weekly shop in Sainsbury's when she bumped into him. He was looking very handsome in casual clothes and she very nearly didn't recognise him without his white coat.

'Hello,' he said, his blue eyes burning into hers. 'Do you live round here?'

She told him where she lived, feeling rather proud of the fact that it was a rather refined looking house in a tree lined street. He wasn't to know it was an attic flat she rented or that she shared it with her husband, a hospital porter.

It turned out that he lived a few streets away, also in a large Victorian house.

'I'm just buying wine. Dinner party tonight. I hate them; I'd rather just settle down with a good book but my wife seems to enjoy them. Bye for now.'

A few weeks later she was standing at the bus stop, waiting for the bus home. The weather had been stiflingly hot and close for weeks, but had now erupted into a violent thunderstorm She had gone to work in a cotton dress which was now drenched and clinging to her body. A sleek Sunbeam Talbot slid to a halt, sending up a spray of mud. She jumped back, her face contorted with anger until she recognised the driver.

'Jump in. I'm going your way. You'll drown, standing there.'

She gratefully accepted the lift, embarrassed that her hair was hanging in rats' tails and her mascara had run. She kept sneaking looks at his profile and was acutely aware of the smell of his aftershave mingling with the damp from her own body. Their conversation was stilted; she felt acutely shy sitting beside him in the steamy, cramped space. It seemed so intimate.

'If I pass you on the way home again I'd be very pleased to give you a lift. There's no sense you walking. Unless you want to, that is.'

'Well, if it's no trouble,' she said.

When he brushed her knee as he leaned over to open the door she felt her skin burn. She was trembling as she climbed the stairs to the attic flat. She had never felt like that with Graham.

Every time she left the house after that, she was aware that she was looking for him or his car. She was interested to see what his wife looked like or whether he had any children. In the hospital, they often seemed to arrive at the staff canteen together, which she was sure didn't happen by chance. He now sat with her almost every day in the canteen and he was giving her a lift home more and more. She began to worry that people had started to notice but, she reasoned, nothing's going on so what did it matter? She never met Graham as his dinner hour was before hers. They had to stagger the dinnertime sessions to avoid long queues and each department had its appointed times. This rule didn't apply to doctors, who needed to fit in their meals between the demands of their patients.

They had started talking about the hospital and the characters who worked there, then progressed to their families. He now knew that she was married to a hospital porter and had no children. He had a son of seven who was going through a difficult phase. She wondered if he was happily married but he never talked about his wife.

'You seem to be getting a bit friendly with that good looking young doctor.' She and Brenda, one of the other receptionists, were having a bit of a natter when there was a lull in the flow of patients. 'Aren't you afraid there might be gossip, especially with your Graham working here too.'

'No, why would I?' Caroline was sure she was blushing. 'He lives near me, us, and sometimes gives me a lift home from work. I walk in with Graham in the morning but he doesn't finish till six. If David gives me a lift home it gives me time to get the tea on so I can have a hot meal ready for Graham when he gets in.'

She felt this explanation was inspired. And it was perfectly true. On second thoughts, was she giving a bit too much information?

'Well, just saying. You need to be careful, that's all.'

And you need to mind your own business, thought Caroline. All this is totally innocent.

David was waiting in his car in the hospital car park. He wound the window down and smiled at

Caroline.

'Want a lift?'

'Yes, lovely.' she said, climbing in. 'I thought doctors worked all hours,' she said.

'It depends which department we're assigned to. 'I'm doing a rotation in pathology so I work regular hours. You don't have emergency calls or long hours.'

They were chatting about their day at work, when he suddenly said,

'I don't suppose you fancy a bite to eat? My wife's out and I have to forage for myself tonight.'

She thought of Graham, coming home to an empty house and the half a pound of mince in the meat safe. She thought of the long, boring evening ahead. Her heart was pounding with indecision, the fight between what she wanted, more than anything, and what she knew she should do.

Chapter 10

Maggie was kept in hospital overnight. Her face and upper body were badly bruised, she had a black eye and her nose was broken. Theresa stayed by her bedside and Maggie wondered if it was entirely out of concern for her or whether she wanted to make sure that she didn't tell anyone what had really happened. Maggie had been so angry at first that she had been determined to tell everyone, including the police, what her father had done to her. Theresa, however, persuaded her that no one would benefit from that. If he was sent to prison there would be no money coming into the house. Maggie saw the sense in that but she now felt that she had the upper hand and was determined to use it to her advantage.

'I promise I'll keep my mouth shut,' she said with difficulty, through swollen lips, 'if you tell Dad that if he ever lays a finger on me or Gina again I will go to the police. I don't know why you have to tell him every time we do something you don't like. Why can't you just deal with it yourself?'

She would have never have dared to speak to Theresa like that in the past.

'All this stress isn't good for my health. My doctor said....'

But Maggie had turned over and shut her eyes.

When questioned by the hospital staff, Maggie said she had tried to intervene in a fight between two teenage girls on the way home from work, got in between them and came out the worst. She didn't know who they were and wasn't likely to recognise them again. They decided there was no point involving the police. Maggie hoped they didn't talk to the ambulance men, who had been given a different story.

When she came home, Alf ignored her. Theresa gave her some soup, which was all she could manage to eat, and Auntie Ruby settled her into bed. Gina sat with her while she did her homework, bringing her drinks and helping her in any way she could.

After a week, the bruises hardly showed with the panstick make up that Maggie artfully applied. Her nose was still very painful but there was no treatment for it. It would heal in time. The rift between her and Alf did not.

'He won't speak to me or even look at me,' she told Gina. 'It's him in the wrong, not me.'

'I expect he feels guilty. You know what he's like, dead stubborn. You'll never get an apology out of him. He can't just ignore it and pretend it never happened so he just ignores you.'

'Well I bloody hate him. I'd like to flatten his big rotten nose. Let him see how it feels.'

She went back to work, telling them the story about her getting caught in a fight between two teenagers. She kept her head down and got on with her job.

'Looks painful. Does it hurt?'

Maggie looked up from her typewriter, raising her hand instinctively to cover her nose.

'A bit. Quite a lot really.'

'You were very brave, or maybe a bit stupid, to intervene in a fight.'

'A bit stupid, but you can think me brave if you like.'

William cleared his throat and lowered his voice.

'Do you think a trip to the cinema might cheer you up? You'd be in the dark so no one would notice.'

'Is this an invitation? I look like the wreck of the Hesperus.'

'I suppose it is, unless you already have a boyfriend.'

'There's a queue of them waiting to take me out, but none with your charm.'

'Tonight then? Unless you were planning to intervene in any more fights.'

'No I'm having a night off. I'd love to.'

She told him where she lived and spent the rest of the afternoon alternating between excitement and terror. It was ironic that she had spent months worrying about her appearance and he chose to invite her out when she was looking her absolute worst.

A week had elapsed since she was discharged from hospital and life was marginally better for her. Theresa appeared to have learned her lesson and had stopped nagging her the minute she walked in the door. Long may it last, Maggie thought. Any communication between her and her father took place through a third person, but mainly not at all. The only people who hadn't changed were Gina and Auntie Ruby. The latter had come up to her bedroom one evening and advised her not to think too badly of Alf.

'Remember he spent four years in a German prison camp during the war. Sometimes we forget the way those cruel Jerries treated him. Starved and beat him they did. Nearly killed him. He was a different man afterwards. You might not remember but he was little more than a skeleton when he came home.'

'Well it wasn't my fault. He shouldn't take it out on me,' was all Maggie could say.

'I don't want any tea, thanks,' she now said to her mother and Auntie Ruby. 'I'm going to the pictures.'

Alf carried on reading the paper.

She was too nervous to eat but also she wanted to spend the time getting ready. She washed and curled her hair and changed her outfit three times before she was satisfied. She then carefully applied more panstick over her bruises and went outside to wait for William. She didn't want him to meet her family. On top of her injuries, it was just too much. He was late. She paced up and down trying to calm herself with slow, deep breaths. Perhaps he wasn't coming. He wasn't the type to be late. She jumped as the garden gate clicked open.

'Sorry. This was so hard to find. What is this place?'

'The grounds of Clayton Manor. My dad's the head gardener. The cottage goes with the job.'

'Very quaint. Nice setting I would think. You'd better hold on to me, it's a bit dark. I don't want you falling over and bruising your face.'

She laughed and clung onto his arm, running

her hand along the rough tweed of his jacket.

The full moon emerged from behind a dark cloud and she saw his face glow silvery white, like an angel. Despite her bruises, her painful nose and her father's silence, she didn't think she had ever felt so happy in her life.

They went to see 'The Curse of Frankenstein,' which she found so scary she had to hold his hand through much of it.

'I could get a part in it,' she said, 'they wouldn't need to put any gruesome make up on me.'

They collapsed into a fit of suppressed laughter and were shushed by a couple in front. This made them laugh even more. They called into a Wimpy bar on the way back and had frothy coffees and a hamburger. She found she was starving and had lost her shyness. He was easy company and they talked and laughed. For the moment she was able to forget her troubles at home. When he returned her to the cottage he squeezed her shoulders, which made her flinch, apologised, and gently pecked her on the cheek. She wondered if he would have kissed her properly if she hadn't been such a sight.

Chapter 11

'I'll have to tell Graham I'll be late,' she said. 'Can you stop at a phone box?'

Caroline's heart was pounding. What could she say? What was Graham going to eat? Was she about to do something she might regret? Would she regret it even more if she didn't go?

With trembling hands she put the coins in the slot, grateful that Mr and Mrs Turnbull had recently installed a telephone in the hall downstairs. It seemed hours before Graham was summoned. She watched David drumming his fingers on the steering wheel.

'Oh, hello, Graham. It's me. No, nothing's wrong. at all. Look, I'm sorry it's short notice but I'm going for a drink and something to eat after work with some colleagues.'

She paused. She had said, 'some colleagues'. With those few words her relationship with David had already stopped being innocent.

'Are you sure?' she asked breathlessly. 'Do you want to get yourself some fish and chips? '

Her knuckles clenching the receiver were white.

'Yes, yes I will. I won't be late. Bye.'

'Everything OK?' David asked as he held the car door open for her. She realised she was trembling and feeling slightly sick.

'Yes, I think so. Graham's going to get fish and chips. He'll enjoy that. It'll be a bit of a treat. We were only going to have shepherd's pie tonight and it saves me cooking.' She was babbling.

They had arrived at a small restaurant on the other side of Wimbledon. She wondered if he had deliberately chosen a small, quiet one down a narrow back street.

There were few customers and the proprietor seemed pleased to see them as he showed them to a table in the bay window.

'Can we have one at the back?' David asked, 'perhaps in that alcove?'

When they were seated he ordered a bottle of wine. 'Beaujolais OK for you?' he asked, smiling at her.

She rarely drank and had no idea whether she would like it or not. She would have preferred a tomato juice but she wanted to appear sophisticated.

'I'll have whatever you choose. The same with the meal. I'm not fussy.' She felt totally out of her depth. She was excited about being in a restaurant with a handsome man, a doctor, who seemed to know his way about, but, at the same time, she was petrified of making a mistake. Supposing she used the wrong knife? Was this a napkin or serviette? What was she supposed to do with it?

He perused the menu. 'I was thinking of having a steak with saute potatoes and garden peas.'

'That sounds lovely,' she said, trying to unclench her hands.

The waiter poured a little wine into David's glass which he sipped thoughtfully.

'Yes I think that will do nicely with the steak.'

The waiter half filled their glasses and took out his notepad. Turning to Caroline, he asked,

'How would you like your steak, madame?'

There was an uncomfortable pause.

'Both medium,' David said decisively.

The waiter left and David took her hand, stroking her long fingers. She wanted to tell him she had never eaten steak in a restaurant but didn't want him to think her naïve. She sipped the wine and felt the warmth of the alcohol seep through her body and she slowly started to relax. She looked round the restaurant where other couples were dining and wondered what they were thinking about her and David. Did they think they were married or could they tell that this was a clandestine liaison? She realised that David was speaking.

'So we're not going to talk about work. Tell me about yourself.'

She told him a little about her childhood home in the grounds of Clayton Manor and even less about her family. They were two worlds that needed to be kept as far apart as possible.

'So, how long have you been married to Graham?'

'Just over a year,' she said. As the unaccustomed wine flowed, the words began to pour out, many of them things that she hadn't admitted to herself.

She found herself telling him that Graham was a lovely man, who treated her well. It was just that they had little in common. They both wanted a family, but if she had to give up work they wouldn't be able to manage on his salary. She felt that her life was work at the hospital and shopping and housework, with little in the way of pleasure. They rarely went out and didn't really have much to talk about. She liked to read and listen to music. He didn't. He didn't have any hobbies, apart from watching television. They both enjoyed the cinema but it was a rare treat. She would love to go to the theatre. She suddenly stopped. He didn't want to hear all this. She felt embarrassed. Luckily, the waiter arrived with their food and refilled their wine glasses. He lit the candle which cast a warm, intimate glow over the table.

'This looks and smells wonderful.' Caroline waited until he had picked up his knife and fork and then did the same, cutting into the juicy steak with the serrated knife.

'Delicious. Good choice. What about you?' she asked. 'Tell me about your life.'

'Well, I've been married for almost seven years. We met when I started at medical school. Penny was doing an English degree and was planning to be a teacher. Then she got pregnant and we had to get married. We have a seven year old son, Michael. She was really fed up when she was unable to teach so she fills her life with a lot of outside interests, tennis club, amateur dramatics, flower arranging, WI. She loves organising other people, including me.' He laughed. 'She's on every committee possible, chairs most of them. Michael's difficult at the moment, possibly due to a lack of attention. I'd have liked more children, especially a daughter, but that would curtail 's activities too much.' He sounded bitter.

She would have liked to ask him if he was

happy, but, in a roundabout way, he had probably already answered that. Instead, she concentrated on the food. She had thought that she would have been too nervous to eat much but the wine must have given her an appetite.

'Would you like a pudding?'

'I don't think I can manage it,' she said, stealing a glance at her watch. It was nearly nine o'clock. 'The meal was delicious. Thank you so much. And I've enjoyed our chat. Unfortunately, I think I should be getting home.'

'Of course. I've enjoyed this evening too. It's good to have a real talk about things that are important.

'I expect I've said too much. I'm not used to drinking wine. Thank you.'

The waiter brought their coats and David helped her into hers. As he drove her home, he said, 'I really appreciate your honesty and your enjoyment of simple things. Maybe I can treat you again.'

They had arrived at her road.

'Would you mind dropping me at the end of the street?'

He stopped the car under a tree where it was quite dark. She turned to thank him again and found she was in his arms and he was kissing her. She responded with a passion she had never felt before and she knew that they had now stepped over the line.

Chapter 12

Over the weekend, Maggie thought of little but William. She hoped it hadn't been a one off because he felt sorry for her. It had been like going out with a best friend; they had laughed and joked and she had felt very comfortable with him. She hardly noticed her father's coldness and she found she didn't actually care. At breakfast he had said to Gina,

'Tell Maggie to pass the salt.'

She almost responded with, 'Tell Dad I'd be delighted, ask him to pass the ketchup,' but she thought that might be going a bit far. Her mother's barbs also bounced right off her.

'You look chipper today,' commented Auntie Ruby as they washed the dishes. You look as though you've found a shilling and lost sixpence.'

Gina asked her how her date had gone with William, as Maggie had confided in her before she went out with him on Friday night.

'Brilliant,' she said. 'He's got a great sense of humour. You'd get on with him. We went to see that Frankenstein film. It was a good excuse to cling on to his hand in the scary bits.'

'Will you go out with him again?'

'He never mentioned another date but at least I'll be seeing him at work.'

'Would it be a bit awkward if he didn't ask you out again and you had to see him at work every day?'

'It would be dreadful. I don't even dare think about it.'

'I'm dreading growing up and going out with boys. It seems so complicated. It also seems unfair us girls having to wait to be asked out. Supposing no one ever wants to go out with me?'

'That's never going to happen. You'll have loads of boyfriends.'

'Do you think Caroline and Graham are happy? She always looks as though she has a dead rat up her nose when they come here. Graham's nice but they don't seem very lovey dovey and they don't ever have a laugh with each other.'

'Has our big sister ever had a laugh with anybody?'

'Spose not. Certainly not with us, anyway.'

Gina suddenly changed the subject.

'How long do you think Dad's going to keep this up? It's really awkward, especially at mealtimes. Doesn't it upset you?'

'Of course it does, but I'm not going to let him know that. I know it makes things awkward for everyone but I'm not going to apologise. I'd move out if I could afford it.'

'Don't you dare. That would leave me on my own. Shall I try and talk to him?'

'Best of luck with that. He won't thank you if you interfere. It puts him in the wrong.'

'He is in the wrong.'

So Gina tried talking to her mother. Theresa was sitting at the living room table, sorting the contents of the biscuit barrel which was used to store all manner of odds and ends. She was untangling small bits of string and individually knotting them.

'Do you want some help?'

Theresa looked up in surprise.

'Not really. I have to decide what's worth keeping and what isn't. It's a habit we all got into during the war. We didn't dare throw anything away. You must be bored if you want to help me sort this lot out.'

'I don't mind. I quite like sorting.'

'You'd be better employed sorting the things in your room then. It's a tip.'

She had to say it now. She sat down at the table.

'Mum, it's awful Dad and Maggie not speaking. Can't you talk to him? They can't carry on like that, it's uncomfortable for all of us.'

'I quite agree with you but your dad's a proud, stubborn man. The longer it carries on the harder it'll be to patch things up. I'll try to talk to him but don't hold your breath.'

Chapter 13

When Caroline returned home, just before ten. Graham was watching the television. The house smelled of fish and chips and the greasy newspaper was screwed up on the kitchen table. For once she didn't use it as an opportunity to criticise him. Instead, she said,

'Anything good on the television? Have I missed anything?'

'Not really,' he replied, turning round to smile at her.

'How did it go?'

'What?' She jumped guiltily.

'The meal with the girls you work with. How did it go?'

'Oh, it was alright. I think it's good to socialise outside work. You see people in a different light. Get to know another side to them.'

She knew he was going to ask her who was there so she quickly changed the subject.

'I'm a bit sleepy. I had some wine so I think I'll go straight up, if you don't mind.'

'Would you like me to bring you up some cocoa?'

'No thanks. You stay and watch the television if you like.'

He was so kind, but so boring. She had been wined and dined and kissed, which had sent her emotions reeling; and her husband was offering her cocoa. She wanted to scream.

She was tired and a bit drunk but she couldn't sleep. Her mind was buzzing as she rewound the conversations she'd had with David. Had she said too much? Did she appear needy? She relived that kiss, the smell of him, the feel of his lips. She wanted more. Then the guilt. What if Graham spoke to the other receptionists and found out she hadn't been with them? What if David wanted an affair with her, did she want one with him and, if so, how could she find enough excuses to spend time with him? She suddenly felt sick and rushed to the bathroom, where she vomited into the toilet. She looked at herself in the mirror, her ashen face and bedraggled hair, and wondered what she had become.

She was still awake when Graham came to bed, but she lay very still and tried to breathe evenly. What was she going to do?

The following morning she was grumpy with a hangover. When Graham tried to question her again about the night before, she said she had to concentrate on getting ready for work.

Once there she found it hard to keep her mind on it. She sent a patient to Audiology instead of Orthopaedics, she miss-spelled names and had to ask patients to repeat questions. Her head thumped and she felt nauseous. She avoided going to the canteen at dinner time. Instead she went for a walk. Nothing made sense any more. She couldn't meet David again. She couldn't not meet him. After work she kept her head down and took a different route home. She made shepherd's pie with yesterday's mince. She forgot to add the onion and had to fry it separately, she didn't put any tea in the teapot and poured Graham a cup of hot, milky water.

'Are you alright love? You don't seem yourself today.' His concern made her guilt even worse. She looked at him and realised that guilt was all she felt. They ate the shepherd's pie, she silent, he trying to make conversation.

'This is delicious. No one makes a shepherd's pie like you. Shall I make a start on decorating the living room next weekend? We could get some of that nice anaglypta. It's supposed to be good at covering up cracks.'

She was screaming inside her head. 'Shut up! Shut up! Let me think.'

Eventually, his attempts at conversation petered out. He was silent for a few minutes, then,

'Have I upset you? Was it the fish and chip wrappers last night?'

She relented.

'No, Graham, it's not you.' He didn't deserve this.

'What is it then? Work?'

'Yes, that's it. I had a hangover and I was sick and had a headache all day. I shouldn't have drunk so much wine, especially when I'm not used to it.'

'No, I suppose not, but you deserved a night out. So who went with you last night?'

'Do you want some peaches and evaporated milk?'

She jumped up and went to the larder. She was trembling and was sure that her face had gone red.

'We're getting a bit low on things but we'll have to manage until I can get to the shops. I wish they stayed open late, then working people like us could do their shopping in the evening. Ouch! I've cut my finger on the peach tin.'

'Here let me open it. Run that under the tap while I get you a plaster.'

He dried her finger and gently put the plaster on. She sat down and put her head in her hands, trying to hide the tears which were welling up, while he put the peaches into two bowls and pushed one towards her.

'This'll cheer you up. You know how you love tinned peaches.'

Chapter 14

'Good morning, Maggie. We can't go on meeting like this. Let me look at you. Mm, it's healing up nicely. No one would guess you had two rounds with Henry Cooper. Have you recovered from seeing Frankenstein?'

'Didn't sleep a wink afterwards. Every time I closed my eyes I saw Frankenstein's monster coming at me.'

'I did tell you it would take your mind off your injuries. Well, I'd better get some work done, I suppose.'

William arranged the papers from his briefcase on his desk and began shuffling through them.

Maggie started on the first letter, feeling disappointed, but not really knowing why. She was finding it difficult to concentrate, whereas William seemed completely lost in his work. She was forgotten. Throughout the day she was acutely aware of his presence but he barely spoke another word to her. When five o'clock arrived, he packed his briefcase, collected his coat and said a general goodbye to everyone in the office. She watched the door close behind him and wanted to cry.

She wandered listlessly to the bus stop, disappointed with William's apparent indifference. Not feeling like like going home, she boarded the first bus that came along, wanting to getting as far away as she could. Maggie didn't know or care where it was going or what she was going to do when she got there. She slumped back on the seat and closed her eyes.

'Where to, Miss?'
'Where are we?' she asked the conductor.
'Just coming into Wimbledon.'
'I'll get off at the next stop.'

She bought a ticket and pushed her way down the crowded bus. She could go and see Caroline and Graham. Caroline wouldn't be pleased to see her. Apart from their not having a close sisterly relationship, Caroline hated unexpected visitors. She liked to be fully prepared. She couldn't go and see Caroline.

She got off the bus and walked past the brightly lit shops and restaurants until she came to a pub. It looked warm and cosy and welcoming. Never having been in a pub on her own before, she felt nervous as she went up to the bar, feeling she had hit rock bottom. It seemed dim after the bright lights outside and she scanned the room hoping there were other women drinking there. There were a few men in groups having an after work pint and a young couple who looked very intimate in a dark corner. The woman looked a bit like Caroline. It couldn't be because the man definitely wasn't Graham. The woman suddenly stood up and went through to the next room, presumably to go to the toilet. She was briefly illuminated by a lamp on the table and Maggie saw with a start that it was definitely Caroline. Maggie ducked behind a pillar. She scrutinised the man left sitting at the table. Even in the poor light she could see that he was very handsome. He didn't look at all comfortable. He kept looking round the room, shiftily, as though afraid to be seen. She hoped that he couldn't see her staring at him and retreated further behind the pillar.

'Are you waiting for someone?'

The barman was approaching her, polishing a glass with a tea towel.

'No, sorry, I think I'm in the wrong place,' she said, and fled.

Caroline was having an affair.

She hurried across the road and headed for the bus stop to wait for the bus to take her to Clayton Park. She couldn't make any sense of what she had seen. Maybe it was a business meeting. Perhaps it was her boss. Then she remembered the way the couple had been looking at each other. Her sister was having an affair. After barely a year of marriage. Poor Graham. He was doomed. He would never be good enough for her. The bus arrived and she climbed the stairs to the top deck which was thick with cigarette smoke. She wished she smoked, it looked so grown up and relaxing. She thought about her family and wondered what else could possibly happen to cause even more unhappiness and discord. She didn't know what she was going to do with the information she had gleaned about Caroline.

'Where have you been? Your dinner was on a low light for an hour but it's now in the bin. I've told you time and time again to tell me if you're going to be late.' Theresa was stretched out on the sofa watching Armand and Michaela Dennis. Large, gaping, gulping fish swam lazily in and out of rocks and corals.

'I'm sorry. I went to see Caroline.'

'Went to see Caroline? Now I've heard it all. Since when did you and Caroline become bosom friends? I thought you couldn't stand the sight of each other.'

'I wouldn't say that. We don't have much in common, that's all. I just thought it would be nice to see her.'

'I expect you passed a phone box. Couldn't you have rung?'

'I had a horrible day at work. I wasn't thinking. You're right and I'm sorry.'

She looked at her father who was not taking any part in this conversation. He probably had his newspaper upside down.

'I'm putting the kettle on. Can I make anyone a cup of tea?

'No thanks,' Theresa said, plumping up the cushion behind her. 'We've all had a cup of tea after our steak and kidney pudding. Make sure you wash the cup and saucer after.'

Maggie could hear her stomach rumbling at the mention of steak and kidney pudding. She was starving. Her mother went berserk if they took food without asking so she wondered if she could sneak a biscuit or a slice of bread and butter without anyone noticing.

On her way out to the kitchen, she heard her mother's voice, 'So how was she?'

'How was who?'

'Princess Anne. Caroline of course. How was she when you went to see her?'

'She was out.'

'Wasted trip then.'

Maggie wondered why it always had to be the Spanish Inquisition. She was over twenty one. It was about time her family stopped interfering in her life. Auntie Ruby followed her into the kitchen, closing the door behind her. In a low voice she said,

'I expect you're hungry. I take it you've had nothing to eat.'

'Starving.'

'I'll make you a little sandwich. Ham alright? I'll put lots of real butter on it. It's really just for your mother but she won't notice if I spread the rest out in the dish. You go and get changed and I'll bring it up to your room.'

Thanks Auntie Ruby. If you're sure. I've had a horrible day and a horrible evening. I feel quite down.'

'Things must be bad. You're usually happy as a sand boy. Now off you go.'

Maggie wearily climbed the stairs, pulled off her high heels and changed into comfortable slacks. She and Gina often said they wished Auntie Ruby was their mother. She was kind and generous, unlike Theresa, who's main interest these days was in herself. Ruby sometimes had a look of Theresa and Maggie thought they might be related in some way. Gina poohpoohed it, saying they might look similar but they were chalk and cheese in personality.

There was a rap at the door.

'Maggie, are you decent?' Her voice was unnecessarily low; the television was blaring out piped laughter from the living room.

She opened the door and held it for Auntie Ruby, who handed her a tray with a ham sandwich, a cup of tea and two biscuits. Clearing a space on Maggie's bed, she sat down with a sigh.

'Do you want to talk about it or you can tell me to mind my own beeswax.'

Maggie was dying to get what she had seen that evening off her chest. Her mother would explode, her Dad wouldn't be interested, if he had been talking to her, and Gina was too young to discuss things like that. She had friends she could confide in but they weren't here when she needed them.

'I'd like to talk about it,' she decided.

Auntie Ruby made herself comfortable.

Maggie took a large bite of her sandwich and said, 'I was a bit upset by something that happened at work and I didn't feel like coming home to face Dad's silent treatment so I just caught a bus randomly. I ended up in Wimbledon and walked into a bar and you'll never guess who I saw.'

'No. Who did you see?'

'Caroline, with a man, and they seemed very lovey-dovey. I don't know what to do.'

Auntie Ruby absent mindedly took a biscuit and began munching it thoughtfully.

'You're sure it was your sister?'

'Definitely.'

'And you're sure it wasn't Graham?'

'Positive.' She took another sandwich. 'It looked nothing like him and anyway, have you ever seen her and Graham being lovey-dovey? She's cold as a fish when she's around him.'

'I see what you mean.' Auntie Ruby picked

up the second biscuit and then put it down again.

Maggie reached for another sandwich. She felt really hungry now.

'I feel sorry for Graham. He's so nice. Much too nice for her. Oh dear, that's not very kind, I know.'

'Keep your mouth shut, that's my advice. It could be innocent and if it isn't then it might blow over.'

'Or I can tell Caroline what I saw.'

'I wouldn't. Least said, soonest mended. Just forget about it. It's not your problem. Now do you want to tell me what's wrong at work?'

'Not really. It's not something I can talk about, but you're right about Caroline. I'll just try to forget it.' She finished the food and drank her tea. 'I'll wash these.'

'No you won't. I'll take them down. You look as though you need a good night's sleep. Thanks for telling me. A trouble halved is a trouble shared. Things will look better tomorrow.'

Chapter 15 August 1961

A week had elapsed and Maggie had given up hope of another date with William. She arrived at the office, sat at her desk and got on with her work. When she glanced up at him from time to time he seemed to be doing the same. They exchanged pleasantries and talked about work but she hadn't the heart for the easy banter of before. He seemed to be exactly the same as he always was. Her face had healed, and there seemed to be no permanent scarring, but her nose was still extremely tender. She had tried to put on a pair of sunglasses one sunny morning but the pressure of them on the bridge of her nose had been excruciating. She was devastated at William's disinterest and found herself scanning the small ads to try to find another job. During her lunch hour she scoured the newspapers on the coffee table in the clients' waiting room.

One day she found an advertisement for a job which immediately attracted her. It was in a local travel agents' office and she would be typing letters, invoices and reports but there was also an opportunity to train as an assistant travel agent, advising customers about holidays. There were even possibilities for trips abroad so that she would be able to give first hand advice about different resorts and hotels. It looked a million times more interesting than working in a drab solicitors' office and she wouldn't have to see William every day, knowing that he had only taken her to the cinema out of pity. She stayed in the office after everyone else had gone home and typed a carefully worded letter of application.

She couldn't stop thinking about what she had done. Every time she saw William she wondered how she would survive without the trembling anticipation of seeing him every day if she got the new job. She would miss the buzz of excitement when the door opened and he walked in. Then she countered this with the thought that he obviously didn't feel the same way about her and she needed to get on with her life. She had been aiming too high. What would a trainee solicitor with a good education want with a girl who had left school at fifteen? She had been mad to even think she'd have a chance. She stopped having early nights and took the minimum amount of care with her appearance. Maggie Langham was going to let go of her silly dreams and face the truth. If she didn't get this job she would apply for another.

'Maggie there's a letter for you. Looks official.'

Gina was waving an envelope at her across the breakfast table. Maggie's hands were shaking as she ripped it open. It invited her for an interview the following week. She would have to call in sick at work.

Sod it, she thought. Sod William, sod the solicitors. She was going to go all out to get this job. Her life needed a damn good shake up. Instead of typing up reports on house conveyancing, legal battles and divorces she would be selling dreams.

She was shaking with nerves when she

arrived for interview at Capital Holidays, but the manager, Mr Wilson, was warm and friendly and she soon relaxed. When he asked her why she wanted to leave her current job, she told him that she had a very outgoing personality, better suited to dealing with the public. She loved the idea of giving clients the opportunity to broaden their horizons as well as her own. She assured him she was a hard worker who was eager to carve out a career for herself in the leisure industry.

The first person she told was Gina, after she had handed her a second letter in a similar envelope to the first.

'I got it! I've got a new job! I'm going to train as a travel agent!'

'Wow that's exciting,' Gina replied. 'I didn't know you hated working in that solicitor's office so much. Wasn't there a man working there that you quite liked?'

'Yes, but it appears that he didn't feel the same about me so I'm going to forget him and start a sparkling new career. I might even get a chance to travel myself.'

'Oh! Will you take me with you?'

'I might, if you behave yourself. Imagine going to Paris or Rome!'

The following day she handed in her notice.

'We'll be very sorry to lose you, Miss Langham. You've brought a breath of fresh air into this place and you're a good typist.'

Mr Harris had emerged from behind his stack of papers. 'We're probably a bit dry and boring for you here, eh? I expect you'll find it much more to your taste at a travel agents. What to you think. William? We'll miss her won't we?'

William was staring at her intently.

'We certainly will,' he said. 'This place will be very dull without you. I hope you'll come back and see us from time to time. When are you actually going?'

'I just have to give a week's notice,' she stammered. 'I start a week on Monday. I'm really excited about it. I'll be typing reports and letters to begin with, but they said if I show an aptitude and interest there might be an opportunity to train as an actual travel agent. I might go abroad and everything.' Maggie was aware she was babbling nervously and tailed off.

'Well I'd better get this finished,' she said, not feeling nearly as enthusiastic about the new job as she sounded. It was ridiculous to hope that he would look upset and beg her not to go.

All too soon, her last day at work arrived. There were no speeches, no present, no party. It was a tiny office, with only three of them working there, so she hadn't really expected any fuss, but she still felt completely flat. She finished as usual at five o'clock, put on her coat and said her goodbyes. William didn't even look up from his desk. She closed the office door for the last time and hurried down the high street, unshed tears stinging her eyes.

Chapter 16

Maggie laid out the clothes she was to wear the next day and decided to have an early night. Just like when I knew I was going to see William in the office. The thought of him gave her a sharp pain in her gut as though she had been kicked. She couldn't believe how stupid she had been, thinking a man like him would be interested in her. Now she was doing it in preparation for the first day in her new job.

She caught the bus to the travel agents' office the next morning. She was excited and apprehensive about the new challenges and meeting her new workmates, but these were overshadowed by the thought that William was no longer part of her life. however tenuous.

'Good morning, Margaret, welcome aboard. Make yourself a cup of tea and I'll introduce you to the others.'

Mr Wilson introduced her to the other members of staff. He gave her their full names but it wasn't made clear if they were called by their Christian names. She would have to wait and see before she used them. There seemed to be a lot of camaraderie between them and she was looking forward to being part of the team, although she knew that she was last in the pecking order. She had a desk in the small office at the back, which she shared with another young girl called Heather. Her face was young but Maggie thought she looked old before her time, with her sky blue twinset, string of pearls and permanent wave. Maggie self-consciously smoothed back her own dark, unruly hair.

Mr Wilson came through and placed a pile of forms and letters to type on each of their desks. He spent the next half an hour giving her detailed instructions,

'Any problems, ask Heather. She'll put you right.'

The rest of the staff worked in the front and dealt directly with clients. Their room was bright and airy, the walls covered in large posters of blue seas, palm trees and cities with exotic buildings. It was a far cry, she thought, from the dingy solicitors' office, with its heavy dark furniture and shelves groaning with dusty books. And William. She had to forget about William. That was over, but it didn't stop her heart plummeting every time she thought of him. She wondered whom they had found to take her place and whether the new typist would fall head over heels in love with him like she had. She was grateful when Heather's voice interrupted her thoughts.

'So is this your first job, Margaret?'

'Oh, please call me Maggie. My mum calls me Margaret when I'm in trouble. Which is most of the time,' she added, laughing. 'No, I've worked in a solicitor's office since I left school.'

'Ooh, sounds a bit dull. It's nice here. We're all friendly, sometimes even go out together for a drink after work, that kind of thing. I've been here since I left typing school. The two girls in the front, Stella and Jill, are thick as thieves but they're OK if you can get a word in edgeways. The boss is fair as long as you toe the line and put the work in. You got a boyfriend?'

'No,' replied Maggie. 'Not yet.' She didn't want to tell her about William, and anyway, what was there to tell? 'Have you?'

'Oh yes, me and John have been together for two years. I knew he was the one for me as soon as I clapped eyes on him. Getting married in the spring. This is him.' She smiled happily and proudly took from her desk a framed photograph of an earnest looking young man with neatly combed sandy hair, wearing a suit and tie.

'Lovely,' said Maggie, hoping her voice conveyed an interest she didn't feel. 'You're very lucky. Well, I'd better get on. I don't want to make a bad impression on my first day.'

She didn't want to hear about girls getting married. She hoped that Heather wasn't going to bang on about it all the time.

They both settled down to work. Occasionally she asked Heather for advice. She was very serious. It wasn't going to be a barrel of laughs in the back office. Mr Wilson popped in and out and complimented Maggie on the standard of her typing. Hand written notes and forms appeared on her desk in a steady stream which kept Maggie busy. The morning flew by.

Do you want to take your dinner now? It's one o'clock. I'm going to eat mine at my desk.'

Heather fumbled in a drawer and took out a box of Ryvita, a Dairylea cheese triangle and an apple.

'I'm trying to lose a stone before the

wedding. The trouble is I'm always hungry. You're so lucky to be so skinny. I only have to look at a doughnut to put on five pounds.'

'Yes I imagine it must be difficult to diet when you're hungry. I can't seem to put weight on. I could do with a few curves. Right I'm off. I think I'll go out and buy something to eat. I forgot to bring a sandwich with the excitement of my first day. I could do with stretching my legs. Can I get you anything?'

'Yes, a Cadbury's fruit and nut please.'

Maggie thought she was joking but it appeared she wasn't.

'OK if you're sure.'

She went through to the front to see Mr Wilson in the cubby hole he called his office. He had a serviette tucked into his shirt and was drinking soup from a thermos. Stella was reading Woman's Own which was scattered with crumbs from the Cornish pasty she was devouring while Jill was polishing off a jam tart.

Maggie bought two bars of fruit and nut and ate one as she wandered up the High Street. She found herself outside her old office and lingered there for a few minutes, but there was no sign of William and she didn't dare go in. What was she thinking? He was patently not interested in her. Taking a deep breath, she strode back to her new office, determined that this was the last time she would waste her time thinking about something that was never going to happen. Jill and Stella, still keeping up their constant chatter, had returned to their adjacent desks. Heather wasn't at hers but soon appeared, red faced and out of breath, a few minutes later.

'I decided to go out shopping after all,' she said emptying her shopping bag on to her desk, proudly displaying the set of tea towels she had bought for a knock down price. 'My mum always says you can never have enough tea towels.'

She refolded them and packed them neatly back into their paper bag before tearing off the wrapper from the chocolate bar.

'I expect I've used up the calories walking round the shops,' she said, by way of justification.

The rest of the day Maggie gave all of her concentration to her work and was surprised when Heather put the cover on her typewriter and collected her belongings. The hours had passed quickly.

'Right I'm off. John will be waiting for me. We've just got half an hour before "Brighter Homes" shuts. We're looking at three piece suites.' she said excitedly. 'See you tomorrow.'

Maggie put on her coat and went through to the front. Everyone was getting ready to go.

'How was your day? Settled in?' Mr Wilson was turning the sign on the door to 'Closed'.

'Good,' said Maggie. 'I found the work very interesting.' She gave a grin, 'I'll definitely be back tomorrow.'

'That's the spirit. See you at nine a.m. sharp.'

As she left the building she noticed a man lurking in the shadows. It couldn't be.

Chapter 17

'William? What are you doing here?' Her heart was beating so fast she thought she might faint.

'I've come to walk you to the bus stop. I thought you might get lost on your first day, or get into a fight.'

'Well you're the last person I expected to see. You didn't even say goodbye the day I left,' she said and immediately regretted it.

'That's because I didn't want to say goodbye. Look, can we talk? Perhaps go for a walk, or a drink? Maybe it's a bit cold and damp for a walk.'

She was in shock and didn't know what to say, so she fell into step beside him.

'Come on, this pub looks OK.'

He held the door open for her. She went in and paused. It was dark and smelled of stale beer and cigarette smoke.

'Where shall we sit?' she asked, looking round at the groups of men who were looking her up and down, pints half drunk.

'Over there by the window.' He helped her out of her coat.' I know it's not very salubrious but that's a biting wind out there. Now, what can get you?'

'No idea. I don't really drink.' Oh dear that didn't sound very sophisticated. She said the first thing that came into her head. 'I know, a vodka and tonic please.'

She had recently seen a film where a glamorous woman had ordered a vodka and tonic in a smart hotel bar. It had looked so, well, glamorous.

'Right, coming up.' She thought he looked faintly amused. She should have asked for an orange juice. Supposing she didn't like it?

While his back was turned at the bar she quickly got out her compact, dabbing powder on her nose and putting on some lipstick. She tried to push her long curly hair, which had gone frizzy in the damp air, into some sort of order.

He carried the drinks to the table and set the vodka and tonic in front of her. She took a small sip and tried not to wrinkle her nose in disgust. It tasted very bitter and unpleasant.

'I need to explain.'

She stayed silent, waiting.

'I wanted to ask you out.'

He pushed the lock of brown hair back that had fallen over his face. She had never seen him look awkward before.

'You're funny, friendly, kind. But,' he paused. 'I felt I couldn't take it any further with us working together, not to mention that it's company policy.' He smiled.' Staff are forbidden to fraternise with each other and I couldn't risk it, especially when I'm still articled. Also, if our relationship didn't work, it would be so embarrassing having to see each other, wouldn't it, working in that tiny office? But now that you've left... oh this is awkward. Maggie, will you go out with me?'

Maggie realised she had been holding her

breath. She thought this was the most wonderful moment of her life. It was what she had always dreamed of. In fact, was she dreaming?

As she exhaled she felt a feeling of relief, of rightness. She tried to keep her voice steady; she thought she was going to cry.

'Of course, William. I'd love to go out with you.' She took a large gulp of her drink. It didn't taste that bad really.

Now it didn't seem to matter that her dad wasn't talking to her, that her mum was a nag, that she didn't get on with Caroline.

He smiled at her. 'I've been rehearsing that speech all day, then it all came out in a rush. Do you fancy a bite to eat?'

'I'm expected home. My mum goes up the wall if she's cooked a meal and I'm late.'

Then she thought, What the hell, I'm twenty one. What have I got to go home for? Another boring night in with my insufferable parents. Or would I prefer a night out with William? Stupid question.

'Wait a tick. I'll go and ring them, there's a call box outside.' She finished off the drink in a large gulp.

'Are you sure? I don't want to get you into trouble.'

'It'll be fine. Wait there.'

It wouldn't be fine but she didn't care. The vodka had made her reckless.

She went outside and felt a bit woozy as the fresh air hit her. The phone box was empty. Trembling, she inserted four pennies and waited, hoping that it wasn't her father who answered. That would make things difficult. She'd just have to ring off. It wasn't likely, he rarely answered, or even used, the phone.

She pressed button A.

'Hello Auntie Ruby. Sorry to be a nuisance but I won't be in for my tea tonight.'

'Oh dear and I've made a nice steak and kidney pie.'

'Can you put it in the larder and I'll have it tomorrow?'

'Everything alright?'

'Everything's wonderful. William was waiting for me outside my new office and he's asked me out.'

'Well that is wonderful. I'll tell..'

But the pips were going and they were cut off. She returned to the warmth of the pub and William, who was sitting there watching the door.

He looked up and smiled.

'Everything OK? I hope you didn't get into trouble.'

'Everything's fine. The only thing between going home and going out with you was steak and kidney pie, which I said I'd eat tomorrow. My family still thinks we're living in the war and it's a crime to waste anything.'

'Mine's much the same. It not a bad attitude to have. So what do you like to eat? You'll not want steak and kidney pie if you're having it tomorrow.'

Maggie laughed. 'I'd be happy with fish and chips. What do you fancy?'

'Fish and chips. Well you're cheap to take out. I thought you might say fillet steak and champagne.'

'Overrated,' she replied, having never tasted either. 'You can't beat the nation's favourite food.'

'We'd better find one where you can eat in with a pot of tea and a plate of bread and butter. I don't fancy sitting on a park bench in this weather.'

They finished their drinks and braved the harsh wind in the high street, a slap in the face after the cosiness of the pub. He took her hand and they walked briskly along the road towards a brightly lit shop emanating inviting smells of fish and chips. As they settled in a window seat, Maggie's mouth watered. She had eaten little lately, thinking that William had broken her heart, and now she was ravenous. When the waitress brought their meal she fell upon it hungrily.

'I see you're not one of these modern young girls who are always on a diet and swear that half a piece of toast is filling.'

Maggie laughed and slowed down. 'You must think me a pig. I didn't realise how hungry I was.'

'It'll be the alcohol. It gives you an appetite, especially if you're not used to it.'

'What you said about girls always dieting. I have the opposite problem. I've always been stick thin. I wouldn't mind putting on a bit of weight. Get a bit of shape.'

'I like you as you are. Anyway, as the infamous Mrs Simpson said, "You can never be too rich or too thin."'

'Well I suppose one out of two isn't bad.'

They walked back along the river, holding

hands and chatting. Maggie felt comfortable with him, her shyness forgotten.

'Well here we are.'

Maggie thanked him and said what a lovely evening it had been. The banter had flowed between them and the time had sped by.

'Do you want to come in?' she asked, her voice trembling slightly. She didn't want him to meet her family but didn't want to seem rude. She realised that she was holding her breath, dreading his answer.

'Thanks, perhaps another time.'

There was an embarrassed silence.

'Well, thanks again,' she said. 'Leaving that job was clearly a good decision.'

'The best,' he said, leaning towards her. At that moment, the curtain was pulled back and the round moon of her mother's face was at the window, peering into the darkness.

'Looks like your time is up,' he said, forcing a smile. 'Shall I phone you?'

'Yes, OK,' she replied, taking a notebook out of her handbag and scribbling her number on it.

'Or you could meet me after work again.'

She didn't want him to phone in case someone else answered. She didn't know what he would make of her family. He dressed smartly and had a posh voice. What on earth would he think of them? Her dad would probably ignore him, and her mother would no doubt interrogate him and monopolise the conversation. When Gina had the misjudgement to bring one of her grammar school friends home, their mother had put on an embarrassing pseudo posh accent and wouldn't stop talking. She couldn't bear that to happen with William. It might completely put him off and she'd never see him again.

'Are you free Wednesday?'

'I'll just check my diary.' She pretended the notebook was a diary.

She scratched her head as she thumbed her way through. 'Hmm. If I postpone my date with Gary Cooper and cancel my trip to Harrods, I might be able to squeeze you in on Wednesday.'

He laughed. 'Maggie. I've never met anyone like you. Most girls would have played hard to get. Say they're washing their hair or pretend they're seeing someone else. I know where I am with you, as long as I can elbow Gary Cooper out of the running. What about the same time on Wednesday? We'll have to think beyond fish and chips or I'll end up looking like Billy Bunter. Look I'd better go. The curtains are twitching again.'

He suddenly grabbed her arm and yanked her behind a tree. Taking her in his arms he kissed her. 'That's to keep me going until Wednesday. Night night.'

She watched him go, her head reeling and her heart pounding. There was a clink of milk bottles and she saw that her mother was on the doorstep.

'Come in, you'll catch your death.'

Maggie went in without a word. Catch her death? It was late August for heaven's sake. She didn't care that her mother hadn't asked if she'd had a good time or that her dad wouldn't talk to her. She didn't care about anything. Except William. He had kissed her. She floated up to her bedroom and threw herself onto her bed, pulling the gold, silky eiderdown around herself in a hug. If she looked in her dressing table mirror she would see a young woman with a flushed face, sparkling eyes and a stupid big grin. William had kissed her.

Chapter 18 January 1962

Caroline knew she had her faults but she was usually honest. She didn't want to hurt Graham but she couldn't see herself spending her life with him. It wasn't the life she wanted and she realised they had just drifted into marriage. They had met at the hospital at a Christmas party. He had looked very handsome, was easy to talk to and seemed popular with his fellow workers She didn't make friends easily and she wasn't close to Maggie, who was only two years younger that her. They were as different as chalk and cheese. Maggie had idolised Gina as soon as she was born and they had always been close. She barely talked to Gina whom she thought a bit of a spoiled brat, especially when she had won a place at the grammar school. She seemed to be excused from most of the household chores because of homework and didn't she milk it? Her mother was totally self centred and her dad didn't have much time for anyone.

When she had met Graham he appeared to fall for her right away. She felt that at last she had someone on her side and was grateful for his attention. They had been going out together for about six months when he had proposed to her. It had been so romantic and she was sure at the time that it was what she wanted. Addicted to romantic novels, she liked nothing better than to curl up with a book or magazines, which painted seductive pictures of married life. Housewives were done up to the nines in chiffon scarves, wavy perms and lipstick. They cooked delicious meals in shiny kitchens and were pictured putting steaming plates of perfect food in front of their husbands. They had through lounges with contemporary furniture and men who bought them flowers on pay day. Caroline felt it was all she ever wanted to make her happy.

They had had a small engagement party after which she began to plan the wedding and collect things for her bottom drawer. She and Graham would talk endlessly about where they would live and the names they would call their children. After the wedding, when the excitement had subsided and they were scraping an existence in the Turnbull's attic flat with little money and little left left to say to each other, she wondered what had happened to all those hopes and dreams. Life had become as mediocre as before. Graham seemed happy enough with his lot which meant he had no aspirations to make things better. He never talked about going to night school and she suspected that he had said that he would just to placate her.

David represented the life she wanted. She didn't plan to use him as an escape route but she was slowly drawn into a full blown affair with a man who made her feel the way she felt she deserved to feel.

She had to find excuses for evenings out, a trip to the cinema with a friend, a late night shopping trip. She had to find out what the film was about beforehand in case Graham questioned her, and buy items in her lunch hour and hide them away in case she needed to show him what she had bought. She pretended to join the WI so she had a regular excuse. Then she and David wanted more, nights in hotels and weekends away. She invented distant relations and sick school friends she had to visit. Then she had to dissuade Graham from visiting her parents too often in case these fictitious relatives and friends were brought up in conversation. She told him that it would make sense for her to visit her family at the same time that he visited his. This arrangement suited her because she found his family a bit common. Visits to them brought dirty jokes and raucous laughter and intrusive comments about their sex life and whether they would ever be hearing the patter of tiny feet. She knew they thought she was cold and standoffish and that she thought herself superior to them, so there was no love lost there.

Without realising it, she became more and more critical of Graham's speech, his table manners and untidiness. Through it all he remained steadfast and long suffering, which infuriated her further. He had no backbone. Now and again they talked of children, but at that moment there was no way they could afford another mouth to feed, especially as she would have to give up work. She felt utterly trapped. Seeing David was the only thing that kept her sane.

Then she missed her period, and then another one and she was sure that David was the father. She and Graham had been taking precautions the few times they had sex, but, just once, she and David had had unprotected sex.

Chapter 19 January 1962

Caroline looked in the wardrobe mirror, turning this way and that. Her stomach looked quite flat in the charcoal pencil skirt. The corset was doing a fine job although it was getting less comfortable and made her feel very hot. She stood in the bedroom, taking deep breaths, trying to quell the feeling of nausea. She couldn't leave it any longer. The problem wasn't going to go away.

She arrived at the hospital the next morning, looking outwardly calm. She sat at her desk in reception and dealt with the constant stream of patients in her efficient manner. Usually sure of herself, today she felt unable to make a decision that could possibly be completely life-changing. The clock dragged on to midday. She was relieved from her position by another member of staff and made her way to the hospital canteen. She joined the queue but when she reached the counter the nausea returned and she knew she couldn't face any food; she filled her glass with water, which she took to an empty table.

'Hello Caroline.'

She looked up with a start and there he was, smiling down at her. He put his bowl of Windsor soup on the table next to her and slid into the seat beside her.

'How are you today?' He stared at her glass of water 'Not eating?'

'I'm pregnant.' Her voice was flat.

David went as white as his lab coat. He had been about to spoon some soup into his mouth, but dropped it. The thick brown liquid splashed up his lab coat and spattered the formica table.

'Is it mine or Graham's?'

'I'm pretty sure it's yours.'

'Oh God!' He looked furtively round the room. 'Look, we can't discuss this here,' he said. 'Can you meet me tonight in our usual bar and we can talk about this? Are you sure you're pregnant? Have you had a test?'

She nodded. 'I'm sure,' she said, quietly. 'Yes, shall I meet you at five thirty?'

'Five thirty,' he agreed and turned away. She had hoped he would be at least a tiny bit pleased. Perhaps it was shock and he needed some time to think about it. She went to look for Graham in the cubby hole where he and his fellow porters met for a cup of tea and a smoke.

'We don't often see you down this way, love? Can't you wait till you get home to see your Graham? Lucky devil.' One of the other porters was smiling as he looked her up and down. 'He's on his way.'

Graham looked pleased to see her.

'Hello love, have you forgotten your key or something?'

'No,' she said, trying to hide the tremble in her voice. She couldn't look at him.

'I've got to work late tonight so can you fend for yourself until I get back? It's some sort of staff training programme. I won't be late.'

She was dreading the meeting with David. She had no idea how he would respond to her news.

He had never really talked about his relationship with his wife but she assumed he must be unhappy, like her, if he risked having an affair. If he did want to leave his wife and begin a new life with her she knew she would leave Graham like a shot. As she stroked her stomach she knew she would certainly feel bad about it and would let him down gently, but things had now changed dramatically. She didn't care what her parents' reaction would be. They would just have to lump it. And Graham was young and handsome; he'd soon find someone else who would suit him better.

She dealt with the patients and paperwork like an automaton, her thoughts constantly straying to the new life she would live as a doctor's wife. David would be on a good salary and money wouldn't be a problem, even supporting his wife and child. She saw a white painted detached house with a large garden, their child playing on a swing. She would buy her clothes in Bentalls or even Harrods; she would host cocktail parties and they would holiday in Italy.

'Excuse me, are you deaf? Or rude? I've got an appointment in outpatients at four thirty.'

She was brought back to the present with a start. An old lady was tapping her walking stick impatiently.

'Oh, I'm so sorry. Oh yes.' She ran her finger down the list in front of her.' Your appointment is with Dr Williams. Please take a seat along the corridor.'

Chapter 20

Caroline's heart was pounding as she entered the dimly lit bar. David wasn't there yet so she ordered a Babycham, in the hope that it would give her some Dutch courage, and went to sit in 'their' alcove. There was an overflowing ashtray on the table that was making her feel queasy so she put it on an adjacent table. Her life was about to change. She was beginning to feel self conscious about sitting alone in a bar when he finally arrived. His usual smile at the sight of her was absent.

'Hello. Sorry if I'm a bit late, I'd better get drinks in,' he said. 'Another Babycham?'

She nodded and watched him go to the bar and order their drinks. There was something confident and commanding about his manner which she found very attractive. He returned to the table setting down the drinks.

'How are you?' he enquired solicitously. 'You look very pale.'

'Tired,' she said. 'Worried.'

He took her hand and stroked it.

'I've thought of nothing else since you told me. What do you want to do?'

'I don't know,' she said. 'What can I do?' She looked at him hopefully. Surely there was only one thing they could do.

'Well, I've been thinking and these are the options. The first is that you have an abortion.'

'What?' She snatched her hand away. 'I'm not going to murder our baby. How can you even think that?'

'No, I didn't think you'd like that idea.' She thought he looked shifty. 'Is there any way you could pass it off as Graham's? After all it might be his.'

'Even if I did,' her voice was hard with disbelief, 'I told you that Graham and I couldn't afford a child. He's just a porter on a very low wage and I'd have to give up work. We wouldn't have nearly enough to live on!' She thought she was going to faint. This wasn't what she had expected.

'I could help you out financially. I wouldn't expect you to do this without my help.'

Caroline couldn't believe what she was hearing. He had said he loved her but now there was no talk of his leaving and marrying her. What a fool she had been. She started to cry. She hadn't wanted it to happen like this. She had dreamed that they would spend the rest of their lives together and now that life had well and truly slipped from her grasp. All she could see now was a future of bringing up a child who wasn't her husband's and living in poverty. How had she got herself into this? She got up. She had to leave.

'Sit down, Caroline. This is a complete mess and I haven't been entirely honest with you. I gave you the impression that Penny was always out and had no time for me and Michael. That was how she used to be, full of energy and enthusiasm for life. Then she was diagnosed with multiple sclerosis after Michael was born.'

Caroline looked at him with horror.

'Why didn't you tell me?'

'Because I didn't want you think that I started having an affair with you because my wife was an invalid.'

'And was that the reason?' Her tone was icy.

'No, of course not. She's well at the moment. Her symptoms are very mild and she can lead a fairly normal life. She tires easily and has to pace herself. But of course the disease is progressive. It will get much much worse and I'll end up looking after her.'

He tried to take her hand again but she snatched it away.

'Can't you see, that although I love you and want to be with you, I can't? I can't leave her. She has no family apart from a married brother in New Zealand. This is why she engages in so many activities. She says she wants to do as much as possible while she still can.' He put his head in his hands and said in a low voice,

'You must think me a bastard. I should never have let this happen. I could say it was the stress and uncertainty about the future, and that's certainly part of it, but that's not the main reason. I was attracted to you. OK I know I shouldn't have let it happen.' He tried to take her hand again but she put them both on her lap. He sighed. 'Believe me, I do love you, but I can't leave her.'

'Then there's nothing more to be said. now I have no option but to pretend it's Graham's. And yes I would like you to help support the child if you can afford it.'

Her tone was icy. She had to leave. The bile was rising in her throat and her eyes had filled with tears of anger and frustration.

    'I can afford it. Penny inherited a great deal of money from her parents. That's the least of our worries. Caroline!'

But she had gone.

Chapter 21 January 1962

Caroline could barely see through her tears as she trudged through the gloomy streets. She was on her way back to the tiny flat to break the news to Graham that she was going to have a baby. If David was going to help her out financially, she'd have to invent a story about where the extra money was coming from. She barely recognised the person she had become. She had prided herself on being scrupulously honest and upright, but since she had met David she had done nothing but lie and the lies would have to continue. There was no going back. She could never tell Graham the truth. He didn't deserve any of this. She stopped as she crossed the bridge over the river and looked down at the dark, swirling water.

'Don't do it. It can't be as bad as all that.'

The voice belonged to a smartly dressed young man who was smiling at her.

She turned round, guiltily.

'No. I don't think I have the guts to do it. Also, I'd be killing two people not just one.'

'Oh, that's it, is it? I was joking. Actually, I didn't really think you'd jump. Now I feel embarrassed. Would it help to talk about it?'

'Why do you want to get involved in my problems?'

'I don't, but now you've told me I can't very well walk away, can I? If you jumped down there as soon as my back was turned I'd have your death on my conscience, wouldn't I?'

'No, really, it's alright. I've had a shock and I just need to think things through.'

'Sure? I'm a good listener.'

'I'm sure, but you can go away thinking you may have saved my life.'

He shrugged. 'All the best then.'

She watched him walk away and wondered why she hadn't confided in him. She needed to talk to someone. This was too big to deal with on her own. Her mother would make a big song and dance about it, apportion blame, be no help at all and would probably make things even worse. She couldn't talk to Maggie. She might be sympathetic and would possibly give her some good practical advice, but they just didn't have that sort of close, sisterly relationship. She thought of her small group of friends. They thought her a paragon of virtue. She had always made known her views on women with questionable morals. She certainly couldn't tell anyone at work. That was too close to home. She ran after the retreating figure.

'Stop! Please!' Panting, she caught up with him. 'It would help to talk if you don't mind.'

'I wouldn't have offered if I minded. It's too cold to stand around here. There's a tea room just around the corner which does pots of tea and a lovely Victoria sandwich.

'Thanks, but you must let me pay.'

'I wouldn't hear of it. You're the perfect excuse to have some cake. Come on, let's get out of this cold wind.'

The cafe was almost empty. Caroline sat down at a table as far away from the waitress as possible and looked through the steamy windows. The street was deserted except for an old man walking his dog. Other people's lives went on as normal while hers was in turmoil. Her companion went to the counter and ordered tea and cake from the bored looking woman who was glancing at a newspaper.

'Sit yourself down and I'll bring it over to you and your wife. Bit brass monkeys out there tonight.'

She brought the tray to the table and lingered, eager to make conversation. The man politely but firmly told her that would be all and she went back to her newspaper with an audible tut.

'I don't know where to start. I feel so stupid telling my problems to a stranger.'

'It's sometimes the best way. I'm not biased.'

He poured the tea and pushed piece of cake towards her. The waitress had given up pretending to read the paper and was openly staring at them.

'Hang on a minute,' he said, standing and rattling the change in his pocket.

She watched him walk over to the juke box and insert some money. The deep voice of Helen Shapiro singing, 'Walking back to happiness' echoed round the room.

Ironic, thought Caroline, sipping the hot tea.

He sat down, grinning. 'That should stop her earwigging.'

She managed a weak smile. 'I don't even know your name.'

'If I tell you my name I won't be a stranger. I won't tell you mine and I don't want to know yours. That way there's complete anonymity. It'll make it easier for you.'

She smiled for the first time and nibbled on the piece of cake.

After a faltering start she found him easy to talk to. She felt immense relief as she poured out her problems. He was right, he was a good listener. His eyes never wandered from her face and he nodded encouragingly in all the right places.

'So,' she concluded, 'the father can't be with me so do I pretend it's my husband's?'

There was a pause as the stranger considered his reply.

'How do you think he would take it if you told him the truth?'

'He'd be devastated. I don't think he'd leave me, but he might.'

'What about your family? Would they help?'

'If you ever had the misfortune to meet them you would know that that isn't an option. My father barely communicates, my mother is self obsessed and I don't really get on with either of my sisters.'

'Oh, that's sad, why is that?'

'I don't really know. We're just different that's all. They get on very well with each other and I feel excluded. Graham is the only person who understands me and has time for me.'

She had thought that about David until tonight.

He chased the cake crumbs round the plate with his forefinger. He looked confused.

'Can I ask you why you were tempted to have an affair then? If he is the only person who understands you?'

She drank her tea and stayed silent. She couldn't tell him that she thought Graham wasn't good enough for her. That life with him was disappointing. That she would never have the chance to be the person she wanted to be. That sex with Graham was dull, but sex with David had felt so right and had been exciting. Even though he was a stranger, she realised that she didn't want him to think badly of her. She wanted him to see her as a victim. She finished the tea with a quick gulp.

'I've taken up too much of your time. You have been so kind.' She stood up.

'Has talking about it helped?'

'It hasn't solved my problem but at least you've stopped me throwing myself in the river.'

'Do you think you would have?'

'Probably not. Thanks again for your company. I hope we don't meet again. You know too much about me.'

He stood up too. 'My lips are sealed.'

She smiled as she gathered her things and left. She wondered why she couldn't have met someone like him. He seemed to be absolutely perfect.

Chapter 22

Caroline trudged up the the narrow stairs to the flat. Her heart and body felt as heavy as lead. As she had walked home through the cold, dark streets, examining her options, she knew she had none. At some point she had to tell Graham she was expecting a baby. She would not tell him it wasn't his. She felt drained, disappointed and deeply unhappy.

She could hear raucous laughter from the living room. Graham was watching a noisy game show on the small television they had rented.

'Hello, darling,' he said, turning to look at her with a sympathetic smile. 'You've had a long day. I didn't know what you planned for us to eat tonight. I haven't had anything. I'm starving.'

The last thing she wanted to think about was food. Why couldn't he feed himself for once?

'Couldn't you have made yourself cheese on toast or a sandwich? I'm tired. I don't feel like cooking.'

She knew her voice was sharp and that she was taking her desolation out on him.

'I'm worn out and I don't feel well. I think I'll go to bed.'

'I was waiting for you. I didn't know how late you'd be. Do you want to get into bed and I'll bring you some tea. Shall I make you something to eat?'

His concern was making her feel even worse.

'Tea will be lovely. Nothing to eat. You make a sandwich or something for yourself.'

'What's the matter? Do you need a doctor?'

'Please stop fussing. I'll be better after a good rest.'

Tomorrow she would tell him about the baby. That would explain her feeling unwell. Meanwhile she needed to be on her own to think. She had to plan what she was going to do with the rest of her life. She took off her clothes and threw them on a chair. Normally she would have hung them up and carefully taken off her make up with cold cream and rubbed Nivea on her face and hands. Tonight she threw herself into bed and blinked back the tears. She would allow herself to cry when Graham had given her her cup of tea and gone back downstairs. She thought back to two years ago when she had been so glad to leave home and have a place of her own. Now it felt like a prison that she was never going to escape from.

'Here you are love, get this down you. You'll soon feel better. Sure I can't get you anything else?'

'Sure, thank you.'

She took the tea and sipped it. Graham was still hovering.

'I'm alright. Best leave me alone.'

'Night night then. I'll be quiet when I come to bed.'

At last he left. She could still hear the television downstairs. The cup rattled in the saucer as she put it on the bedside table. How would she explain the extra money coming in from David? Graham knew her parents couldn't afford to support them. If she invented a well off relation who wanted to help, she was bound to be found out. She had to be seen to earn it. She would no longer be able to work at the hospital once she started to show so she would have to think of something else. Perhaps she could pretend she was doing some typing for someone at home, during the day when he was at work. She sighed. Once you started to lie you had to keep going. Maybe she should have thrown herself in the river. She thought about the kind young man who had taken the time to listen to her. It was a pity she hadn't met someone like that. Not only was he kind, he was quite good looking, smartly dressed and well spoken. Much like David. She wondered who he was and whether their paths would ever cross again.

    She stroked her stomach that was just starting to swell. In there was David's baby. She squeezed back the hot tears pricking behind her closed lids. She loved David. She probably always would. His invalid wife would die one day and he would come back to her, where he belonged. She just had to be patient.

Chapter 23

The weak sun streamed through a gap in the curtains and Caroline reluctantly woke from a fitful sleep. She had spent many hours going over what she was going to say to Graham. Today was Saturday and the empty weekend stretched ahead of them. She had to tell him today. His head poked round the door.

'Hello, love. Just came to see if you were awake. How are you feeling this morning? You've had a nice long sleep. Cup of tea?'

'I feel a bit better today. A cup of tea would be lovely, thanks, you're so kind.'

His face broke into a grin. He wasn't use to receiving compliments from her.

'Anything for my beautiful wife. The kettle's on, I won't be two ticks.'

He came in with the tea and sat down on the bed.

'What would you like to do this weekend?'
'We need to talk first.'

His face fell, expecting bad news, or criticism.

'I'm pregnant, three months, and I don't know how we're going to afford it.'

She looked at him helplessly. His expression had been serious, guarded .Now his face lit up.

'A baby! Our baby! Oh Caro, that's lovely, brilliant news. I'm going to be a dad. I can't believe it.

Yes we'll be short of money but I'll look for something better, with prospects, I promise. I'll spend the weekend looking in the papers for jobs and you must take it easy. Do you want to stay in bed?'

She was already irritated. 'No, please don't fuss, Graham. I'll get up now and make some breakfast.'

By the time she had washed and dressed, she was feeling sick.

'Can you make your own? I'll just nibble on some dry toast.'

She had been feeling sick in the mornings for about a month now but hadn't said anything to Graham. Although she had told him not to fuss, she quite liked having a bit of sympathy.

'Can we tell people? My family'll be over the moon.'

'I suppose so but I don't want anyone to know at work. The longer we can keep it quiet the longer I can work. It shouldn't show under my uniform for quite a few months.'

'Shall we go and see our parents this weekend and tell them?'

'Yes, good idea. After breakfast we could go and give them a call from the phone box across the road, arrange a visit.'

Well she'd done it. The baby was officially Graham's. He was pleased. She was off the hook. She was just going to have to make the best of a bad job. At least she'd have a baby to keep her occupied. As to explaining where the extra money was going to come from, she'd decided to pretend she was taking in typing and doing secretarial work from home.

Graham wouldn't find out if she went about it the right way. Perhaps she could actually even do some, as well having David's contribution. Things didn't look quite so bleak financially.

Chapter 24

Maggie heard heavy footsteps and then her mother burst into the room without knocking. Theresa was puffing like a steam train and her face was red as she sat down on the end of the narrow bed. Maggie was not going to be allowed to go to bed without her mother cross examining her.

'So this young man you're seeing. When are you bringing him home to meet us?'

'His name's William.'

'You don't tell me anything these days.'

'I thought you weren't interested. You've never asked before.'

Maggie was surprised. Her mother didn't usually take much interest in her life. Perhaps she was annoyed that she hadn't brought him in for the once over.

'He works in that solicitor's office I left a few months ago.'

'Is he a nice boy? I noticed you hanging around with him outside. I hope he doesn't get fresh.'

I notice you're forever gawping through a crack in the curtains.

Maggie sighed. She wished her mother would leave her alone. She didn't want to be interrogated.

'Mum, he's training to be a solicitor. He's a respectable man, not a boy. You've no worries there. I need to go to sleep now.'

Maggie turned over and drew the eiderdown up to her chin. Theresa tutted and heaved her body from the bed.

'Pardon me for taking an interest.' With that she went, shutting the door with what was nearly a slam.

And yes my job is going very well, thank you for asking, Mother.

'Well you sound chipper for a Monday morning.' Auntie Ruby was stirring porridge with one hand and wiping the draining board with the other. 'How's work in that travel agents going?'

'It's really interesting, nice friendly people and a big bright office. Very different from the gloomy old solicitors'. I love it. I wouldn't mind training as a travel agent. They said I might be given the opportunity if I show an aptitude.'

'Well that's lovely. It must be a really interesting job selling houses, having a peek into how other people live.'

Maggie laughed. 'Oh that's an estate agent. A travel agent sells holidays.'

'Oh ! Even better! I do like a lovely trip to Bournemouth or Littlehampton in a charabanc. You can't beat a bit of sea air and sand between your toes. Porridge? There's golden syrup on the table.'

Maggie accepted a bowl of porridge. Gina was already there twirling another spoonful of syrup on to what was left of hers.

'Do you like porridge with your syrup, Gina?' Maggie sat down opposite her.

'Love syrup, it's liquid gold,' She returned to

the textbook propped up against the cruet.

'Not finished your homework by any chance?'

'I've got a French test in about an hour and I don't know anything.'

'You always say that and still manage to come top in everything. I wish I had your brains.'

'No you wouldn't. It's a hard slog. I wish I was working in a nice office earning oodles of money.'

Gina scraped the last of the syrup off her plate and threw the book into her satchel with a sigh of resignation.

Maggie looked at the kitchen clock.

'I wish I did earn oodles of money. I'm going to be late. Got to go. Good luck with the French test, Gina.'

But Gina had gone.

Maggie only just caught the bus and had to hang on to a strap on the platform, it was so crowded. As she jostled backwards and forwards she thought that life couldn't get much better. Well, it possibly could if she could just swap her parents for two reasonable human beings. What was she going to do do about her father? She felt she could never forgive him for the brutal way he had attacked her. Gina had said she had talked to Mum about it but so far nothing had changed. He was so bloody stubborn he was never going to make the first move. The bus groaned to a stop and she jumped off and strode quickly along the high street. Mr Wilson was just unlocking the door.

'Good morning, Mr Wilson. How are you

today?'

He turned the key in the lock and swung the door open, standing aside to appraise her.

'Good morning to you, Miss Langham. All set for another day in paradise?'

'Certainly am.' She smiled as she skipped through the door.

'You know, already I think you may be wasted, hidden in the back room. With your sunny nature you should be dealing with customers.'

Maggie went through to the back, shrugging out of her coat as she walked. He followed her in so she said,

'Any time you want to give me a try, I'd be more than willing.'

'Maybe next week.'

He threw a bundle of papers on to her desk and hurried through to the front. Maggie sat down at her desk, unable to stop grinning. Heather came through from the kitchen with a cup of tea.

'You won the pools or something? I would have made you a drink if you'd been here a minute ago. I don't know about you, but a cup of tea sets me up for the morning. MyJohn always says you can't beat a cup of tea for setting you up in the morning.'

'It's alright, I'll make my own, thanks.'

Maggie hurried through to the tiny kitchenette, humming. She didn't want to tell Heather about her having a trial with the customers next week in case Heather hadn't been given the same opportunity to advance. Or maybe she wasn't interested. All she seemed to talk about was getting married to 'my John' who appeared to get more boring by the minute. She decided to keep her trap shut until she saw how the land lay. She thought about William. No one could call him boring. Just thinking about him made her smile and her heart do a backward flip.

At dinner time she bought a packet of bourbon biscuits from the grocer's on the High Street, made a cup of tea 'to set herself up' and sat in the empty office reading holiday brochures and any literature she could lay her hands on, stuffing several into her bag to go through at home. She was going to be ready for the next phase of her career.

The day flew by and, as the hands of the clock approached five, everyone started packing up. Heather was out of the door before the clock had finished striking the hour, her paisley headscarf wound tightly round her perm. Jill and Stella came in to get their coats, keeping up their constant stream of chatter.

'Well we could have a room each.'

'Yes but one's a double. It would be a waste and we can't really afford it. Let's keep looking. There might be somewhere cheaper.'

'Or we could get someone else to share and we could take the double. It's so handy for work, we wouldn't even have to catch a bus.'

'Do you know anyone? If we advertised we wouldn't know who we were getting. She could be really untidy and have no end of nasty habits.'

'Look who's talking!'

Their voices and hoots of laughter grew more distant as they went through to the front without saying goodbye to anyone.

'Are they usually that rude?' asked Maggie,

putting on her coat and hat.

'Who? Tweedledum and Tweedledee?' Mr Wilson was turning off the lights.'They live in their own little world, those two. They're alright when you get to know them. They don't mean to be rude. In fact they're perfectly normal when they're on their own and they're both good workers. When they're together no-one else gets a look in. Well, goodnight.'

'Yes, bye.'

Maggie checked she had the brochures in her bag and made her way to the bus stop. She thought of home. If only she could move out. A germ of an idea started to form.

After tea, Theresa put a cup of tea in front of Maggie and said she wanted a word with her. Maggie sat down at the kitchen table. She knew what the subject of conversation was likely to be.

'How's the job going?'

'It's really good. I enjoy working there much more than at the solicitors'. It's a nicer office and there's scope for advancement if I want it. It could be a bit of a career rather than just a job.'

'Is it more money that the last job? How much are you earning?'

'Five pounds ten a week take home pay. Ten shillings a week more than my last job.'

'Well maybe you could pay a bit more towards your keep, then. Let's see, you were giving me two pounds before, do you think two pounds ten is fair? It still leaves you with three pounds a week, which would be plenty for the bits you need to buy for yourself. Gina needs more and more things for that grammar school and my doctor said I need special food to keep my strength up.'

There was a silence while Maggie worked out what she wanted to say.

'It's not as simple as that, Mum.'

'What's not simple?'

'Can you imagine what it's like living in a house with a father who won't talk to you? This has been going on for months now. Will it ever end? I'm sick of it. I'm old enough to move out and that's what I'm planning to do. That is, unless he apologises and starts acting normally.'

Theresa had gone pale and was staring at her, open-mouthed.

'What do you mean, move out? Where do you think you can go? It's not something to do with that boyfriend, is it?'

'Nothing to do with him at all. Two of the girls at work have found a flat they want to share and they need another girl to make it affordable.'

'And how do you think we'll manage without your contribution? The whole family relies on what you bring in. It's not a fortune, I know, but it helps us to make ends meet.' She clutched at her heart. 'My doctor says I'm not to have unnecessary stress. It'll be your fault if I have a heart attack and die and then where would you all be?'

Don't tempt me to answer that question.

'I've already explained, it's not up to me, it's up to Dad. I'm not going to live here any longer than I have to if things don't change. I'll leave it with you to talk to him about it. I'm going up to my room now. And see what I need to pack,' she added for good measure.

Maggie knocked on Gina's door. She could hear Radio Luxembourg playing at low volume. Gina was sitting at the dressing table.

'Do you think my hair would suit me shorter, like this?' She held up the long golden plait.

'Yes, you'd look like a cheeky urchin. How did the French test go?'

'Oh I winged it. Most of the words I revised at breakfast came up.' She turned back from the mirror. 'I could hear raised voices. Have you and Mum been having a bit of a ding dong?'

Maggie went in and sat on the bed, closing the door. She gave Gina a synopsis of their conversation. Gina came and sat beside her, looking worried.

'You're not serious, are you? About moving out? Oh Maggie, I'd hate it if you did that. I can see your point though. This thing with Dad is ridiculous. These girls at work. They hardly know you and you don't know them. Supposing...'

Maggie interrupted her, whispering, 'They haven't actually asked me and to be honest I don't know that I'd enjoy living with them. The boss calls them Tweedledum and Tweedledee. They don't seem to have time for anyone else. They were talking about a third girl to share though. Basically,' and she lowered her voice so it was barely audible and Gina had to shuffle along the bed to hear, 'I'm blackmailing Mum and Dad. If they don't do what I want then I'm pretending I've got an option.'

'You cheeky mare. What happens if they call your bluff?'

'Don't know, I haven't thought that far. I'll

have to play it by ear.'

'Well I thought you said I was brainy but there are certainly no flies on you, big sister.

And I've got to go and revise now. Not French, but holiday brochures. I'm planning to get ahead of the game.'

Chapter 25

There was a tentative knock on the bedroom door.

'Enter at your peril.'

Maggie thought it was Gina coming to find out what she was revising. She looked up from her brochures in surprise. Filling the doorway was her father, clearing his throat and rubbing his hands nervously.

'Dad.' She mouthed the words.

'Can I come in for a minute? You look busy.' His voice was gruff, as though he'd got out of the habit of speaking.

'Of course.' Maggie stared at him. He looked haggard and uncomfortable. The ticking of the clock seemed unnaturally loud as the silence grew.

'How's the job?' he finally managed.

'Oh that. I love it.' She held up the brochures. 'I think I've got the chance of training as a travel agent rather that just be a typist so I'm trying to learn as much as I can.' Stop babbling Maggie.

'Well that's good. Maggie...'

Gina burst into the room. 'Oh sorry. I just came to see.. .' She gulped nervously.

'I'll come back later.'

'No, no.' Alf didn't try to hide his relief. 'I'll leave you two to it.' With that he turned and walked swiftly down the stairs.

'Well you could have knocked me down with a feather,' said Gina leaping on to the bed, which made all the brochures spring into the air and scatter across the floor.

'So are you and Dad best mates now?'

'I'm not sure what happened there. He may or may not have come to apologise but didn't actually say much apart from asking me how the job was going.'

'Oh dear, sorry. I interrupted didn't I?'

'Don't worry, we were both relieved. I think he's made a start and will probably now behave as though none of that horror ever happened. Communication has never been his strong point.'

'Understatement of the year. Do you think your little attempt at blackmail did it?'

'I'm sure of it. I think Mum panicked about me leaving home and the prospect of a bit of a drop in income and so she put in her two pennyworth.'

'So what about you? Will you start speaking to him again?'

'I think so. We couldn't go on like that. It was ludicrous. Gina, do you remember all the times I tested you when you had to revise?'

'Message received and understood.' Gina gathered up the scattered brochures and randomly shuffled through them.

'OK, now let me see. So you work for Capital Holidays. Who started the company?'

'Aubrey Morris.'

'Correct. What is meant by a package holiday?'

'A package holiday is where a tour operator puts together a holiday, flights and transfers, or coach travel, along with a hotel.'

'Word perfect. What's the difference between a tour operator and a travel agent?'

'A travel agent sells the tour operator's holidays to the public.'

'Good, good.' What are the most popular holiday destinations abroad?'

'Now, let me think. Spain, Mallorca, Switzerland, um..'

'Italy, Corsica, Sardinia. I've never heard of the last two.'

'Now let me see. What's a charter flight?'

'No idea I haven't got that far.'

'Better leave you to it then. It looks a lot more interesting and useful than Latin declensions which is what I'm doing. Good about Dad, I think.'

'Yes it's better than nothing, I suppose. Now, charter flights.'

Maggie had never been what anyone would call academic and she was surprised at how interesting and easy it was to absorb the information about the travel industry. She learned about the increasing unpopularity of the British seaside and the thirst for cheap holidays where sunny weather could almost be guaranteed. She discovered that flights abroad had become cheaper and more available but the hotel industry hadn't kept up with the pace. She read about the cost and duration of flights, world climate and popular landmarks. The more she learned, the more excited she became. Not only had she met the man of her dreams, she had also found her career. And, it seemed, her father had at least made a move towards rebuilding bridges between them. She fell asleep dreaming of Paris and Rome and the huge world beyond.

'Yes, I'd like a grandchild as long as you don't expect me to look after it. It would be too much for me these days.'

Theresa was lying in her usual place on the sofa, puffing away at her usual cigarette. 'When's it due?'

'July 25th. It's a nice time to have a baby, when it's warm.'

'And I'll be Auntie Gina. I like the sound of that. What do you think, Auntie Maggie?'

'Sounds very good to me. Congratulations, you two. I'll babysit. I love babies.'

'So do I,' said Auntie Ruby. 'I remember the day Gina was born like it was yesterday. Such a little speck of a thing. I don't how she got such a big brain.'

'I nearly died giving birth to her. I hope you have a better time of it than I did, Caroline.'

Graham put his arm round his wife and patted her shoulder.

'You'll be fine my love. Your mum had a heart problem. You look after yourself.'

Theresa snapped, 'It wasn't a case of not looking after myself. I had rheumatic fever which affected my heart.'

'I didn't mean that,' Graham stammered, 'I just didn't want Caroline worrying about the birth. It's different altogether.' He had gone red.

'There are worse troubles in the sea,' said Auntie Ruby. 'Or do I mean, don't meet your troubles halfway? Piece of Victoria sponge anyone?'

'How do you feel about being a grandad,

Dad?' Caroline turned her attention to Alf who hadn't said a word so far.

'If it's what you want, then it's good news.'

'Of course it's what we want,' said Caroline. 'Isn't it, Graham?'

Graham rubbed his hands together and grinned.

'You bet. We'll be a proper family.'

But Alf hadn't finished.

'All I'm saying is, it's a lot of responsibility, being a parent, and there's no turning back. Best of luck to both of you, although I don't know what you're going to do for money.'

'When debts come in the door, love flies out the window,' added Auntie Ruby darkly, clearing away the plates.

Maggie followed her into the kitchen and shut the door behind her.

'Do you remember me telling you I'd seen Caroline with another man a few months ago?' she whispered.

'How could I forget?' Ruby mouthed. She dropped the plate she was drying and stood to face Maggie, mouth agape.

'You don't think...'

'Your guess is as good as mine, but Graham obviously thinks it's his.'

'Nothing more to be said then. It's a secret that stays between you, me and the gatepost.'

The reception at Graham's parents was a lot more enthusiastic They were over the moon about the prospect of another grandchild. They already had a grandson of two whom the whole family adored. There was much patting on the back of Graham and kissing of Caroline on the cheek, which she not very subtly tried to avoid.

'This calls for a drink,' said his father, fetching bottles of beer from the shed. 'I hoped it wouldn't be too long before we heard the patter of tiny feet.'

He thrust a bottle towards Caroline. 'Can I tempt you? Sorry we've got nothing posher, like Babycham or fizzy wine, but can get you a glass.'

Bottles were opened and bets were placed on whether it would be a boy or a girl. Graham puffed out his chest with pride at his clever, beautiful wife and impending fatherhood.

He was about to open another bottle of beer when Caroline said,

'Can we go home now? I'm feeling a bit tired. Sorry to break up the party.'

Suddenly they were all solicitous, fetching her coat and bag and entreating Graham to look after her and the precious baby. Graham brought the car to the door and helped her in. She hated herself and wondered how she was going to keep up the pretence, but she knew she had no option. The die was cast.

Chapter 26

On the way home from his parents' house, Graham stopped at a newsagent and bought a copy of all of the local papers. He spent the rest of the weekend combing the job sections. He knew he was limited by his lack of qualifications and experience, having left school at fifteen without sitting any O levels or CSEs. The only job he had ever had was working as a porter in the hospital. He became more and more despondent, especially with Caroline asking if he had found anything, every five minutes, it seemed.

'I think I've found something,' he finally told her and read out the advertisement.

Chauffeur required to drive clients to meetings, etc. in central London. No previous experience required as training will be given. Must have a clean driving licence and a willingness to work at any time. Generous basic salary and tips. Uniform provided. Please apply in writing t0 "The manager, Elite Cars Ltd, Tooting Broadway SW 18."

'What do you think, love?'

'It's worth an application. Do you think you'd like a job driving people about?'

'Driving rich people about. It wouldn't be like being a taxi driver. I like driving and I think I'm good with people. Not that different to what I do now, wheeling patients about.' He gave a half laugh to show that he was joking, 'I'd certainly like to give it a go.'

Caroline helped him word his letter of application and checked his spellings and grammar. She read it through and wasn't happy with his handwriting, which was uneven and messy. She said that she would write it for him. It was very important to make a good first impression.

A week later he told his supervisor that he had a dental appointment and attended an interview in Tooting. He wore his wedding suit and impressed the boss with his easygoing manner, enthusiasm and willingness to work irregular hours. The pay was more than he had expected and he would receive tips on top of that.

He and Caroline went out for a meal in Wimbledon to celebrate. Stupidly, she chose a restaurant that she had sometimes visited with David. If the waiter recognised her, he showed no sign as he showed them to their seats, but she immediately began to feel hot and uncomfortable. As the waiter took her coat and pulled out her chair, she glanced up to see David at a table over the other side of the restaurant. He was sitting with a woman she assumed to be Penny. Caroline picked up the menu, holding it in front of her face until Graham said,

'Have you chosen yet? I'm going to have the steak and kidney pie and chips.'

She hadn't even looked at it and knew that she would barely eat anything. He took the menu from her and pointed to the roast lamb.

'What about that? You're always saying how fond you are of lamb.'

'Yes, the lamb, lovely.' She hoped he didn't

hear the tremble in her voice.

He nodded at the waiter who arrived with a notepad. Did she imagine the knowing look on his face?

She glanced across at David while Graham was giving the order, and she had time to appraise his companion. She was very slim and fashionably dressed in a simple apple green shift dress. Her golden hair was stylishly swept up into a sophisticated French pleat, which showed off her small, sparkly diamond earrings. Caroline felt a huge jolt in the pit of her stomach and put her hands protectively over their baby. She felt drab and lumpy in comparison with his petite, bejewelled wife in her elegant clothes. He suddenly caught sight of her and half raised his arm in recognition then immediately dropped it. She could see a flush suffuse his face.

'Who's that?' Graham asked, tucking his napkin into the collar of his shirt. 'I don't think you heard a word I said, so I ordered peas, roast potatoes and carrots with the lamb. Are you alright? You look a bit queer.' K8

'I'm fine. Tired.'

She wished he wouldn't tuck his napkin into his shirt collar. It was so common.

'You were staring at that man over there. Is it someone you know?'

'No-one, really. A doctor from work. Don't you recognise him?'

'Oh yes, vaguely. His wife's a bit of a stunner.'

He looked embarrassed and quickly amended it to,

'Nowhere near as beautiful as you, though. You'd look much better than her if you had her expensive clothes and hairstyle.'

She smiled at this back handed comment through gritted teeth and quickly changed the subject.

'So are you excited about your new job?'

'Well, I'm on three month's probation, don't forget. I've got to memorise the map of central London and show I can get from A to B in the shortest possible time and show that I can talk to customers in a professional manner.'

'Well you were always good at sweet talking patients. You get on with everyone.'

She was aware of David, looking across at them, his expression unreadable. She smiled at Graham, taking his hand in hers.

'We'll buy an A to Z and you could learn a section every night and I could test you.'

He put his hand over hers and leaned across the table to give her a kiss. She looked up to see David helping on with her coat. He glanced at her briefly and she saw a grim expression on his face, set like granite. As the door closed behind them she felt as though someone had switched off the light. A soundless sob escaped from her. The forkful of lamb she had just put into her mouth felt and tasted like cardboard.

Chapter 27

It was Friday. Mr Wilson came into the back office to give Maggie and Heather their wage packets.

'Check them now because once I walk away I can't do anything about it if the amount's wrong.'

Maggie counted the notes. 'I didn't realised you paid me for a job I really enjoy,' she said, smiling, then thought perhaps it sounded like she was crawling.

'Well, we make sure you earn your money here. We like to get our pound of flesh. On that subject, you'll find you'll be working harder next week. You'll be having your trial in the front for one hour every day, but I expect you to do your job here as well.'

'That shouldn't be a problem,' said Maggie. 'Now that I've found my feet with the work here I should be more efficient. Which hour will I do?'

'I can't say at the moment. We'll see where we can fit you in.'

When he had left, Heather asked coldly, 'So what's all that about? Are you working with the customers already? I've never been asked if I wanted to work on the shop floor.'

"Have you ever asked if you could?"

'Did you?' Heather looked aggrieved.

'Yes,' Maggie lied, 'it looks really interesting and I thought I'd like to have a go.'

'Hmph. There's not much point now. I'll be

leaving in May, as soon as I get married. MyJohn says a woman's place is in the home. He doesn't expect me to have a career. Mine will be to look after him and the family we hope to start soon.'

'Well you're very lucky,' said Maggie kindly, thinking exactly the opposite. The thought of spending one's life with Boring John was the last thing she'd choose for herself.

'Anyway, I might not be suitable. It's only a trial.'

'Well as long as I don't have to do your work as well as mine. I have quite enough to do as it is, thank you. And it's early days. You might not be up to it yet.'

'Of course. That's why it's a trial. And you heard what Mr Wilson said about me doing my own work as well.'

Maggie was getting fed up with trying to be nice to Heather. It wasn't her fault if Mr Wilson didn't think Heather was cut out for dealing with the public. She tended to agree with him.

Maggie combed her dark curls and adjusted the red spotted neckerchief in the mirror in the staff cloakroom. She swivelled the knot round so it was was on the right hand side, as she had seen Jill and Stella do. The borrowed blue and red uniform hung off her slight frame, but she thought she looked very professional. The girls smiled a welcome as she nervously came through to the front of the shop. Mr Wilson showed her to her work station behind the counter and pulled out several drawers containing holiday brochures and forms, explaining what they were for. She had her own telephone, a scribble pad and a jar of pens and pencils. She felt nervous but excited as she lowered herself into the office chair on wheels.

'I've put you next to Stella. Today I just want you to watch closely how she deals with the clients. You'll see that first of all you ask them if they have already chosen a destination and if not, you ask them what they would like from a holiday. Then you tell them their options. You can advise and recommend but the ultimate choice is theirs. It's not your responsibility to tell them where to go.'

Maggie had only seen Stella and Jill nattering nineteen to the dozen like a couple of schoolgirls. She was surprised to find that, with clients, Stella was the ultimate professional, smoothly guiding a couple along a path until they had found exactly what they wanted. She made phone calls with one hand and filled in forms with the other. The couple, bearing a brochure, a receipt and satisfied smiles, left the shop with a spring in their step. Stella turned to Maggie.

'So that's how it's done. Just by asking the right questions you get a good idea of what people want even if they don't always know themselves when they walk in the door. You're selling dreams.'

'I like the idea of selling dreams,' Maggie smiled. 'You're really good at it. Does it take long to train?'

'Depends on your aptitude and attitude,' replied Stella. 'We'll know that when you've tried a few yourself. The business is expanding and Mr Wilson was talking about advertising for another member of the sales team.'

'Well, if I play my cards right he might be looking for another typist instead, or two when Heather goes.'

'How are you getting on with her?'

'Oh, OK I suppose.'

'She's not exactly a little ray of sunshine, and if you think she's dull, you should meet John.'

'Oh, I thought he was called, "MyJohn." He seems to have a lot of opinions.'

Stella laughed. 'You'll get on with me and Jill. I hope you get the job.'

'Me too. Did you two get the flat? Sorry, I'm being nosey, I overheard you saying you were hoping to share digs with Jill.'

'Nothing's been signed. It's a bit too expensive really. It wouldn't leave us much to spend on ourselves and groceries and the like. We really need to find a third person to share. We don't want any old person. It would have to be someone fun who we both get on with. Look, are you free to go for a drink with us after work, just the three of us, I mean?'

Maggie wasn't seeing William that evening and she was quite keen to get to know her workmates.

'I'll have to ring my mum. She gets het up if I don't let her know if I'm not in for tea.'

'If you lived in a flat you wouldn't be answerable to anyone. Listen,' Stella looked furtively round to check that Mr Wilson was in his office. 'if you're quick you can use the office phone while we don't have any clients.'

Maggie spoke to her mother, who did a bit of sighing but thanked her for letting her know before she had put the fish fingers on.

Heather heard Stella tell Jill about the pub visit and hissed at Maggie when she went to retrieve her coat, 'I see you're thick as thieves already with those two.'

Maggie decided to ignore her. She was sick of pretending to be nice. Heather was becoming quite insufferable.

Jill bought a round of port and lemons and after the second, bought by Maggie, it was as if they had known each other forever. As women tend to do, in the space of an hour they had swapped life histories. Jill was twenty two and Stella twenty three. They each had a boy friend. but nothing serious. She told them about her relationship with William and, after the third port and lemon, she found herself talking about her family, particularly about her father. They were both horrified.

'I don't know how you could bear to be around him,' said Stella. 'They sound really strict, your parents. He sounds a bully and she sounds like a controlling hypochondriac. So you have an older sister who's pregnant and a younger sister who's a complete brainbox, but you still manage to get on with her.'

'Cheeky mare, thash the reason I shtay. Can't leave her wiv 'em,' slurred Maggie. 'Not fair.'

'God, I can tell you're not used to alcohol. Better have a black coffee in the caff up the road and then we'll walk you to the bus stop. Come on.' Jill pulled her up and linked her arm.' We're a bad influence. I hope you don't get into trouble.'

Jill bought them all a coffee.

'I shpect I'll be right by the time I get home. Fresh air. Had lovely time. Good friendsh.'

They marched her to the bus stop and stood with her until the bus came.

'Now get off at the right stop and get home safely. Do you want us to come with you.'

'I'm not six,' retorted Maggie, falling unsteadily onto the bus, helped by the two girls, who unceremoniously pushed her on.

She managed to fumble in her purse and randomly give a handful of coppers to the bus conductor who gave her a filthy look, shaking his head disapprovingly. He counted out the fare, thrusting the change back into her hand.

'You need to be careful, missy.'

She couldn't reply as her head was spinning.

'Where do you want to get off?'

She attempted to tell him and he helpfully escorted her off when it was her stop. She wasn't too drunk to realise that she'd be in deep trouble if she went home in the state she was in. She decided to go instead to her grandparents' house. Mary, her grandmother, was never judgemental, and George didn't do much but puff at his pipe and grunt.

'Oh Jesus and all his holy angels! You do look in a state, Maggie.'

Mary, who had lived in England since she was fourteen but still had more than a trace of an Irish accent, held the door open for her. 'What on earth has happened to you? You look as though you've been dragged through a hedge backwards.'

'Hello Grandma, Grandad.'

He grunted a hello which turned into a fit of

coughing. She slumped into the nearest armchair.

'Sorry about this. I went out with the girls at work in my new job. We went to a pub. I'm not used to drinking. I can't go home like this. Sorry. Sorry.'

'Easy done. You weren't to know. I'll make you a nice cup of tea and you can have a little lie down. You go up and rest on the spare bed. I'll bring it up.'

When Mary brought up the tea she found Maggie snoring on top of the bed, her mouth open. She took off her shoes and threw a woollen blanket over her. Taking the tea back down again she put it on the table and slipped on her coat.

'George, I'm away over to the phone box to ring Theresa. Would you like the tea?'

'Hello Ruby. Just tell Theresa that I've got Maggie here. She dropped in for an unexpected visit and she's crippled with period pains. I've put her to bed with a hot water bottle on her tummy. Yes I'll see how she is in the morning.' She put the phone down and raised her eyes to heaven. 'Sorry, Lord, I told a little white lie. But it'll save a lot of fuss. Least said soonest mended.'

The following morning Maggie came down to breakfast, holding her head. Mary had put two aspirins next to a cup of tea.

'How are you feeling? Drink the tea and take the aspirins. Can you manage a bit of toast?'

'I'm not too bad really. I'll have some toast thanks. I've got to go into work. I daren't have a day off in my second week. Does Mum know I'm here?'

'I spoke to Ruby last night and said you had

bad period pains and I'd put you to bed.'

'You're the best. I've certainly learned my lesson. What are you two up to today?'

'I'm doing some baking and your grandad says he's going to mend the shed roof. Water gets in every time in rains and his tools are getting rusty.'

'What are you doing mending shed roofs, Grandad? You're eighty six. Dad could do it.'

'And so can I. I'm not in my box yet.'

'Stubborn as they come. It'll be the death of you.'

Maggie was gathering her things together.

'Better rush.' She kissed her grandmother's soft, papery cheek.

'Thanks Gran, I love you. You be careful, Grandad.'

But he was busy scouring his pipe with a pipe cleaner.

Chapter 28

Caroline heard Graham's tread on the stairs. He used to trudge wearily up the two flights after a day at the hospital, but now she opened the door of their flat to see him taking the stairs two at a time. He strode through the door, sweeping off his chauffeur's cap in an exaggerated gesture and executed a deep bow. It was the first time she had seen him in his uniform.

'You do look very smart and handsome. How was your first day?'

'Have a look out the window,' he said excitedly.

She looked out of the attic window down to the street below. A large shiny car was parked outside the house.

'Is that a Rolls?' she gasped.

'Certainly is. I've got a pick up at 5am so they let me bring it home.'

'I bet it's a dream to drive. So have you done many trips today?'

'Only one. I picked up a businessman from the airport and took him to The Savoy. I spent most of the day finding my way around the cars, getting my uniform, talking to the boss and stuff. He tested me on the London routes and seemed quite impressed with my knowledge. All that learning and you testing me really paid off. What's for tea?'

'Lamb chops, peas and mash. Why?'

'After we've eaten do you want a short spin

in the Rolls round Wimbledon?'

'Can we? Do you think you should?'

'A short trip won't hurt.'

'Keep your uniform on then. I can pretend I'm rich.' She laughed.

He laughed with her. It was so long since they had done that, in fact, he couldn't remember the last time.

'OK I'll even wear the cap and you can sit in the back like Lady Muck.'

He was delighted that she was so excited. Things hadn't been going too well between them for some time now. All he wanted in life was to make her happy.

She put on a smart outfit, including a rather worn fur coat that she had found in a second hand shop. She arranged herself elegantly on the spacious back seat that smelled of leather polish, and looked through the gleaming windows. Graham took his place in the driver's seat and the Rolls purred away from the kerb.

'Where to, madame?'

'Uh, better not drive far. They might see the extra mileage. Let's just cruise round here.'

He drove up and down the streets. Pedestrians stopped to stare, trying to get a glimpse of the fur coated lady in the back. Some of the houses were quite grand but there were no Rolls parked outside. A man and a boy were playing football in a large garden. With a jolt she saw it was David playing with his son. He was totally absorbed in the game, oblivious to the sleek limousine that was gliding past, oblivious to the woman carrying his child sitting, now hunched, on the back seat.

'Let's go back,' she said, dully. Her excitement at the ride, at Graham's happiness in his new job, had quickly dissipated. All she could feel was her loss, and disbelief that David's life could just carry on as though nothing had happened.

'Aren't you feeling well?' Graham was solicitous.

'No, I feel a bit sick. I think I ate my dinner too quickly. If you don't mind I think I'll have a little lie down. Sorry. The car's lovely. Perhaps we can do it another time.'

When they went into the hall, Mrs Thomas came out of her living room.

'Oh hello. I just need a few words.' Caroline knew what was coming. 'Sorry to have to ask this, but are you expecting a baby?'

'Yes,' said Caroline. 'Is it a problem?'

Mrs Thomas shifted from one foot to the other.

'You are ideal tenants but I'm afraid the flat isn't suitable for a baby. They'll be a pram and the crying and everything. Sorry.'

Caroline looked at Graham who was biting his lip. He knew there was no point trying to sweet talk her. They couldn't promise that the baby would be quiet.

'We'll look for another place straight away,' she said, and, fighting back the tears, hauled herself up the stairs. Things couldn't get much worse.

Graham closed the door and took Caroline in his arms.

'We'll find somewhere. She's right, you can't

lift a pram up the stairs and she wouldn't want it left in the hall.'

'I know, but it's our home. You painted it and we chose the pictures and ornaments. I love my blue and white kitchen and I love this street. The houses are so elegant.'

'We'll find somewhere better,' he said with a confidence he didn't feel. We'll move out of Wimbledon, somewhere with green space for our baby to play. We could put our name down for one of those nice new council houses in Clayton Park. They've got big gardens. I'll put our names down tomorrow,'

Caroline lay down on their bed and wept.

Chapter 29

When Maggie arrived home the following evening no-one asked her about her staying the night at her grandparents' house, or supposed period pains, because something far worse had happened. Theresa had gone to Clayton Hospital with Mary. Ruby told her that George had climbed a ladder on to the shed roof, which had collapsed. Mary had found him with most of the roof on top of him and had called an ambulance.

'What a daft old codger he is, thinking he can climb on the shed roof at eighty six. What does it matter if the rain comes in and his tools go rusty? He's not going to be using them much longer. I don't think he broke any bones.'

'I suppose no one's phoned to say how he is?' asked Maggie taking off her coat. 'I'm starving. Is it awful to think about food?'

'Course not. We've still got to eat. Life goes on and marches on its stomach. I've made a casserole with a bit of scrag end. I expect you'll want yours now.'

'Lovely. Are you having some?'

'You bet. Can't beat a nice bit of lamb on the bone. I've done mash and swede to soak up the gravy. Your mum had a phone call from Caroline today. She and Graham are coming over tomorrow. Looks like they're having to leave that flat in Wimbledon. The landlady says it's not suitable for a baby. Talking about putting their names down for a council house.

'Lady Caroline won't like that. She'd have to live amongst the common folk', said Maggie. 'I don't suppose the common folk would like her much either.'

'You don't like your sister much, do you?'

'It works both ways. She doesn't much like me. There's never been any love lost there. It's the way it is. Where's Gina, the light of my life?'

'Gone to Jane's house, she says, to do her homework.'

'Well she probably is. Jane's a swot even if Gina isn't. That was lovely, thanks, Auntie Ruby. I'd offer to wash up but I'm meeting William tonight. We're going to the pictures.'

'How's it going with William. When are you going to bring him home to meet the family?'

'I want to keep him as a boyfriend, thanks. It'd be the kiss of death bringing him here.'

'Get on with you. But I can see your point.'

'I feel bad going out enjoying myself with them all at the hospital. Do you think I should go there instead?' Maggie paced up and down, She could meet William and tell him she couldn't go to the pictures.

'You can't do anything. Go to the pictures and we might know more when you get back.'

William was waiting for her outside the Odeon. As they queued for their tickets, she briefly told him what had happened.

'I can understand your concern. What can you do if you go to the hospital? They'll be doing tests and I doubt whether they'll be much news tonight. But if you think you should go and support your family then I'll drive you.'

Maggie suspected she was being selfish, but she was going to go to the pictures. She decided that Auntie Ruby and William were right, she couldn't help by going to the hospital. She'd only be doing it to make herself feel better and to avoid criticism. She decided these weren't valid reasons. William put his arm round her and she put her head on his shoulder and tried to concentrate on the film. As soon as it was finished she jumped up and started to make her way to the exit before the National Anthem, William not far behind. One or two people tutted as they stood back to let them pass. William left her at the gate but didn't go in with her. He kissed her briefly.

'I hope he's OK. I'll ring you tomorrow.'

She hurried into the house.

'You know Grandad has had a serious accident?' Theresa glared at Maggie as though it was her fault.

'How is he?'

'Lots of bruises, nothing broken, but they're keeping him in because they're worried about internal injuries. And his age is very much against him.'

Alf was boiling a kettle and Theresa was looking in the larder.

'There's a bit of stew but it would take too long to heat up. I think I fancy a ham sandwich. Do you want one Alf?'

He nodded as he poured the water into the teapot.

'I didn't come to the hospital because I thought there was nothing I could do and I'd only get in the way.' Maggie's voice was defensive. 'I'll visit him after work tomorrow. I take it he's in Clayton General. Will he need me to bring anything in?' Now she was eager to please, to make amends.

'That would be a good idea,' Theresa said, starting to make the sandwiches. It always fascinated Maggie that her mother buttered the loaf before slicing it, standing the loaf on its end.

'He'll need pyjamas and toiletries but expect Gran will be seeing him again tomorrow. Ruby's gone back to the the house with your gran to make sure she's OK.'

'How did he seem?'

'Hard to tell,' said Theresa, her mouth full. 'He doesn't say much at the best of times.'

The harassed nurse showed Maggie to the geriatric ward, where George lay pale and inert. There was a sharp smell of carbolic that didn't quite mask the smells of urine, and dinners that had been kept warm for too long.

'Hello, Grandad,' she brushed his rough, unshaven face with her lips. He had cuts and bruises and a black eye

'Fetch me my pipe,' he growled.

'I don't think you're allowed your pipe in here. Are you feeling sore?'

'Pain everywhere. Where's Mary?' He started a bout of coughing and was struggling for breath. 'Help me sit up,' he wheezed.

She felt scared and helpless as he continued to cough and fight for breath. A nurse came bustling in, her shoes squeaking on the wooden floor. She gently pushed Maggie to the side.

'Come on, let's have you sitting up, it'll be easier to get your breath. That's it, breathe nice and slow, in, out, in, out. There, that's better.'

She could have been speaking to a six year old.

The racking cough mercifully stopped and her grandfather lay slumped against the white pillows, utterly exhausted. He looked at her with his faded blue eyes. She had seen pictures of him when he was a young man. He had been very handsome, with his fair hair, neat beard and twinkling eyes, which had apparently been turquoise. Mary had been a slip of a thing with curly red hair, an elfin face and a cheeky smile. They must have made an attractive couple. He was fourteen years older than her grandmother but she had definitely ruled the roost. Mary had told her stories of the tricks he used to play on people, of his disarming way with women that had made him irresistible, when he was the life and soul of every party. The Great War had changed all that. The shell shock had made him silent and morose, but Mary had stuck by him. It can't have been easy for her. Maggie looked down at the grey shell of a man in the narrow bed. Life could be so cruel to some people. It was just as well you couldn't look into the future. She wondered what was in store for her and William. Would they get married and have children? She didn't want a future without him. Her grandmother must have felt for Granddad what she felt for William.

George had drifted off to sleep, his life behind him.

Chapter 30

When Maggie arrived home the next day, they were all sitting at the table apart from Alf, who was leaning against the wall, smoking a cigarette. Auntie Ruby, red faced, was taking roast potatoes out of the oven, while Theresa was carving a chicken. They didn't usually have a roast on a weekday but then she saw that Caroline and Graham were there.

'Hello you two. How are you?' she asked.

'Oh you know, not so bad, but we've got a bit of worrying news.'

'Later, Graham. How's Granddad?' Caroline glared at him.

'I've just come from the hospital,' said Maggie, hanging up her coat. 'He looks awful and he had a terrible bout of coughing while I was there. Couldn't get his breath.'

'It's that pipe,' said Alf, stubbing out his cigarette. 'He's never without it.'

'Did you see a doctor for any results? Who wants leg and who wants breast?' asked Theresa putting some chicken on each plate.

'I'll have whatever anyone else doesn't want although I always think the dark meat has more flavour,' said Auntie Ruby, dishing out the steaming, golden potatoes.

'No,' Maggie replied, 'but they were just about to take him in for an x ray. Maybe we'll know more tomorrow. So what's your worrying news? It's not the baby is it?'

'No, the baby's fine,' said Caroline, stroking her swelling stomach. 'Mrs Turnbull wants us out. She says the flat's not suitable for a baby. I don't think she wants to listen to it crying.'

'She's got a point, though. You can't get a pram up all those stairs and she's never going to let us leave it in the hall. I said we should put our name down for a council house. There's been a bit of building round here lately.' Graham was eating his roast dinner with relish. 'New estates going up all the time.'

'That'd be nice, said Auntie Ruby. 'Everything nice and new, and handy for babysitting. How long would you need to be on the waiting list? Or is the answer, '"How long's a piece of rope?"'

'That's a question,' said Gina, reaching for a plate, 'and the expression's, " How long is a piece of string?"'

'String, rope, what's the difference?' countered Auntie Ruby good naturedly. 'Pass the redcurrant, will you?'

'So what will you do, meanwhile?' Alf sat down and took a plate. 'You've got to live somewhere.'

'That's the problem,' said Graham.

'You could stay here for a bit,' said Theresa. 'Gina could go in with Auntie Ruby in the attic and you and Graham could have the room you used to share with Maggie. You'd get a small cot in there and your rent would help us out. The pram could go in the shed.'

'I need my own bedroom to do my

homework.' Gina's voice was verging on a whine. 'So Maggie gets my room. Why can't Maggie share with Auntie Ruby?'

'Well I won't stop you doing your homework,' said Auntie Ruby. 'I only sleep in my room. You can have it to yourself all evening. Your big radiogram won't fit but we could get you one of those transvestite radios.'

Gina forgot her annoyance and laughed so hard she nearly fell off her chair and Maggie spluttered gravy all over the table.

'That's brilliant, Auntie Ruby,' Maggie managed. 'It'll always be a transvestite radio from now on.'

'Well, I'm glad I amuse you. It'll be a bit cramped with all of us in this small cottage, six by my reckoning. I think Theresa's right. Maggie should have a room on her own. She's a young lady now.'

'Seven,' said Gina, 'I expect you forgot to count yourself.'

'You can see why Gina got to the grammar school,' commented Maggie. 'Any more roasties Auntie Ruby? You can cook even if you can't count.'

'Cheeky,' said Auntie Ruby. 'It's easier to count people when you can see them.'

'Well if everyone's OK with it, it would certainly get us out of a hole. But I don't know how long it would be for. We might be on the waiting list for years.'

'If you go down to the council offices and say you're living in a cramped cottage with six other people and a baby, they'll bump you up the list. And if not, then it will give you a bit of breathing space to fine another rented place if you stay here.' Theresa was reaching for more potatoes.

'Are you sure you all don't mind?' Caroline was tearful, absent mindedly rubbing the swelling in her stomach with a circular motion.

'Let's see how it goes,' said Theresa. 'If it doesn't work we'll have to think of something else. Are we ready for pudding?'

Auntie Ruby went to the stove and lifted what looked like a mis-shapen sausage, fashioned out of grey material, from a large pot. She carefully unwrapped it and it flopped on to a chopping board.

'I've made a nice Spotted Dick,' she said, carving it into thick, steaming slices and pouring custard into a jug. 'This'll put hairs on your chest.'

After tea had been cleared away, Maggie left Alf and Theresa to their cups of tea and cigarettes and knocked on Gina's door.

'Can I come in?' she asked, without waiting for an answer, and sank onto the bed with a sigh.

'So what do you think of the latest turn of events? I know this is really unchristian but imagine having Caroline back living with us again.'

Gina threw the heavy textbook on to her desk with a bang.

'I'm thinking the same. Then there's Graham and then there's the mewling, puking infant in its mother's arms, who will probably scream round the clock. How on earth are we all going to fit into this cottage? I'm planning to run away.'

'I think I'll come with you,' Maggie laughed. 'You know I told Mum that some girls at work had asked me if I'd like to share a flat with them. Well at the time I was just using it as a lever to get Mum to make Dad start talking to me again. Now I'm actually thinking of doing it. Where's mewling, puking infant from or did you make it up? I love it.'

'It was William Shakespeare,' Gina replied, retrieving *The Complete Works* and waving it at Maggie.

'Well, wasn't he good with words?'

'Please don't leave me. You're my only ally in this house. It'll be purgatory if you move out. Oh I wish I was old enough to get a flat as well. I don't think I could stand it. Can't we get a flat together?'

'And how are you planning to pay your half of the rent?'

'A detail I'll have to give further thought to. Mind you, the plus about your moving out is that I can keep this room.'

'Well, every coat has a silver lining, as Auntie Ruby would say. I'd better leave you to your Shakespeare. I've got to study holiday brochures.'

Chapter 31

When Graham came home from work there was no smell of cooking coming from the kitchen. His stomach was rumbling.

'Caroline? Is something the matter?'

She was kneeling on the floor in the living room, packing books into a cardboard box.

When she looked up he saw that her eyes were red.

'What's wrong love? What's happened?'

'Mrs Turnbull wants us out by the end of the month, which is only two weeks away. She's got someone lined up for our flat.'

'Well she can't do that. She has to give us a month's notice.'

'I know. I let slip that we were moving in with my parents so she said in that case it wouldn't really matter when we moved. If we gave her a month's notice we'd have to pay for another whole month. She banged another book into the box. 'So we might as well go at the end of this month. She's right. What difference will it make?' she added hopelessly.

'Well we'll go down the council offices tomorrow and get our names down. We could tell them we've been evicted.'

When Caroline started crying again he sat next to her and took her in his arms.

'Imagine a lovely new house with a garden. You wouldn't have all those stairs to climb or worry about the baby making a noise. And we'd have our own front door. Imagine that. And there'll be other young parents around and we might make some nice friends.' He looked around the room. 'It would be so much better than this.'

She knew he was right. They couldn't stay here, even if it were possible. A council house wasn't what she wanted but it was all they'd be able to afford. She thought of David and his wife in their elegant Victorian three storey house in a tree lined street. She would never have that. She looked at Graham and knew, deep down, she should think herself lucky.

'I expect you're hungry.' Her voice was soft.

'Starving. I could eat a horse sandwiched between two bread vans. Shall I nip down the road and get us fish and chips? We deserve a treat.'

'If you like,' she replied. 'I'll go and warm some plates.'

'We could eat them out of the newspaper with our fingers. Or perhaps not,' he amended, when he saw the look on her face.

After they had eaten and the plates were washed, Caroline suggested they went to see her parents to make arrangements for the move. Now that it was inevitable, she wanted to get on with it.

Maggie answered the door.

'Mum and Dad are at the hospital with Granny. Visiting's over at eight if you want to wait.'

They followed Maggie into the kitchen where Auntie Ruby had the chairs up on the table while she washed the floor.

'Hello,' she said. 'We didn't expect you tonight. Go and sit down and I'll make some tea, Everything alright?'

'Not really. We've got to be out in two weeks so I was going to talk to Mum and Dad about the move.'

'Well it never rains when it pours. You two homeless and your poor grandad in the hospital.'

'How is he?'

'Grumpy. But that's nothing new. I think they're doing some tests on his chest. He can't get his breath.'

'Well he's had his three score years and ten,' said Caroline thoughtlessly, ignoring Maggie's glare.

Your poor granny's worried sick. What the silly old bugger was doing on the shed roof, I'll never know. He's no spring chicken. When he gets home she'll need some help nursing him I expect. Where that's going to come from I've no idea.'

'I could help,' said Maggie. 'They've got a spare bedroom. I could go and live there and help look after him until he's better, That would make more room for you and Graham. I take it your moving in is only temporary.'

'We're going to put our names down for one of those nice new council houses they've just finished building in Clayton Park, aren't we darling?' Graham said brightly, smiling at his wife.

'I suppose so,' she said. 'I don't see what else we can do.'

'You know, that's not a bad idea, Maggie.' Auntie Ruby said. 'Graham and Caroline could have your room and the rest of us could stay where we are.'

Maggie was beginning to regret her impetuosity. If she was going to help look after grandad, how was she going to go to work, let alone see William?

'I'll have to think about how it would work,' she said, heedlessly spooning sugar into her cup.

'I could pop in during the day while you're at work,' Ruby said pouring a cup for herself. 'We could all do our bit.'

Highly unlikely, thought Maggie. Theresa would claim her doctor said she shouldn't exert herself, Gina would have too much homework, and as for Alf, well, she couldn't see him being much help. He barely lifted a finger in the house. That was women's work. The best part though was that she wouldn't have to live in the same house as him or Caroline.

The front door banged and Theresa and Alf burst into the room.

They all looked up expectantly.

'How is he?' asked Auntie Ruby.

'Not at all well,' said Theresa. 'It looks like he's got lung cancer and it's inoperable. Its a shock. I need a cigarette.'

Alf shook his own cigarette from the packet in his pocket and lit it with nicotine stained fingers. He took a deep drag and cleared his throat.

'They're not giving him any treatment at all apart from what they can do to keep him comfortable and they're discharging him at the end of the week.'

'Oh dear. That's terrible news. How's your mum taking it?' asked Ruby, putting the kettle on and taking cups and saucers from the dresser.

'She seems to be taking it surprisingly well,' answered Theresa, 'but knowing her she's putting on a brave face for Dad. I don't know how she's going to manage. I wish I could do more to help but I'm limited, what with my heart.'

'I wondered about moving in with K11 Gran and helping out and Auntie Ruby said she could help Granny during the day.' Maggie was pouring the tea into cups. 'It would mean Caroline and Graham could have my room.'

'That's a good idea,' said Theresa, tapping her cigarette into her saucer. 'Good idea all round. Don't you think so Alf?'

'Certainly solves a few problems. Do you think you could nurse a dying man, Maggie? It might be upsetting.'

Maggie was becoming less sure by the minute, but knew she had now backed herself into a corner. She wasn't as attached to her grandad as she was to her gran but she dreaded the thought of him dying on her.

'I s'pose so. It seems the best plan.'

'Thanks, Maggie, you're a good daughter, isn't she Alf?'

Alf nodded. 'Not afraid of sticking your neck out and doing something that not many people would offer to do. I'm proud of you.'

Maggie could feel the tears pricking her eyes. For once she seemed to be doing the right thing.

'I'll go and see Gran tomorrow and see if it's alright with her.'

'Well I can help, too,' put in Caroline briskly, resenting Maggie being in the limelight. 'As long as I don't have to do any heavy lifting,' she added, cradling her stomach.

'Well I could do the heavy lifting,' put in Graham, always eager to help.

'And I could drop in after school and see if they need any shopping or anything,' said Gina.

'That's good. If we all do our bit, we'll get through this,' said Theresa. 'Let's see what your gran thinks about it and then we can make plans. Is that alright with you two?' asked Theresa, looking at Caroline and Graham.

'Of course,' said Graham. 'Let us know what's happening when you've talked to Gran. Are you ready to go Caroline?'

Caroline was already putting her coat on.

'Give Granny our love,' she said, 'and tell her how sorry we are. I'll look in on him in my lunch hour. And thanks, Maggie.'

Maggie smiled and nodded, pondering on the fact that it took an imminent death in the family to make them pull together for once.

Chapter 32

Mary called round the next evening after her visit to the hospital. There were black rings under her eyes and the lines between them had deepened. Her voice sounded tired and defeated.

'Maggie, It would be really helpful if you came to stay, if it's not an inconvenience. Sure, I'd be glad of the company. George is being discharged on Friday so do you want to bring your things over before then? I'll have the spare room all ready for you. I don't know whether the fall from the shed roof made it worse or whether it was bound to happen anyway. I always told him that smelly old pipe would be the death of him but he just told me to stop fussing. He didn't have many pleasures, so what could I say? Well, I'd better get off. There's still such a lot to do.'

'Poor Mary,' said Ruby after she'd gone. 'He doesn't say much, apart from grunting and groaning but she'll really miss him.'

'I know,' agreed Theresa. reaching for the last biscuit to go with the inevitable cup of tea, 'they've known each other since she was fourteen. Imagine that.'

'It's a lifetime', replied Maggie. 'l'll go up and see him tomorrow after work. Does he know he's dying?'

'No, I don't think so,' replied Theresa. 'What's the point in spoiling the time he's got left?'

'I see what you mean,' said Maggie, 'but doesn't he need time to sort his affairs, write his will and all that?'

'It sounds like you picked up a thing or two in that solicitors. Our sort of people don't write wills and sort their affairs. Anyway they've always lived hand to mouth. A bit like us,' she said looking pointedly at Alf.

'I've always made sure there was food on the table for my family,' snapped Alf. 'Talking of which, I need to sort the potting shed.'

So much for family harmony. That was short-lived, thought Maggie.

'Well, I'm off to start packing my things. I take it I'll be giving money to Gran to pay for my keep, rather than to you.'

Theresa looked up, worried, then her face relaxed into a smile.

'Yes. We'll have board and lodging from Caroline and Graham. It'll help us out and be a lot cheaper for them than that flat.'

Maggie managed to get most of her possessions in a small, dusty, cardboard suitcase that she took down from the top of the wardrobe. The room, where she had slept for most of her life, looked shabby and bare. On the bed lay the black pencil skirt and red blouse she was going to wear to work the next day, which would be smart enough to wear in the evening. She and William were going to see West Side Story. Heather at work had said it was the best musical she'd ever seen. She was always humming, 'Tonight' and 'I Feel Pretty' under her breath in the office. They could do a duet after she'd seen it as well, she thought wryly.

Meeting William after work, she told him about Grandad and how she was going to live with her grandparents for the time being.

'I'd be glad to help, when I can. What a sad time for all of you. He must be a bit of a character to attempt to mend a shed roof at eighty six.'

'He's a stubborn old soldier. Doesn't like to be defeated and they couldn't afford to get someone in to do it. He loved his garden. He used to grow all sorts of things, including vegetables and fruit. My gran got him interested after he got shell shocked in The First World War and it became a lifetime hobby. I remember going round and Granny giving me a bowl of redcurrants with sugar and top of the milk. I can still taste them now.'

He smiled at her and squeezed her hand.

'Lovely memories. Talking about food, let's find somewhere to eat before the pictures.'

They found a quiet restaurant where they ordered a quick snack of Welsh rarebit so that they would have plenty of time to get good seats for the film.

On the way home they walked by the river, singing snippets of the catchy tunes from West Side Story. The evening was mild and the sharp, fresh green smell of new mown grass filled the air.

As they crossed over the bridge, William told her about the young woman whom he had met a month before in that very spot.

'She was crying. I almost thought she was going to jump.'

'Oh my God, did you persuade her not to?'

'She said she didn't think she would have. I could see she was at the end of her tether, though, so I took her for tea and cake in that little cafe along the High Street and she poured out her problems.'

She waited but it seemed he wasn't going to tell her and she didn't like to ask. Instead, she said, 'So what was she like, this woman?'

'Young, very pretty. I think she just needed someone to talk to.'

Maggie put her hand on his arm, thinking what a lovely person he was.

'Was she OK afterwards?'

'I think so.'

'How awful to be that desperate and feel you have no one to talk to.'

'That's what I thought. I suppose some problems are too embarrassing to talk about with people you know.'

'You ought to think about joining the Samaritans,' she laughed, then her voice became more serious. 'We all have our problems some time or another. I suppose some people are better at dealing with them than others.'

'What would you know, Maggie? You don't appear to have a care in the world. That's what I like about you. Apart from your grandfather, that is.'

If only, she thought, smiling up at him.

'You never talk about your family,' she said. 'I don't even know where you live or whether you have any brothers and sisters.'

'I live in Belbridge. I have a car, but it's so easy on the train, just three stops, so I prefer that. I can read the paper on the way to work. I have an older brother, Bob, who's a doctor and a younger sister called Fiona who's reading modern languages. I get on well with both of them although my brother used to tease me mercilessly when we were young and we hated each other.' He laughed. 'My father is a solicitor, which is how I got into the business. Eventually, I'll be expected to work in the family firm. My mum is a chemistry teacher at Belbridge High and can be a bit bossy, a lot bossy. We're a very ordinary family. I expect you'll meet them before long.'

Maggie's blood ran cold. They sounded far from ordinary, as different from her own family as they possibly could be. She wondered what they would think of her if and when she ever met them. Would they think her good enough for their son? Not a chance. The evening had soured. She looked sideways at William in his well-fitting suit and expensive shoes, and then at herself in her C&A coat and cheap skirt and blouse from the market. He didn't appear to mind, but would they? Should she save up and buy a quality outfit? Should she try to get elocution lessons?

'You've gone very quiet, Maggie. Are you thinking about the girl on the bridge or your grandfather?'

'My grandfather,' she replied miserably, her voice barely a whisper. They were approaching the cottage. She had never been ashamed of her home and family, unlike Caroline, who always gave the impression that she deserved better. But now, with this new knowledge about William's family, she couldn't help putting herself in their shoes. She felt awkward. Would he wonder why she wasn't asking him in? She couldn't keep them apart forever. She felt sick. Should she stop seeing him? It was only going to end in tears. She was sure of it. They had arrived at the door.

Chapter 33

Nearly everything was packed, apart from things that were needed for the next two days. The tea chests, each neatly labelled with a list of contents, were stacked against the living room wall and the flat was beginning to look as it had when they moved in, devoid of all the things that had made it a home. Caroline stood up and rubbed her aching back. She hoped that most of them could be stored in her in-laws' shed until they had their own home, and the rest would have to be squashed into what had been hers and Maggie's bedroom. She sat on on a tea chest and surveyed the flat. She had been happy here when they were first married. It had been their own little haven. Now she wasn't that sorry to leave it, especially with David living just around the corner with his wife and child. His other child.

It was a pity that they had no choice but to live with her parents. Her stomach knotted at the thought. When it had first been suggested, her main thought was the money they would save. Now she pictured what their lives would be like. They'd have to be in the living room with her mum and dad, who sat and smoked themselves to death all day long. The baby would stink of smoke. It wouldn't be able to breathe. They wouldn't be able to breathe. Her mother would lie full length on the sofa so no one else got a look in. Then when the baby was born they'd be even more squashed in and with a crying baby to boot.

What on earth had she been thinking? How had her life got so complicated?

At the back of the wardrobe she found the soft cloth bag. From it she withdrew a crumpled menu, which she unfolded and smoothed with trembling fingers. It was from the first restaurant David had taken her to. She held up the fine silver necklace he had given her, which she had never dared wear, and a clean, ironed handkerchief he had lent her and which she had never returned. She held the handkerchief to her cheek, her throat thick with tears.

She heard the door to the flat slam and then his cheery voice greeting her. Shaking, she pushed the items back into the cloth bag and buried it deep into the nearest box, as Graham burst into the room.

'How's my gorgeous wife?'

'Hello, David,' she said.

'David? Who's David? I've only been away a few hours and you've forgotten my name.' His smile was uncertain.

She reddened. 'I've been listening to the wireless,' she stammered. 'Just turned it off. It was a play with David Niven. I got rid of it as I couldn't concentrate. Look how much I've done. Are you alright with a corned beef sandwich? I've just about packed everything else.' She was talking too fast.

'You alright? Perhaps you're doing too much. Of course a sandwich is fine. I love corned beef. Did you leave out the Branston pickle?'

'It's in the sandwich already, with tomato.' She thought of the bag a few feet away containing her shattered dreams. She sat down opposite him at the kitchen table and cut her sandwich into quarters. He attacked his pile of sandwiches while giving a running commentary about his day at work. She excused herself and wretched into the toilet.

When she came back, he was sitting at the table, his face pale.

'Are you feeling ill, love? Look there's no hurry to finish the packing. You might feel better if you try to eat your sandwich. I'll put the kettle on, then we'll sit on the sofa and make some plans. You're coming back from a day at work and then doing all this.'

'It's finished now,' she said tiredly. She pushed three quarters of the sandwich towards him.

'I've lost my appetite. You eat it. You haven't had much.'

She moved to the sofa and put her feet up. It reminded her of her mother. She took them down again. He made her a cup of tea and sat down beside her.

'I've been thinking about us moving in with my parents. It'll be horrible. I can't face it.'

'Do you want to find another place to rent while we're on the council waiting list?'

'Yes. Tomorrow we'll get all the local newspapers and see what there is and whether we can afford it.'

'Anything's better than living with them.' She started to cry. He shuffled along the sofa and put his arm round her.

'Just think, My pay's a lot better in this new job and I've had some generous tips.'

'I know. That's good, but soon we're going to lose my wage.'

Graham couldn't think of an answer. He was sure something would turn up. As long as he had Caroline he could put up with anything, even her family. He suspected she didn't feel the same about him, even though he would do anything to make her happy. With a deep sigh he switched on the television for her.

'These damned indoor aerials are more trouble than they're worth,' he said raising it towards the ceiling. The picture stopped rolling. 'It would be fine if I just stood here and held it up high like this.' He grinned, but Caroline's face was thunderous. He replaced it on top of the TV, wiggling and adjusting it to no avail.

'That'll do. Just leave it,' Caroline said snappily. The picture was blurry and the sound distorted. 'We might as well pack it, the signal's really poor tonight.'

'Oh it might improve,' said Graham and went into the tiny kitchen to wash the two plates.

The following day, which was a Saturday, they scoured the papers for flats, putting a ring round the ones they thought they could afford. They went across the road to the phone box and rang each number systematically. It was the same story every time. They were sorry but they couldn't accept children. There was just one who said she was happy to offer them some rooms so they made an appointment to view it on the Sunday.

Caroline dressed carefully and told Graham he had to wear his suit. It was important to make a good impression. They were early for the appointment and decided to walk round the area.

'Well it could be worse,' said Graham, trying to hide his disappointment.

'It couldn't,' replied Caroline. 'Look at that rusty old pram in that garden and those overflowing rubbish bins at the back.'

She jumped as a huge dog threw itself against the fence next door, barking loudly.

'Come on, let's go.'

At that moment the door opened and a middle aged woman, wearing a floral overall and head scarf, knotted at the top, was standing on the doorstep, beckoning them.

'You come to view the rooms?'

'Yes, that's right,' said Caroline. 'But...'

'Well don't stand on ceremony. Come on in.'

Caroline looked at Graham, who shrugged.

'We'd better look at it now we're here,' he whispered.

'Scuse the smell of cabbage. It's the Sunday dinner cooking. My Stan always likes his roast of a Sunday.'

She led them through the house which looked in need of a good clean. Two-way Family Favourites was on the wireless. Caroline could see a layer of dust on the skirting board and a heap of old newspapers lying in a corner.

'You'd have the use of the back parlour for your sitting room and bedroom, next to the kitchen. It's what's called a studio these days. You'd have to share the kitchen and bathroom. The bathroom's upstairs but everything else is on the ground floor so you'd be alright with a pram. We could sort out a rota for the shared rooms. Me and Stan keep ourselves to ourselves. This space is a waste now my mother's passed away. These were her private quarters.'

She opened the door to the parlour and ushered them inside. It was a reasonably sized room, furnished mainly with shabby utility furniture. The sofa had been re-covered in a lurid nylon material and there was a winged fireside chair that reminded Caroline of an old people's home. An open fireplace was furnished with a dull brass fender and companion set. Beside the fireplace were alcoves fitted with dark-stained shelves.

'Full of books they was. A great reader my mother.'

These were now empty, apart from two matching table lamps with torn fringes and scorch marks. There was a small double iron bedstead pushed against the wall and in the corner sat, horror of horrors, what looked like a commode. There were stains on the worn floral carpet and, was it her imagination, did the room smell of stale urine? The woman followed Caroline's shocked gaze.

'Oh that, Don't worry, that'll go. My mother couldn't get to the toilet upstairs towards the end.'

Caroline was going to be sick.

'Thank you, Mrs Evans,' she said quickly, 'but it's not really what we're looking for. We would need our own kitchen and bathroom and a separate bedroom. What with the baby and everything.'

'Well really! You've not seen the rest of the rooms. We had the bed properly cleaned after Mother died. You'd be hard pressed to find a flat where they'll accept babies. I love them meself, but me and Stan was never blessed. The rent is very reasonable. Only a fiver a week. You'll not do better.'

'Sorry, we must go. Thank you.' Caroline fled back through the house, a handkerchief to her mouth, and was violently sick in the front garden. She wiped her mouth and carried on walking as fast as she could. She heard Graham mutter an apology, saying they had to go as his wife wasn't well. They heard her scream,

'Good riddance to bad rubbish, you stuck up bitch!' before she violently slammed the door.

Graham caught her up.

'I agree it was awful. We couldn't live there. Are you alright.'

'I am now,' she replied taking deep breaths. 'What a dump. I bet it had rats. Well, it looks like we're moving in with my parents. Suddenly it doesn't seem quite so bad.'

Chapter 34

Maggie was allowed to deal with one or two clients on her own, closely supervised by Stella. She proved that she had a natural flair with people and the more she learned about the work, the more she liked it.

'You'll be getting more commission than me and Jill put together, soon,' joked Stella, putting the phone down on a successful sale with a satisfied click. 'Have you talked to Mr Wilson yet about transferring full time? We've got more work than we can handle here.'

'I did, a day or two ago,' said Maggie, straightening her desk at the end of her hour in the front. 'He said he's pleased with my work but with Heather leaving to get married he needs me in the back office. He's advertised for Heather's replacement.'

'I'll be glad to see the back of her,' muttered Jill under her breath. 'I'm sick to death hearing about rosebud-sprigged bridesmaid dresses and whether she should wear a tiari with her sodding bouffant veil. I notice we all got invitations to the wedding, this morning. Who's going? Are you Stella?'

'Wouldn't miss it for the world,' Stella replied. 'I can't wait to see how twee a wedding can possibly be. She's probably hired a pumpkin-shaped horse drawn carriage like Cinderella.'

'And there'll be a choir of angelic schoolboys wearing smocks, singing sickly love songs in falsetto voices,' replied Jill.

'And the wedding dress will have an enormous train carried by flower girls who'll scatter rose petals in front of her,' said Maggie, warming to the theme.

'They can't scatter rose petals in front and carry the train behind her,' said Jill reasonably.

'No, you're right, the page boys in purple velvet knickerbockers will be carrying the train.' said Maggie, pealing with laughter. They were all getting a bit noisy and hysterical when the door to the back office was flung open and Heather was standing at the door. They looked from one to the other like naughty schoolgirls, suddenly mortified that they may have been heard.

'What's all the hilarity for? Am I missing something?'

Maggie recovered first. 'We were just imagining what it would be like if the three of us shared a flat. Sorry.'

'Well just because Mr Wilson had to go out there's no need to be so unprofessional. Supposing a client had walked in? Oh I don't know why I bother.'

She swivelled on her heel and shut the door none too quietly, clearly miffed that she had been left out. The other three looked at each other, trying to contain their laughter.

'Do you think she heard any of that?'

'If she did we'll be struck off the guest list then we'll never know about the wedding. What shall we give her as a wedding present?' asked Stella.

'I think a set of garden gnomes would be very appropriate,' said Maggie, standing up to return to the back office. 'Or a crinoline doll to hide the spare toilet roll.'

'Before you go, Maggie, have you given any thought about sharing a flat with us? Think what fun we'd have.'

'I have,' said Maggie, 'and yes, it would be great, but things have changed.' Her tone was now serious. 'We've just heard that my grandad is dying and I'm going to move in with my grandparents and help look after him.'

'Oh bad luck. That's awful. Let us know if we can help in any way.'

'I will,' said Maggie. 'Sorry my news has destroyed the hilarious atmosphere.'

'Just as well, I think,' commented Stella, as Mr Wilson came through the door.

At the same time that Caroline and Graham were neatly packing up their life in the flat in Wimbledon, Maggie was throwing her clothes and toiletries into a suitcase. She didn't know how long she would be staying at her grandparents but she had to clear the room so Caroline and Graham had every inch of space for themselves. Every evening after work she took a few more things round until, by Thursday, all that was left were what she needed for work the next day. Grandad was coming out of hospital on Friday, and Caroline and Graham were to move in at the weekend.

When Maggie arrived at her grandparents house on Friday after work, she was welcomed by Mary and the savoury smell of Irish stew. Her gran emerged from the scullery, wiping her hands on her apron, her face pale, the lines set into a worried frown.

'Hello love. Grandad's in his bed upstairs. He's exhausted. I'm hoping that he can get down tomorrow and sit in his chair. It looks so empty without him.'

'Shall I go and see him, or is he asleep?'

'I wouldn't disturb him. I've made his favourite dinner. I thought he might like a wee bit after that hospital food, although I think they must have starved him. I mince all his food with him having no teeth but they just stuck a plate in front of him with tough bits of meat on.'

'Did he get upstairs alright?' Maggie was taking off her coat and hanging it on a hook in the hall.

'The ambulance men carried him up, although I think he can still walk. Anyway, how was your day?'

Maggie wasn't used to being asked this question, at least not by Theresa, who usually kicked off the conversation by moaning about the state of her bedroom or cataloguing her woes. She smiled gratefully.

'Good. Every day is good. I love the job and the people who work there, apart from one, but she's leaving soon. You've made my room look very cosy, Gran. I'm going to love living here with you. I'll do my best to keep it tidy.'

'Oh, get along with you. You can do what you like with it. It's your space. Now sit yourself down.' She placed a bowl of steaming stew in front of

Maggie. 'There's rhubarb and custard for pudding'.

Maggie didn't get as far as the pudding as there was a loud knocking on the floor.

'Oh that'll be your grandad woken up. I gave him his walking stick to bang with.'

'I'll go,' said Maggie, pushing her plate to one side and jumping up.

George was struggling to raise himself, red in the face from coughing. She straightened his pillows and, with an enormous effort, helped him sit up. She passed him a glass of water from the bedside table. The coughing finally eased.

'Hello, Grandad. How are you feeling?'

'Bloody awful, what does it look like? What are you doing here?'

'I've moved in with you and Granny to help her look after you.'

'I've only got cuts and bruises and a bit of a cold and cough. I'll be up and about in no time. Mary does fuss. There's life in the old dog yet. There's no need for you to be here.'

'Yes, well, there is another reason. Caroline and Graham have moved back home while they wait for a council house so I haven't got a room anymore.'

'I notice no one asked me.'

'Don't you want me here, Grandad?'

'Better than that hoity toity sister of yours. If Mary finds you useful....'

The coughing started again and he spat into a handkerchief. She saw gobbets of blood splattered in the sputum. Surely he must know. When the coughing had abated, she said, 'Can I get you anything? Cup of tea? Some lovely Irish stew?'

'Later. Now go away and let me sleep. You can leave the pillows up. Easier to get my breath.'

She saw his eyes were closing and went downstairs. Her gran was filling the old stone sink with hot water.

She turned round, the furrows between her eyes deepening.

'How is he? I heard all that coughing.'

'I gave him some water. He doesn't want anything else so I propped him up a bit and he's gone back to sleep.'

'Do you want your rhubarb?'

Maggie looked at the chunks of rhubarb, the colour of blood, embedded in the yellow custard and felt sick.

'No thanks. I'm full after your lovely stew.'

'Maybe Grandad will take a wee bite later. You know, I don't mind if you want to see your young man. I'll be alright.'

'Not tonight. I'd planned to stay with you and keep you company. Shall I make us a cup of tea and we'll see what's on the telly?'

'You can always bring him here. I'd like to meet him.'

'I will. Look, it's Dixon of Dock Green. I always fancied that Andy Crawford.'

Chapter 35

Ruby had pushed the two single beds together in the middle of the room, which made it look even smaller. All of their clothes were piled on top. Caroline looked at it helplessly.

'If we're still here when the baby's born, heaven forbid, where are we going to put it? It'll have to sleep in a drawer.'

Graham put his arm round her.

'When the time comes, we'll put the two beds back against the wall and the cot can go in the middle.'

She laid her head on his shoulder and sobbed.

'Look what we've sunk to. Three of us will be stuck in this cramped room. This is going to be our home for the foreseeable future.'

'It's only temporary. It'll be alright. At least we won't be short of babysitters.'

But she wasn't to be mollified.

'How can you be so optimistic? You've never tried living with my parents.'

'It might not be as bad as you think. Give it a try.'

'What choice have I got?' she cried.

'Look, you go and make a cup of tea and I'll start putting this stuff away.'

She returned with a large tray bearing two cups of tea and two plates with shepherd's pie, carrots and peas, swimming in puddles of greasy gravy, which she set down on the bed.

'What's this? We haven't got to eat all our meals sitting on the bed have we?'

'No, of course not. I just can't face sitting with them tonight. I need to acclimatise slowly. I said we needed to get ourselves organised. Anyway, Mum's having a go at Gina about the state of her bedroom. She's got a point. I just put my head round the door and it looks like a bomb's hit it. It's like Maggie all over again. I had to put up with her mess all my life.'

She looked in the wardrobes and drawers. I think your things should be on the left and mine on the right, the same side as we sleep, then we'll know where everything is. And I usually fold up the jumpers like this.'

He sighed as he balanced the plate precariously on his lap.

'I knew whatever I did, it would be wrong.'
Kangaroo

On the Monday they both took an hour off work to go to the council offices to put their names down for one of the new council houses. The officious clerk, a po-faced woman with pursed lips and her hair scraped into a bun, shuffled through their papers, then looked them up and down as though she didn't like what she saw. They held their breath as they waited for the verdict.

'You have quite a lot of points,' she said, 'living with your family in cramped conditions and a baby on the way.' She didn't try to disguise her glance at Caroline's stomach.

'The waiting list is long. Is there anything you can add to this?' she asked, not unkindly, 'that might help to push you up the list? You haven't said who's living in this cottage. It has three bedrooms?'

'Yes,' said Caroline, not mentioning the converted attic space where Auntie Ruby slept.

'There's my mother and father, a teenage sister and my aunt, as well as us and the coming baby. The cottage isn't very big and it's damp, not at all suitable for a baby. There's a bathroom and an outside toilet. There was an inside toilet too, but she didn't mention that either. She hoped no-one would come round to check.

'Well, this extra information may help your case. Anything else?' Caroline thought for a minute.

'Everyone smokes all the time which makes me ill. I don't want my baby having to breathe that in. And,' she blurted out, 'my father can be violent and because of him my other sister had to go to hospital, and now she's had to move out because of that and because there's just not enough room.'

'Oh dear me,' the woman said, now looking at them pityingly. 'I'll see what I can do.'

'I think you went a bit far telling them about your dad.' Graham said when they were out of earshot. 'It's not as though he ever laid a finger on you, is it? Or did he?'

'Well, no, but I never gave him cause to. I know I went a bit far with that but you could tell that she didn't think we had much chance to begin with. I don't even want to live in a council house but the quicker we can get out of that cottage the better.

We've been used to having our own space; it's going to be horrible having to share a kitchen and bathroom again.'

'I know, darling, but at least we've got a roof over our heads.'

'It's alright for you. You'll be out driving your posh cars all day long. Once I give up work I'm going to get it full time. Anyway, talking about work, we'd better get ourselves there. See you tonight.'

'What's happening about cooking?'

'I think Mum or Auntie Ruby will do it. Mum likes to be queen of the kitchen. At least we don't have to worry about shopping or getting it ready.'

When she arrived home, the smell of burnt sausages and onions greeted her. So her mother was cooking tonight. Theresa had a knack of overcooking everything. Anything fried or grilled was slightly black, and anything boiled, reduced to mush. Cabbage was soggy, cauliflower had no shape and, for some reason, she always insisted on buying tinned carrots, which were slimy.

'What time does Graham get home from work?' her mother asked through the habitual pall of cigarette smoke. 'This won't keep forever in the oven and Ruby needs to clear up.'

'I've no idea,' replied Caroline, wearily taking off her coat and hanging it on a hanger in the hall, 'he works all hours, whenever they need him, so don't cater for him. I'll do him something when he gets back, or heat it up for him.'

'Well as long as you clear up afterwards. This isn't an all night cafe.'

'Of course I will. I always do.'

Caroline tried to unclench her teeth as she climbed the stairs. She had no idea how she was going to cope with her mother's daily onslaught. The bedroom was neat and tidy, the way she had left it, and she gratefully sank down on the bed as she felt the baby kick. She put her hand on her stomach and felt the tiny flutters. For the first time, she thought of the baby as a little person growing inside her, and felt an unexpected surge of love.

Chapter 36

Mary's cooking was very different to Theresa's. She had a light hand with pastry and cakes, and cooked her, admittedly limited, repertoire to perfection; a testament to her years working as a scullery maid, then cook, in the kitchens of Clayton Manor. It was always good, wholesome food made from scratch.

'I've no truck with instant meals and tinned this and packaged that. George would never touch them,' Mary told her. 'Your mother thinks everything they show on the telly is better than humble home cooking because it costs more and someone tells you it's good. I'm old school, not likely to change my ways now.'

'You're a great cook, Gran. I'd love you to teach me how to make your pastry and cakes.'

'Just in case your young man pops the question?'

Maggie began to feel the heat on her face and neck.

'Ooh, it's early days. He's talking about me going to meet his parents. I get the impression they're ever so posh.'

'Don't let that worry you. It doesn't make them better people. When they meet you they'll be delighted with you. You're a lovely girl. Look how you're helping me out now. Your William's a lucky man, so he is.'

'I'll just nip up and see how Grandad is. He's

not tapped on the floor for over an hour.'

Maggie quietly opened the door and put her head round. He was propped up, his pale eyes staring into space, as though he was already leaving this life. She walked into the room.

'Are you alright, Grandad?'

'Alright? I'll never be alright. When I try to breathe, a pain goes right through my chest like a knife. I'm for the knacker's yard.'

'I'm here to help you get back on your feet.'

'Well you're wasting your time. Do you and Mary take me for an old fool? I've had a good innings but now my time is up. Come and sit down on that chair.'

He reached out for her hand. It was the first time he had ever touched her and, she thought, that was probably the longest sentence he had ever said to her.

'I know I'm a grumpy old bugger, but..'

His sentence was punctuated by a desperate bout of coughing. She could hear the phlegm bubbling in his chest.

'Pass me that bowl,' he gasped.

She placed the chipped enamel bowl in his trembling fingers and he spat noisily into it. She tried not to look at the dark flecks of blood in the sputum. He handed it to her and fell back, exhausted, on the pillows. His voice was a low rasp.

'See that? It's cancer. Mary keeps going on about when I'm better, but who's kidding who? I knew I had it before I went through that roof.'

'I'm so sorry, Grandad, but you ought to be talking to Gran.'

'Can't talk to her. She'll be upset.' The staccato sentences came in a short rush as he fought for breath.

'Just join in the game. I want it that way. She wants it that way,' he managed.

'OK Grandad. I won't say anything. Can I get you anything? Soup? Cup of tea?'

'Cupatea.'

But by the time she had made it and brought it up to him, he had fallen asleep.

She went slowly back downstairs, trying to weigh up whether it would be breaking a confidence to tell her Gran about this conversation. She hated this pretence on both of their parts. Each thought that they were protecting the other. Surely it would be better for both of them to be able to talk about it? But was it her place and hadn't she just promised Grandad that she wouldn't?

'How is he?'

'He was asleep by the time I took the tea up. Would you like it?'

'Might as well. Make yourself one, then we'll sit here and have a little chat. There's a tin of newly baked shortbread in the pantry. I know he won't eat it but I have to keep myself busy.'

'Tell me about when you first met Grandad. Did you know straight away that he was the one for you?'

'I was a little wisp of a thing. Only fourteen and I knew nothing of the world. You couldn't learn much about real life from the nuns in that orphanage in Ireland. It was all about hell and damnation. I went into service at Clayton Manor and almost the first person I met was George. The only men I ever saw before that were priests, tradesmen, gardeners and the like. He was a first footman and I thought he looked like a god, with his blond hair and blue eyes. He liked the ladies and they liked him.'

Her grandmother's tired eyes twinkled and her face lit up as she stared back into the past. She was fourteen again.

'I was a scullery maid, the lowest of the low. I never thought I'd get a second look.'

She dreamily dunked the shortbread into her tea.

'So how did you? Get to marry him, I mean?'

'Oh it's a long story. I was much too young for him, or anyone else for that matter. I had to watch him marry a pretty girl called Agnes. It near broke my heart. Then when he was away fighting in the Great War she took up with someone else. He was sad and I... I comforted him.'

Maggie could feel herself getting hot with embarrassment and she pretended to concentrate on picking the fringe on a cushion. She didn't want to say anything in case she'd got the wrong end of the stick. If her Gran meant what she thought she meant, Maggie was shocked. Her gran always seemed so correct, so religious; she never missed Mass, even now. The grandfather clock ticked loudly, the traffic hummed outside, a tap dripped in the scullery.

'I was,' Mary eventually continued, 'what's that word? Naïve. I didn't even realise how you got pregnant. Next thing I'm feeling sick and putting on weight. Mrs Thompson, the cook, got me a place in a convent for unmarried mothers. Oh! The nuns were cruel and we all had to work our fingers to the bone.'

She stopped speaking abruptly. Maggie looked up and saw there were tears trickling down her face. She rushed over to her and put her arms around her.

'Oh don't upset yourself, Gran. You don't need to tell me all this. It wasn't your fault.'

'It's alright. It's just that I haven't ever talked about it to anyone, except Mrs Thompson and George. You think as time passes that you get over things, but you don't. It stays buried and then, one day, years later, the memories come flooding back and they're just as painful as the day they happened. They say it's good to talk about painful things. Its supposed to get it out of your system.'

'What happened to the baby. Is it Mum?'

'No. Those nuns wrenched my baby off me; it was a little girl, and she was adopted. You, know, I've never said this to anyone before, but I look at Ruby, and there's something about her, something, I don't know, familiar..' Her voice trailed off.

'You mean, you think Auntie Ruby might be your daughter? Blimey, that would be a co-incidence. Have you talked to her about it?'

'No, it's a stupid thought. Every bit of her name is different. Our daughter's name was Annie O'Brien. They promised me they'd keep the name Annie. It can't be her.' Her gran brushed away a small tear. She took a ragged breath.

'It's not that stupid. Do you know, Gran, I've never thought to asked her about her past. She doesn't look much like mum, though. She's dark and mum's fair, for a start.'

'I know. I'm just being fanciful.'

'So, how was it that you and grandad got married, when he was married to this Agnes?'

Maggie was desperately trying to get away from the story of the cruel nuns and the adopted baby. She had never seen her gran so upset.

She thought she would perhaps talk to Ruby about her parentage some time.

'Agnes went to America and died soon after.'

Maggie nodded. She was sure that her grandmother was keeping something back, but that was up to her. She said, 'So was he the only man you ever loved?'

'He was,' she replied wistfully, 'but he wasn't the same man when he came back from the war. I wish you could have known him then, when he had the gift of the gab and could have charmed the birds off the trees. That was the man I fell in love with.'

'Well you stayed with him, which can't have been easy.'

'That was my path and I followed it. People these days get married, then they get divorced when things get a bit tough.'

'Well, marriage is supposed to be for better or for worse and in sickness and in health. If you love someone you should love them, whatever, I suppose,' said Maggie, thinking about Caroline and Graham. She suspected they weren't going to stay the course. If she married William, she knew she would stay with him, whatever happened.

There was a faint banging from upstairs.

'It looks like he's woken up. I'll go,' Maggie said, jumping up.

She looked at her dying grandad, lying in his bed, old, pale and unshaven, his chest rattling. She tried to imagine the first footman with the turquoise, twinkling eyes and silver tongue, that her gran had fallen in love with.

And somewhere, out in the world, was their other daughter, an aunt she would probably never know.

Chapter 37

Caroline's poor baby would come into this world with a smoker's cough. The living room was thick with smoke from her parents' cigarettes. Theresa was lying full length on the sofa, a tartan rug over her. Alf was in his usual chair beside the fire. That left one armchair for Caroline and Graham. Naturally, Graham always insisted that she sat in it and he had to make do with a hard chair at the table. They were watching an Ealing Comedy, or at least, were trying to watch it. It was impossible to follow the plot with Theresa punctuating it every five minutes with comments like: kangaroo

'Isn't that old whatsername who was in that other thing we watched the other day, you know that actress who married him who had the heart attack? I think he was alright but she never worked again.'

No one actually replied but that didn't stop her. Alf had his head in a crossword, Gina was in her room and she could hear Ruby's sewing machine whirring in the kitchen. Caroline wanted to scream. Not only did they have no say in what they watched but they had to listen to Theresa blathering on night after night and taking up the entire sofa with no regard for anyone else.

'We'll get our own TV,' Graham said as they went to bed much earlier than they ever did in the flat. 'I'll rig it up in here and we can decide what we want to watch.'

Caroline surveyed the room.

'It'll be a bit funny lying on the bed in the evening, but I suppose we could dig out the cushions we have in storage and make it into a sort of settee I tell you what, we could separate it back into two singles and have like a corner settee.'

Graham's face dropped.

'I like the double bed.'

'OK, so then we could push them back at night. But to be honest, what's the point? You know I couldn't dream of having relations when there's a paper thin wall between us and them.'

Graham sighed but knew there was no point continuing the conversation. Caroline had never been enthusiastic about what she called Relations and now she had the perfect excuse. Although he had to admit the situation was more than off putting. They might as well leave them as two single beds.

'At the weekend we'll go shopping for our own TV, then we can be on our own like we used to. We can choose what to watch and sit in a smoke-free room. The only time we'd need to be with your parents would be mealtimes. What do you think?'

He was pushing the two beds apart and setting them at right angles.

'I think that's the best we can do,' she replied. 'I'll get the single bedding out of the airing cupboard. We can get that little coffee table back from your parents' shed and the TV can sit on the dressing table. Yes,' she said, standing back to survey the room. 'I think that's the only way we'll survive staying here.'

'Well, I don't see why you want to spend

your evenings up in the bedroom,' Theresa snapped, taking up even more of the sofa. 'Isn't our company good enough for you?'

'It's the smoke,' said Graham, trying to be tactful. 'With me and Caroline not smoking it's hard to breathe sometimes. And it's probably not good for the baby. You pick up a thing or two, working in a hospital.'

'I thought you used to be a porter, not a doctor.' Theresa was well into one of her argumentative moods.

'Shall I make us all a nice cup of tea?' asked Ruby. 'I think it's a good idea. Caroline and Graham need their own space. And there isn't room for everyone to sit.' She looked pointedly at Theresa's outstretched legs.

'Well I'm sorry if you don't like me putting my feet up. If you had a weak heart like me then perhaps you'd understand. You'd probably be glad if I died then you'd all be able to sit where you like.'

'I'm going to our room before I say something I might regret.' Caroline heaved herself from the chair and made for the door. 'Come along Graham.'

'I find that woman completely unbearable sometimes' she told him when they had firmly shut the bedroom door. He said nothing. He had been trying to watch Waggon Train when this latest row had erupted and was now pacing up and down with nothing to do. Caroline had taken a book from the shelf and had started reading.

'Why don't you read a book?' she asked, knowing full well that she was wasting her breath. He only ever read The Daily Mirror, The News of the World and The Radio Times. She propped herself against the pillows and put her feet up, showing more than a passing resemblance to her mother. He took one randomly off the shelf and flicked through the pages. She pretended not to notice, trying to concentrate on her own book.

At the weekend they bought a small TV and some brightly coloured rugs to make the beds look more like settees. They retrieved the coffee table and a few pictures to replace the ones on the walls, which were old fashioned and had started to lose their colour. Caroline also thought about replacing the curtains with some modern ones, but that would be admitting that they might be staying for some time. Graham installed the TV and they sat back on their settees, placed their cups and saucers on the coffee table and felt that they had made the best of a bad job. Theresa only ever came up to have a bath or go to bed, wheezing audibly as she reached the top, so she rarely disturbed them.

Caroline was starting to show and knew she should think about giving up work. The hospital policy was that you didn't work if you were pregnant. So far she hadn't told anyone there, apart from David, whom she now went out of her way to avoid. She had accepted that her future didn't lie with him, but seeing him still made her want to weep. As she lay in the single bed, in the dark hours of the night, she couldn't help thinking of the life she had imagined she would spend with David. She saw the elegant house and garden and pictured their child on a swing on the lawn, she and David sitting on a bench, drinking coffee, or a glass of wine. Then she returned to her reality, living with her parents, cramped in a tiny room with a man she didn't love, however hard she tried, carrying a baby that wasn't his.

One afternoon, while Theresa was having her afternoon nap, Auntie Ruby knocked on the door.

'Come in.' Caroline sat up and rubbed her eyes

'I just came in for a little chat. You must be bored to tears being stuck up here all day.'

'I am, but don't really know what else to do.'

There was a silence then Caroline continued, 'I suppose I should offer to do some housework or something. You do so much for everyone.'

'Oh I'm not bothered about that. You lay the table and wash up and do your own washing and ironing. The housework needs to be done whether you're here or not. No, I wondered if you'd like to go for little walk or we could go to the shops. We could go and see your granny and grandad.'

Caroline suspected that this was the purpose of the conversation. Maggie, on her weekly visits, said that Grandad was getting weaker and that he wasn't expected to last much longer. Ruby was right. She needed to get off her backside and visit him before it was too late.

'I wouldn't mind walking round to Granny and Grandad's but you don't have to come with me. I know you go and help out several times a week. I've got very lazy since I stopped work. I don't seem to have the energy or the inclination to go out.'

'Well, come on then. Hanging around up

here won't get the parsnips battered. No time to like the present. You might want to change into a nice dress and put some lipstick on. Your hair looks as though you've slept on it.

'That's because I have. Give me ten minutes and I'll see you downstairs.'

She threw some water on her face, applied some lipstick and a lick of powder and changed her clothes. Her hair needed washing but looked passable after she had backcombed it and sprayed on a bit of lacquer.

Auntie Ruby appraised her. 'You look a different woman. Now just stick a smile on your face and you'll be the belle of the ball.'

Mary was delighted to see Caroline and busied herself pouring tea and delving into the biscuit tin.

'So, how are you Caroline? Excited about the baby? A new generation. I'm really looking forward to my first great grandchild.'

Caroline wasn't exactly excited, but since she and Ruby had started preparing for the baby it had become more of a reality. She was slowly turning from feeling she was in limbo, to almost looking forward to having something useful to do with her life. She wasn't sure she actually liked babies but she supposed, hoped, that an instinctive bond would occur when you had one of your own.

'Yes, Gran, I'm really looking forward to it. I just wish that we had somewhere of our own to live.'

'Yes, let's hope the council comes up with one of those nice new places soon.'

Mary opened a work box beside her and brought out the most exquisite christening shawl.

'I've been working on this since I heard you were expecting. I hope you like it. It's helped to keep me busy when I've been downstairs on my own in the evenings.'

'Oh Gran, that's absolutely beautiful. Thank you. How is Grandad?'

'Well, he's not getting any better, obviously. The coughing is very upsetting. Sometimes it sounds as if he's bringing up his entire lungs. I feel so helpless. When he's having a bad turn he looks at me with those pleading, desperate eyes. Sometimes I wish he'd just get on with it and die. I can't bear to see him in so much pain. Is that awful of me?'

'No, no. It's perfectly understandable. I expect he feels the same.' She was suddenly consumed with guilt that she hadn't been to see them before. 'Shall I go up and see him?'

'Yes. Creep up and look round the door.'

'Very well, I will.'

Her grandfather's eyes were closed, but he awoke with a start when she opened the door.

'Is that you, Mary?'

'No, Grandad, it's Caroline. I came to see how you are.'

'Well you can see how I am,' he managed, his voice barely audible. 'Not likely to be mending any more shed roofs. You been ill? Haven't seen you for weeks.'

'No, Grandad. I apologise. I think I've been feeling a bit sorry for myself.'

'Sorry? What have you got to be sorry about?

You've got your whole life ahead of you. Come where I can see you properly. Always was a looker. Puts me in mind of Mary when she was expecting Theresa. She didn't feel sorry for herself. Busy right up to the confinement.' He burst into another fit of coughing which left him breathless and wheezing.

Caroline had an inspiration.

'Don't talk if it's painful. Would you like me to read to you?'

'Do you know? I would. There's a Daily Mirror over there.'

Caroline read to him for half an hour, stopping when she saw him beginning to drift off.

'Well you've been a long time,' said Ruby. 'How is he?'

'Sleeping. Gran, I'll come over every day and read to him for a bit if that suits you.'

Chapter 38

'So how's it going, looking after your grandfather?'

Maggie and William were walking hand in hand round the park.

'I don't really do very much. I take his meals up, make him cups of tea, change his bed, that sort of thing. I'm dreading it when he can't get to the toilet and I have to help him with that. It'll be so embarrassing for both of us. At the moment he can get himself there and back with his stick.'

Maggie went on to tell tell him about her grandparents thinking they were protecting each other from the truth.

'I don't know whether to tell them so it's all out in the open.'

'What would that achieve?' William asked thoughtfully. 'Also you gave him your word.'

'If I was Grandad I'd want to talk about what I was going through. Reminisce perhaps, talk about what I would like at my funeral. Stuff like that.'

'You've got a point, but that's your viewpoint, not theirs.'

'I suppose so. I'll just have to keep my mouth shut.'

Maggie felt very frustrated, but she suspected that William was right. She respected his opinion more than her own.

'Does your grandmother look after him by

herself when you're at work?' kangaroo at work?

'Mostly. She's quite a bit younger than he is and pretty agile. Auntie Ruby pops in most days and Gina helps her with her shopping, when she remembers, which isn't often.'

'I thought she was the brains of the family? No offence. I'm just repeating what you said.' He laughed and squeezed her hand to show he was joking.

'Offence taken,' she replied. 'Gina is very good at school work. Comes top in everything, but she's also very scatty. Barely remembers anything in everyday life. She once went to the shops with a broom because they're kept in the same cupboard as the shopping bags.'

William guffawed with laughter. 'Your family seem a really interesting bunch. I can't wait to meet them.'

'I'm sure you will eventually but it's not the best time with Caroline and Graham moving in, and me living with my grandparents.'

'Yes of course. My family has been hinting that they'd like to meet you. Shall I arrange a time for you to come over, perhaps for a meal?'

Maggie could feel butterflies erupt in her stomach. She knew she couldn't put it off forever. It was so awkward. She didn't want to meet his family in case they didn't think her good enough and she didn't want William to meet her family in case he was put off. She couldn't face either situation.

'Of course. That would be lovely, but shall we leave it a bit while my grandad is so ill and Caroline and Graham are busy moving in?'

She knew this was totally illogical as she was out with him now. It wasn't as though her gran expected her to spend every minute at her grandad's bedside. She was then worried that William might see through her excuses. What a coward she was. She took the nightmare a step further and imagined their parents meeting each other.

'I know. Why don't you come back with me this evening and meet my gran? She's a real sweetie.'

When they arrived at the door, Maggie said, 'Do you mind if I just pop in and warn her in case it's not convenient?'

'Of course not. It's a tough time for you all at the moment. She might not want visitors.'

He waited on the doorstep, smoothing his hair and straightening his tie.

Mary came to the door.

'What on earth is my granddaughter thinking, leaving you on the doorstep? Come on in. I've heard so much about you and here you are, large as life and twice as handsome.'

He held out his hand. 'Good things I hope and I don't know about being handsome. I'm really pleased to meet you.'

'Well take off that smart coat and take that seat by the fire, Make yourself at home while I put the kettle on and see what's in the biscuit tin.' She hurried out to the kitchen.

'Oh, she's lovely,' said William, settling himself into George's chair. 'Where's your grandad? In bed?'

'Oh yes. He doesn't come down anymore. Too weak.'

'Well now, this is nice.' Mary placed the tea and a plate of home-made Shrewsbury biscuits next to his chair. 'I've been looking forward to meeting Maggie's young man and I can see you're every bit as nice as she said.'

'Gran, you're embarrassing me.' She pushed the plate towards William. 'You must try one of these. Gran's such a good cook. She's started to teach me to bake.'

William bit into it and agreed that Mary was a very good cook indeed. Maggie took one herself and resisted the urge to dip it into her tea.

'Sure, you're a natural, Maggie. She has a lovely light hand with the pastry. Another biscuit, William?'

'They're delicious but no thanks. You know, if you need any help with anything, I'd be only to glad to assist. If you need furniture moving or anything lifting. I've got strong shoulders.'

'Well that's very kind of you. I'll remember that. So Maggie tells me you're training to be a solicitor. That must be very interesting.'

There was suddenly a repeated banging from the floor above.

'Shall I go? I haven't seen him today.'

William stood up and took his coat. 'Well I'd better be off. Thank you for the tea and excellent biscuit. It has been a real pleasure to meet you, Mrs er..'

'Call me Mary. It's been a pleasure to meet you, too. Don't leave it too long.'

'I'll see you on Friday,' he said to Maggie as she showed him to the door, which she drew shut behind her. He kissed her briefly.

'You'd better go.' He looked up at the bedroom window. 'The banging's getting louder. By the way, your gran's a treasure.'

Maggie ran up the stairs two at a time. William had liked her gran. That was one hurdle. He hadn't turned his nose up at the tiny terraced house with its worn carpets, cheap, dated furniture and ornate-framed pictures of the Sacred Heart and Virgin Mary. Gran had won him over with her warmth and kindness. How she ever had a self-centred daughter like her mother she'd never know.

'Took your time. Do you expect me to come down and get me own tea? A man could die of thirst.' He exploded into a fit of coughing, gasping to desperately draw air into his tar-dredged lungs. His faded blue eyes stared at her imploringly.

'Come on, Grandad. Let me help you sit up. You'll be able to get your breath. Here, have a sip of water.'

The racking cough eventually stopped. She managed to wrench his slight frame into a sitting position. He was now all skin and bone. She held the glass to his lips and noticed blood dribbling out of the side of his mouth. She pulled a handkerchief from her pocket and gently wiped it. Her heart was drumming in her chest and she felt light headed. She could hear the cacophony of rattles and wheezes in his chest. It was too hard to bear. He slumped back on the pillows.

'This dying is taking too long. I just want to get on with it. I could hear a man's voice downstairs, who was it?'

'That was William, my boyfriend. He

brought me back so I asked him in to meet Gran.'

'Well don't bring him up here. I'm in no fit state to entertain visitors.'

'Of course not. Is there anything I can get you? Gran has made some lovely chicken broth. Could you manage some?'

'I might try. Good cook, your grandmother.'

'I know, Grandad, She's teaching me how to cook.'

'More sensible than learning from Theresa. She gets everything out of tins and packets and then burns 'em. No way to cook.' His voice was a series of gasps.

'No need to tell me. Right, I'll be back in a jiffy with your soup. Can you manage a bit of bread?'

'No. No bread. Need teeth to chew bread.'

'You could soften it in the soup.'

'No bread,' he growled.

She managed to get him to eat a little and settle him down. She went downstairs to join her gran for another one of their chats. It was such a treat being with someone who actually listened to you and was interested in what you had to say. She had long ago given up trying to talk to her mother.

Chapter 39

Life back at the cottage was as difficult as Caroline had remembered in the two years that she had been away. Her father barely spoke. He seemed content in his own way with his television, his crosswords and pottering about in his greenhouse and garden.

Her mother was becoming more and more lazy, if that were at all possible. She rose after nine, read the paper, drank innumerable cups of tea, wrote shopping lists and jotted down what she spent on scraps of paper in her odd spidery writing, always with a cigarette stuck to her bottom lip, her eyes screwed up against the spirals of smoke. At about eleven she would start to prepare the vegetables for dinner, which was eaten at one when Alf knocked off for an hour. Ruby would clear away the dishes and sweep the kitchen floor while Theresa settled down on the sofa, which put the living room out of bounds for anyone else in the family. Ruby would be stationed in the kitchen like a guard dog preventing anyone going in.

'Your mother's having a little nap so you need to be quiet.'

Ruby seemed to do everything else in the house, the cleaning, ironing, bed-making and often the cooking. The fact that she was so willing, gave Theresa carte blanche to do absolutely nothing if she chose. Caroline thought that if she got off her fat bottom and did something useful she would be less self-obsessed and even perhaps lose a bit of weight. She marvelled at her mother's ability to consume huge quantities of food that would have made anyone else sick.

Caroline was making hers and Graham's breakfast one morning, a boiled egg and a piece of toast each, to find Auntie Ruby preparing her mother's breakfast.

'Surely that's not all for her!' gasped Caroline, surveying the huge bowl of sugar puffs and five slices of toast, next to which was a jar of bloater paste.

'That's what she asked for,' replied Ruby reasonably. 'Your mother said her doctor told her she needed it to keep her strength up. Who am I to argue?'

Theresa was just coming into the kitchen, her face thunderous. It was clear that she had overheard the conversation.

'Ruby! Why on earth have you made all that for my breakfast?' she snapped. 'You know I never eat that much.'

'Good morning, Mother. Apparently you do,' said Caroline sweetly. 'Where on earth do you put it all?'

With that she had swept out of the room, before Theresa could think of an acid reply.

She and Gina had little to say to each other; they never had. Now that Gina no longer had Maggie to giggle with, always excluding her, she mostly stayed up in her room. She sometimes chatted to friends on the phone in the hall, if she could get away with it, and most evenings Caroline could hear Radio Luxembourg blaring out of the radiogram in Gina's room. She had on occasion tried to engage Gina in conversation but old habits die hard and her sister often came up with excuses such as homework deadlines. She stayed in during school nights but was out most of the weekend, catching up with her friends, so their paths didn't cross very much. At mealtimes Gina rushed through her food as though she couldn't wait to get away. Caroline knew how she felt.

The one person who was always the same was Auntie Ruby. She often hovered, asking if Caroline and Graham needed anything washing or mending, or just fancying a bit of a gossip. She was the one person in this household whom Caroline had any time for. She would pass the leanest bits of beef or the freshest slices of bread to Caroline, saying, 'You've got two to think about now,' much to Theresa's chagrin. If Theresa asked Caroline to fetch her cigarettes or make her a cup of tea, Aunty Ruby would leap up crying, 'I'll get it! Caroline's been on her feet all day and deserves a rest'.

Caroline would have hugged her if she had been the type to show affection.

She and her mother didn't exactly not get on. It was just that neither of them thought they ought to compromise. Theresa was always on a short fuse, inclined to snap and snarl at everyone, like a bad tempered dog, and Caroline's behaviour was always measured and just a little bit superior. Unlike her mother, she never lost her temper, but often responded to the criticism and the constant carping with coldly biting retorts, before sweeping out of the room and up to her and Graham's bedsitting room, as she liked to call it. Saying they were going up to the bedroom brought with it entirely the wrong connotations, she told Graham.

'Chance would be a fine thing,' he was heard to mutter darkly. Graham was stoic and never critical. Like Mr Micawber, he was always saying that something would turn up. This situation couldn't go on forever.

Chapter 40

'So what are you wearing to Lady Muck's wedding and are you bringing your dishy solicitor?'

'Dishy trainee solicitor,' replied Maggie. 'I have nothing remotely suitable in my wardrobe and I don't want to spend my hard-earned money on something that I'll only wear once. I'd better get a move on, though, it's a week on Saturday, isn't it?'

'Afraid so,' said Jill in a hushed voice, checking that the door to the back office was shut. I've got a dress and jacket I bought for a friend's wedding. What about you, Stel?'

'Oh I'm not really putting on anything particularly weddingy. I'll dig out a smartish summer dress and wear it with my new burnt orange boxy jacket. I've got a fluffy white angora bolero you could borrow, Maggie, if you can find a dress. It'll go with anything.'

'That'd be good, Stella, if you don't mind lending it to me. I'll go to C&A at the weekend and look for a summer dress that I can wear when I go out with William. Is anyone wearing a hat?'

'I've got a pillbox with a little veil that I bought with the dress,' said Jill. 'You could wear that one with the silk bow at the front, Stella. You look nice in that. And you, Maggie, when you go to C& A you could look at those lovely picture hats with the big floppy brim. It would look stunning with those dark curls cascading underneath. William'll take one look at you and pop the question.'

'If only,' said Maggie dreamily, as the phone rang on her desk.

'Capital Holidays. We make your dreams come true. Margaret speaking. How may I help you?'

They arranged to meet outside the church, half an hour before the start of the ceremony, where they introduced their boyfriends. Stella's was called Tony. He had slicked back hair, narrow trousers and polished winkle-pickers. He walked with a swagger and seemed to think a lot of himself. Apparently he worked in a betting shop. Jill's boyfriend, Peter, seemed a nice chap, quietly dressed and quietly spoken. Maggie warmed to him far more than she did Tony. William, as always, showed his impeccable manners and was dressed smartly. He was friendly and natural with everyone and Maggie had never been so proud of him. They took their places at the back of the church and looked around at the other guests, most of them whom were done up to the nines in elaborate outfits.

Excitement grew as the organ music soared with the opening chords of Jesu Joy of Man's Desiring, and there was Heather, floating up the aisle in a ballerina-length confection of lace and satin, with the much talked about bouffant veil and glittering tiara. She was followed by two tiny bridesmaids, cute as buttons, in pink beribboned frothy dresses and white patent shoes. She looked happy and confident, smiling left and right at her guests, as she processed up the aisle on the arm of her father.

'That organist is eighty five,' Maggie

whispered. 'He's her great uncle, on his way out apparently. According to Heather he promised her that, before he died, he'd play the organ at her wedding.'

They turned round to look at him across the back of the church.

'It looks like he's only just made it,' Stella observed.

Heather had now arrived at the front of the church where 'MyJohn' was waiting for her with slicked back hair and a fixed grin on his face. The congregation were invited to sit and, just as the service was about to begin, there was a crash at the the back of the church, with an abrupt cessation of 'O Jesu.'

'Oh my God! It looks like that organist has fallen down dead off his piano stool,' Jill whispered.

They, and others at the back, turned round to see him lying inert on the floor, his limbs splayed. One of the ushers was entreating everyone to keep calm and quiet so as not to disturb the ceremony that was continuing heedlessly at the front of the church. He was pacing up down, asking in a stage whisper if there was a doctor in the congregation. A young woman came forward and said she was a nurse and she would see what she could do. Several people left their seats to see if they could help and someone said they'd go and phone an ambulance. There were loud whispers of, 'What? Is he dead?' and, 'Never seen the like,' and, 'You'd think they'd have the decency to stop the wedding.' More people were leaving their seats, and now a second usher appeared and was herding them back into the pews and asking if anyone was able to play the organ so the service could continue without the bridal couple knowing what had happened. Peter pushed his way out of the pew.

'I can,' he said in a loud whisper. 'I sometimes play at my church.'

There was a lot more whispering and shuffling of pages of music. Gasps and excited chatter again broke out at the back, which was summarily silenced by the first usher, who entreated them not to spoil the wedding. The bride was not to know. It would ruin the day she had been meticulously planning for two years. It was a miracle that the people at the front of the church appeared not to have heard any of the commotion at the back, but it was a huge church with many pillars. The remaining pieces of music, culminating with, 'Here comes the bride,' were executed quite skilfully by Peter, the body having been carted out of the door and into an ambulance.

Heather beamed her way back down the aisle on the arm of her brand new husband, completely oblivious to the drama that had been playing out behind her as they had stood at the altar.

The guests were beginning to recover, although there was more than the usual amount of whispering as the photographer was lining up the wedding party outside the church.

'Two for the price of one,' said Tony lighting a cigarette as he pointed to the graves. 'We could have the old codger's funeral at the same time.'

Stella glared at him, putting her finger to her lips. The photographer was barking out instructions.

'Bride and groom only. Can we have the

confetti now? Smile, you're not at a funeral. Will the bride and groom's family come forward? Watch the birdie. Come on, say "cheese". Can we have the bride and groom looking into each other's eyes?'

Eventually, after what seemed endless hours of different groups forming and reforming, the last photograph had been taken and the guests piled into cars heading for The Bluebell Hotel, two miles away.

'Well, that was memorable,' commented Tony as they climbed into one of the cars. 'I wonder when they're going to tell her that her uncle popped his clogs at the back of the church while she was exchanging vows at the front?'

'I heard someone say they'd wait until they got back off their honeymoon,' replied Stella. 'They'll probably just say he went home as he was a bit tired.'

'Well it just shows,' said Jill, 'that you can plan a wedding down to the last detail and something's still bound to go wrong.'

'Poor Heather will be devastated. She's done nothing but talk about this wedding for the last year.' said Maggie.

'Yes, I can't say I like her but you wouldn't wish it on anyone, not even Heather,' said Jill.

At the door of the hotel, Heather and MyJohn were there to greet the guests, and a glass of real champagne was thrust into everyone's hands. At first, everyone seemed a bit subdued, but as the alcohol flowed, people appeared to have forgotten about the unfortunate organist. The wedding breakfast was a sit down meal, which was a glorified Sunday roast, followed by thick wedges of lemon meringue pie, after which they had to sit through the interminable speeches.

'No such thing as a free meal,' whispered Jill.

Tony said, 'Let's make it more interesting and bet on how many minutes the best man's speech goes on for.'

'You're a naughty man, but go on then,' Jill replied with a giggle. 'I'll say six minutes.'

Tony got out his watch and pen, grabbing a serviette.

'We'll all put five bob in the kitty and whoever is nearest gets the lot.'

Maggie had guessed nine minutes and it was actually nine and a half so she went home with thirty shillings jingling in her pocket.

'Interesting friends,' said William on the way home. 'I had a good time, did you?'

'Yes. I feel a bit guilty though. The three of us were being really awful about it last week in the office. I've had nothing but wedding arrangement updates since I started there and had to share an office with her. I was sick to death of it. We thought it would be a really extravagant and tasteless affair so it was a pleasant surprise.'

'Apart from her great uncle picking that moment to drop dead in the middle of Jesu. I can't believe the bride and groom were unaware of all the commotion at the back.'

'It was quite a big church and I expect they were wrapped in their own little bubble of love,' Maggie replied sweetly. 'I'm a bit tiddly. That champagne went straight to my head, then I had the wine. I'm walking on air.'

He stopped and wrapped his arms round her.

'I love you, you know.'

Her head was spinning. 'I love you, too,' she breathed. At that moment the world shrank to just the two of them so they were in their own little bubble. She had never felt so happy in her life.

He put his arm round her shoulder and she put hers around his waist as they walked, as one, to her grandparents' house. He kissed her again on the doorstep and said, 'I'd better not come in. It's late. You need to get to bed and sleep off all that alcohol.'

'I wish you were coming with me,' she said, as she went in the door. 'Oh God? Did I just say that out loud?' She giggled and found she couldn't stop.

'Me too,' he said quietly.

Her gran was still up. Maggie's head was beginning to throb and she just wanted to go to bed and dream about William and to mull over what he had said. I love you. She didn't want to talk to anyone. She wanted to stretch this moment so it lasted forever.

'Oh there you are Maggie.' Gran had dark circles under her eyes and her skin was grey. 'I'm so glad you're home. Your grandad has just taken a turn for the worse. Can we take it in turns to sit up with him?'

CHAPTER 41

Now that she had finished work, the days seemed endless, Caroline spent as much time as she could up in their 'bedsit'. She knitted a rather lop-sided matinee jacket and some odd shaped bootees with neither skill nor enthusiasm, but she felt she should do something to while away the hours. It was a bit pointless anyway, as Ruby had never been happier clacking away with her knitting needles as she watched the telly. The little mounds of knitted garments slowly grew into a complete layette, with the nighties Ruby sewed and the shawl she crocheted. She cut down worn sheets to make cot bedding and turned scraps of multicoloured material into a patchwork quilt. Theresa merely said she had never been a knitter or sewer and what was the point when Auntie Ruby clearly loved making things for the baby?

    Most of the time Caroline read library books or listened to music on their radio. Sometimes she flicked through magazines showing slim, lipsticked housewives in their shiny kitchens, carrying steaming home-made pies to the their delighted families, sitting expectantly round the table. This increased her feelings of inadequacy. Now she felt huge and ungainly. She wore shapeless clothes and didn't see the point of makeup. The less active she was, the more tired she felt. Much of the time she slept, blanking out the reality of a life that was going nowhere. Theresa had thankfully given up complaining about her and Graham not spending much time with the rest of the family. Caroline had been adamant neither of them wanted to sit in a smoky environment so they had no choice but to stay upstairs.

In contrast, Graham was in his element with his new job. He loved driving the limousines and chatting to his rich clients, who often gave him generous tips. He still sometimes brought one of the sleek, shining cars home with him if he had an early start. He would try to entice Caroline to put on her fur coat and come for a little drive with him in the evenings, but even this little game of make-believe no longer interested her. He would return home, tired but wanting to chat about his day. Sometimes she pretended to listen but more often she would say, 'Not now Graham, perhaps later.'

His good mood would then evaporate and he would sigh and sit in front of their tiny TV, a tray of warmed-up food on his lap, until it was time to climb into his single bed. He would flick through a newspaper and try to discuss articles he had read but, more often than not, he would receive an unenthusiastic response. Caroline knew she should try harder but couldn't find the energy or enthusiasm.

Alf came up trumps when he found an old cot and pram in one of the outhouses of The Manor and had done a fine job restoring them. His main strength was his practicality. He could repair or rebuild almost anything. The pram was a Silver Cross which, when painted and oiled, looked top notch. The cot was made of carved oak and bore the scuffs and teethmarks of several generations of offspring from

The Manor. By the time Alf had attacked it with emery paper and burnished it with beeswax, it looked fit for royalty.

Under Auntie Ruby's scrutiny, Caroline covered the mattress with some new oil cloth. They made up the cot with the reworked sheets and the patchwork quilt and Caroline tried to imagine David's baby lying in it, staring up at her. She had to admit she was rather taken with the image of a succession of Barclay babies occupying them before her own child. She wondered whether Graham would instantly fall in love with it, or whether he would somehow sense that the baby wasn't his.

In the middle of the night, when the discomfort of her growing belly woke her, she would lie, staring at the ceiling, wondering if David would ever want to see his child. She created scenarios of his seeing the baby and deciding that he wanted to spend his life with them. Sometimes she had nightmares that he had come back to her, and his wife would suddenly appear, trying to tear him away. She would manage to drag them apart and the baby would fly off into the air, land with a thump and the baby would be dead. She would wake, covered in sweat, silently screaming, to discover that her cheeks were wet with tears. Graham would be snoring gently beside her, oblivious of the dramas that were playing out in her head.

Chapter 42

Maggie felt all the excitement of the wedding, and William's surprising declaration, dissipate. She suddenly felt very sober.

'Oh no! What's happened, Gran?'

'I went up to see if he wanted anything and he couldn't stop coughing, and then couldn't get his breath. Oh Maggie, I can't bear it. His chest is rattling so and his lips are turning blue. I've just come down as I heard you come in. I don't know what to do.'

Her gran, usually level headed and capable, whatever the crisis, was clearly now out of her depth. George was difficult these days but she was the only person who remembered the George she had fallen in love with.

'I'll go up and see him. Get yourself a nice cup of tea. I'm so sorry you've had to cope with this all alone while I've been out gallivanting.'

'How was the wedding?'

'Later.'

Maggie took the stairs two at a time and then came to an abrupt halt outside the bedroom door. She realised her heart was pounding and her own breath was shallow. She could hear his gasping and wheezing from the other side of the door. She had to go in. At this moment, she would rather be anywhere than here. Taking a deep breath herself, she opened the door gingerly, bracing herself for what she might see.

He was propped up with three pillows, his face grey, his lips a bluey purple. Every breath seemed an enormous effort. The air whistled and rattled in his chest. He stared helplessly at her through sunken, bloodshot eyes. She stood there, not knowing what to say.

Eventually, 'What can I do for you, Grandad?'

He didn't answer.

She held a glass of water to his lips. He managed a few sips then sank back into the pillows and closed his eyes. She stroked his forehead, and then his hand, and went back downstairs.

'Gran, we should call an ambulance. I think he needs oxygen. As you said, he's fighting for every breath. Oxygen would make it easier for him.'

Maggie didn't know if she was being selfish. What she really wanted was for someone who knew what they were doing to take over, to take the responsibility away from her and Gran.

Her gran nodded. 'You can try to suggest it to him, but my guess is he'll want to die at home.'

It wasn't the first time she thought that her gran could see inside her head.

'I know this is hard, but it's the last thing we can do for him. If he wants to stay here ,then so be it.'

'Shall I ask him?'

'You're determined aren't you?'

'I'm just trying to do the right thing.'

'Sometimes there isn't a right thing. What's right for one person isn't right for the next. Ask him what he wants if you like. It's your grandad's life. And death.

Maggie was so tired and desperate to go to bed and hug the thoughts of William to herself. She trudged up the stairs again and went into to see her grandad. kangaroo

She sank down onto the chair beside his bed.

'I'm parched,' he croaked, his voice barely audible.

'Water or a cup of tea?'

'Cupatea.'

'You fell asleep last time I made you one.'

'Not promising anything.'

There was the vestige of a twinkle in his eye.

'Grandad, if you went into hospital, you'd have special care. You could probably have oxygen, which would help you breathe. You are really struggling and perhaps it would make you more comfortable.'

'Maggie, I know you mean well,' he gasped. 'Want to stay here. Don't want to be surrounded by people I don't know, when I die.'

He fell back with the effort of this long speech.

Maggie sat down and took his hand. Her eyes filled with tears. It might have been the emotion of the wedding, or the wine, or both.

'Then you won't. We're here with you. You're not alone.'

She looked at him and saw that tears were seeping from his eyes too.

'I'll get that tea,' she said awkwardly.

'Maggie,' he began again. 'Look out for Mary. Theresa waste of space. Caroline's alright underneath. Lot on her plate. Not happy. Gina too young. Head in the clouds. You're alright. Hope William marries you. Ruby. Truth. Sleep now.'

His voice, deathly quiet, petered out. His eyes were closed. She wondered if this was it. What did he mean, Ruby. Truth.

'So what did he say?' Mary was sitting staring into the fire.

'He said he wanted a cup of tea but the last time I made it he'd fallen asleep. Shall I bother?'

'If you don't mind. I'll come up with you and settle him down for the night and sit with him. I expect you want to go to bed. You've had a long day. You look exhausted.'

They climbed the stairs and went into his room. George was lying on his back, looking more peaceful than he had been for weeks. The wheezing and rattling in his chest had stopped and now there were just gentle gasps of inhalation and exhalation, the space in between getting longer and longer. Maggie knew she couldn't go to bed. She placed the tea, which her grandad would never drink, on the bedside table. Mary sat one side and she the other, each holding one of his hands.

'Is he in a coma now, do you think?' whispered Maggie, watching the shallow rise and fall of his chest.

'I don't think he'll last the night,' Mary said. 'Did he say anything when you went up?'

'He told me to look after you, which of course I will. Not that you need looking after,' Maggie smiled tiredly. 'He also said something really strange, which I didn't understand. He said "Ruby. Truth." Do you know what he meant, or do you think he was delirious?'

Mary was silent for a while. Then, 'You know I told you that I'd had a baby girl who was taken away by the nuns and adopted?'

'Yes, of course.' Maggie stared at her gran. She suddenly gasped. She couldn't mean..

'George always thought that Ruby could be our daughter. I told him not to be so silly. Our daughter was called Annie O'Brien and she's Ruby Andrews. I wouldn't say she particularly looks like either of us, or Theresa come to that, but sometimes, you know, I catch a look or a gesture.' She shook her head. 'Imagine what a co-incidence it would be. I think he just wanted her to be our long lost daughter. If only,' she sighed wistfully. 'You know, there's not a day goes by when I don't think of her and I dream that one day she'll find me. But I know that's just fanciful. I always remember her in my prayers.'

'If she has a completely different name and doesn't really look like either of you, then it's unlikely, isn't it?'

They were whispering, even though George was clearly unconscious now.

'She has the same birthday as Annie and she would be the same age,' her gran said simply.

'Surely Ruby would have some identification papers, a birth certificate maybe?'

'She thinks she did, but things like that often disappeared in the war, She's no idea of their whereabouts.'

'Well I'm sure her parents could be traced. I think you can go to Somerset House or something. If you felt there was a chance it would be worth it, surely?'

George groaned and she stroked his inert face. They fell into silence and there they stayed into the small hours, until he drew his last unconscious, tiny breath. They reached for each other's hand across the bed as they watched the tension in his face disappear, as his pain-racked body finally relaxed.

Chapter 43

Alf was always an early riser. He liked to be up before seven and would potter about making himself a cup of tea and enjoying his first cigarette and cough of the day before anyone else in the household was awake. He was surprised when the shrill ring of the phone broke his precious hour of peace.

'Hello,' he said tentatively, wondering who on earth could be calling at this hour.

'It's Maggie. Grandad died around two am. We didn't think there was any point waking everyone. He drifted off peacefully.'

'Oh dear. I won't wake anyone. There's nothing to be done at the moment, is there?'

'No. We'll contact the doctor at nine and take it from there.'

'How's Mary?'

'She's still asleep. I think she was exhausted. She didn't say much after he died. You know what she's like. Doesn't want to make a fuss. She's probably a bit relieved. It's horrible watching someone gasping for breath like that. The chest rattles were so frightening.' Maggie burst into tears.

'Maggie. You did a good thing there. I'm proud of you. Let us know what's to be done.

'I will. Bye.'

Alf turned round. Theresa was standing at the top of the stairs.

'Who's that ringing at this hour of the

morning? I was in a deep sleep.'

'It was Maggie. George died last night.'

'Oh dear, no. I see. Your grandad died last night,' she told Caroline, who had just appeared on the landing and was rubbing the sleep out of her eyes.

'I thought that would be it when I heard all the commotion. At least he's at peace now.' She went back into their room to tell Graham.

There were brisk steps from above as Ruby trotted down the attic stairs in her floral dressing gown.

'Well, everyone's up nice and early. Am I missing something?'

'Dad's died,' said Theresa. 'Put the kettle on, Ruby. I think we all a need a cup of sweet tea for the shock.'

'Hardly a shock,' said Gina, appearing from her bedroom. She saw the look on everyone's face and quickly added. 'Look, of course I'm sorry, but we did expect it. Do we have to go round and see his dead body?'

'Well, it would be nice to say goodbye,' said Theresa. 'A mark of respect.'

'Isn't it a bit gruesome? He's not actually there anymore, is he? I wonder if he's in heaven yet?'

'Gina, it's too early in the morning for this,' said Alf. 'Why do you always have to argue about everything?'

'I wasn't arguing, just making a point.'

'I'll make a point in a minute,' replied Alf, sternly. 'Now go back to your room.'

'So everyone gets a cup of tea and not me?'

'Oh, for crying out loud, go and get dressed,

then come down. My heart won't stand all this arguing, and I've just lost my father.' Theresa put her hand dramatically to her head, and then her heart. The fact that no-one else was dressed appeared to be irrelevant. Gina looked as though she was about to say this but thought better of it. She went back into her room and shut the door with what was not quite a slam.

Ruby poured out the tea and one by one the rest of them joined her at the table.

'Alf, we'd better get round there after breakfast. Mum will need our support. And I still think the rest of you should go round and see your grandad before they take him away.'

'I've never seen a dead body before,' said Gina. 'I feel a bit scared.'

'Well don't come then,' snapped her mother. 'But you might regret it later.'

'It's not scary, really,' put in Auntie Ruby. 'People look really peaceful when they're dead. Apart from that, they look the same as when they were alive. But dead,' she added for clarification.

'Alright, I'll come, said Gina. 'It'll be a good experience.'

Theresa tutted and Alf shot her a filthy look.
'Have some respect.'

'Well he had a good innings,' said Graham quickly before another altercation erupted. 'Eighty six is a good age.'

'It's still very sad,' said Theresa. 'Poor Mum will be very lonely, now. She'll need us more than ever.'

'And she'll get it,' said Alf. 'Shall we have

some breakfast or has everyone lost their appetite?'

'I could manage something,' said Theresa. 'I need to keep my strength up. Do we have any bacon, Ruby?'

Chapter 44

At nine o'clock Maggie went over to the phone box and rang Mr Wilson to say she wouldn't be in today, and then she rang the doctor, who said he would visit some time that morning to write the death certificate.

Mary was sitting in George's chair, staring into space, when she returned. Maggie decided not to interrupt her thoughts for a few minutes, and busied herself making them some breakfast.

'Do you want to come and eat something, Gran? I've made us a boiled egg and some toast.'

'I'm not hungry, love. Sorry to put you to the trouble.'

'If this was the other way round you'd persuade me to eat it. It's going to be a long day.'

Her gran gave her a faint smile and came to sit at the table.

'And I'd be right.'

'You always are.' Maggie reached for her hand across the table.

'I won't say he's in a better place or out of pain now. It probably doesn't help. If you want to talk, I'm here to listen, but otherwise I'll just do practical things.'

'Maggie, you're such a good person to have around at this time. You know when to talk and when not, and you're so practical. Thank you.' Her voice ended in a sob which set Maggie off. They sat in silence, which was suddenly interrupted by a persistent banging on the door. Maggie wiped her eyes and went to open it. Their entire family stood on the doorstep.

'Hello. I don't think Gran...'

Theresa was already inside the door.

'We've come to see what's to be done and to say goodbye to Dad. Is it a bad time? You look exhausted, Maggie.' She looked beyond her to where Mary was still sitting at the table, her untouched egg in front of her.

'Come in all of you,' said Mary wearily, starting to clear the plates. 'We're late getting started. It was a terrible night.'

'I'm sure,' said Auntie Ruby, taking off her coat. 'Here, let me do that, Mary and I'll put the kettle on. Sit down and eat that egg or the poor hen will have laid it for nothing.'

'We're waiting for the doctor to sign the death certificate,' Mary said, a catch in her voice. 'Well you'd better all go up. We're in a bit of a state at the moment, as you can imagine.'

Theresa took the stairs slowly, her breathing laboured. The combination of her weak heart and excess weight made everything difficult these days. They arranged themselves around George's bed.

'Come in and close that door, Georgina. Your grandad won't bite.' Theresa broke the silence. She leaned forward and kissed George's bald head.

'Goodbye, Dad.'

Caroline came forward and brushed his cheek with her lips. 'Goodbye grandad.'

'Now you Georgina.'

Even at this solemn moment Gina couldn't

help bristling at the use of her full name. Her mother never called her Gina like everyone else. She had been named after her grandfather and wasn't allowed to forget it.

'Do I have to? I really don't want to kiss a dead body.'

'Yes. You need to say goodbye.' Theresa's voice was firm.

'Can't I just say goodbye? And I can't even really see the point of that. It's not as though he can hear.'

Theresa was obviously about to try to regain control when Alf said,

'No point making her do it if she doesn't want to. Go downstairs, Gina, and see if there's anything you can do to help.'

Gina was off like a shot. Graham stood there wringing his hands, not knowing what was expected of him. Caroline said,

'We'll go down too and let you and Dad have some time with Grandad. Graham rewarded her with a grateful look and made for the door.

Mary assured them that there was nothing to be done at present so they and Gina decide to walk back home.

When the door had shut behind them Caroline said,

'Why do you always have to argue, Gina? Sometimes it's best just keeping your mouth shut. I mostly just walk away.'

'I know. I expect you're right. But Mum comes out with such twaddle sometimes.'

Graham and Caroline laughed. It was a rare

moment.

'I wonder where his spirit is now? wondered Gina, staring up at the sky. 'Will he go to heaven or hell? He wasn't a particularly nice person. Maybe he'll spend hundreds of years in purgatory until God makes up His mind.'

Chapter 45

The funeral service went on forever. It was a requiem mass because Mary wanted to give George a good send off. If George had been asked, he probably would have said that they could chuck him over a cliff into the sea, or get the dustmen to take him away, for all he cared. He had held no truck with all that religious mumbo jumbo. There was nothing really personal about the ceremony; it was all Catholic prayers, half of which were in Latin. Maggie thought once again that it was a pity her grandad hadn't been consulted. But then, on the other hand, funerals were for the living, not the dead.

The wake was at the cottage, the fare quite similar to that of Caroline and Graham's wedding, relying heavily on pork pies and sandwiches, without the wedding cake of course. Instead, Mary had made one of her light and fluffy Victoria sponges and Gina had constructed a centrepiece of a grapefruit covered in foil with cheese and pineapple and cocktail sausages on sticks, like a hedgehog. She had raved about it after going to a friend's birthday party. There were a few of Mary's old friends and, of course, the parish priest. George had no friends to speak of. He had become far too grumpy and insular in the last years of his life. Mary bore up well. There was little doubt that she was a survivor and that she would make some sort of life for herself without George.

In the days after the funeral, she and Maggie

disposed of George's possessions, which mainly comprised a wardrobe of baggy, well-worn clothes, a rack of smelly pipes and a shed of rusting tools. Together, they took down curtains, shampooed rugs and flung open the windows. Mary had endured a lifetime of George's smelly pipes infiltrating the fibres of their life together. Now she wanted fresh air and the smell of lavender. The huge, holy pictures in their heavy frames stayed put. George had hated them and had railed against them all his life, so it had been a compromise; she put up with the pipes and he had to live with her images of the Sacred Heart and the Virgin Mary staring down at him from the living room walls. They had been as stubborn as each other.

  A new regime emerged. Now every week Mary and Maggie went to the cottage for Sunday lunch. This wouldn't have happened in the latter years of George's life. He could never be persuaded to leave his armchair and attempt to be sociable. Added to this, Mary had needed to mince everything so that it resembled baby food. He had retained barely any teeth and had refused to consider false ones.

  'Why would I want a mouthful of plastic that traps all the bits of food underneath? And who wants to look at at a set of teeth snarling at them in a glass of water by the bedside?'

  The extended family ate in the living room instead of the kitchen, and the smell of the roast, chicken, lamb, pork or beef (in strict succession) would greet Maggie and Mary as they walked in the door. Ruby would be rushing here, there and everywhere while Theresa and Caroline would help prepare vegetables, but mainly just get in the way.

Mary always brought the pudding, apple pie or bread and butter pudding (I've put three eggs in it. Three!) and a bowl of proper home-made custard. They would all sit round the table, with both of the extension leaves in place, and anyone looking in would see a seemingly convivial family gathering. It always started promisingly, but would invariably end in some sort of minor fracas.

'Georgina, don't bolt your food, you'll end up with an ulcer.' Theresa.

'I like to eat it while it's hot. If I do get an ulcer I'll slow down.'

'And eat your carrots. They make you see in the dark.'

'That's an old wives' tale. Anyway, that's what lights are for.'

'Gina, don't be rude to your mother or you'll feel the back of my hand.' Alf.

'Violence never solves anything. I should know.' Maggie.

'It would be lovely to eat Sunday lunch in peace for a change.' Caroline.

'Oh! Sunday lunch is it? It's Sunday dinner in this house.' Theresa.

'Lunch, dinner, what does the name matter?' Ruby.

'Ruby, it's absolutely delicious, whatever anyone wants to call it. Now who's for some lovely bread and butter pudding?' Mary.

'Gran's put three eggs in it. Three.' Maggie and Gina in unison.

Chapter 47

The houses were getting bigger and more opulent, the roads wider and lined with more trees. Maggie's heart was sinking with every mile. William's car drew to a halt in front of tall double gates, painted black and gold. He leaped out of the car and flung them open before continuing up the tree lined drive which swept in a graceful curve in front of a mellow-bricked house.

'Here we are.'

He went round to the passenger door and helped her out.

Maggie was paralysed. She wanted to be anywhere else but there.

The front door opened and a tall woman with short iron-grey hair and a no nonsense pleated skirt and twinset, came towards them with a pair of golden retrievers in tow.

'Mum, this is Maggie. Maggie, my mum.'

Maggie wanted to shrink into his side, but summoning up her courage, she walked towards his mother and held out her hand, which his mother either deliberately ignored, or didn't appear to notice.

'Get down, you two!'

The dogs cowered.

'Come on in both of you. Lunch will be ready in about half an hour so I thought we'd have a sherry.'

Maggie, completely tongue tied with

shyness, followed William and his mother into the kitchen. The dogs flopped down in front of the Aga. His father was pouring sherry into glasses on a tray.

'Dad, this is Maggie.'

'Hello,' she said faintly, not risking offering her hand a second time.

'So you're the young lady we've heard so much about. How do you do.'

'I'm very well, thank you,' she said and then blushed, remembering that it was a greeting, not an enquiry after her health.

'Sherry?'

'Yes please.'

She accepted it, thankful for the Dutch courage it offered. She looked round the kitchen. There was an enormous cooker and a u-shaped run of oak cupboards. In the centre was a large oak table cluttered with pots and pans and dishes. The kitchen and living room of their cottage would have fitted comfortably into this room. It was surprisingly untidy. Viewing the house from the outside, Maggie imagined that it would have been more ordered. Although the furnishings may have originally been expensive, they looked shabby and a bit neglected, as though the look of them wasn't at all important to the inhabitants. A smell of damp dog pervaded the air.

'Can I help with anything?' Maggie stammered.

'No thank you. It's all under control. Or it would be if that sister of yours was around,' his mother said in a clipped voice, looking at William with raised eyebrows.

'Fiona!' she bellowed, then turned back to

them. 'She went upstairs to get changed and she's now probably got her head in a book. Reads books in French for pleasure. Don't know where she gets it from. Now hurry along into the parlour while I attempt to get this meal on the table. Do you like venison, Margaret?'

Before Maggie had a chance to reply, William's mother was at the bottom of the stairs yelling for Fiona to come down at once. They followed his father into the parlour, which was as unkempt as the kitchen. The furniture was heavy and old fashioned and the walls were peppered with faded pictures in carved oak frames. Maggie didn't know if they were prints or the real thing. One wall had been reserved for framed photographs of various member of the family in gowns and mortar boards, clutching degree certificates. Maggie's heart was in her mouth, wondering if they would grill her about her own family. She had no doubt that they would.

'After lunch perhaps you'd like to have a walk around the garden, Maggie.' William put a reassuring arm round her shoulders.

'Yes, I'd like that,' she replied, looking out of the window. The view out of her own window wasn't dissimilar, except that the land didn't belong to her family. This 'garden' appeared to go on forever.

William's father was now completely ignoring her, for which she was grateful, and was talking to William about their work. This did seem strange, and slightly rude, however, as William was still living with them. She concluded that he was probably useless at small talk. He was smaller than William, his face florid and his figure rather rotund.

He spoke in a deep, sonorous voice which she could imagine ringing with authority across a courtroom. She noticed he was dressed casually in flannels and a baggy cardigan with leather patches on the sleeves. She slowly sipped her sherry and pasted, what she hoped was, an interested look on her face, as the conversation went completely over her head,

'Lunch is ready!' William's mother's voice boomed from the kitchen.

Maggie swallowed the last of her sherry and felt the alcohol seep warmly into her bloodstream. She followed them into another huge room which was apparently the dining room. Here there was more dark furniture, dominated by another massive table, laid with old fashioned plates and heavy cutlery, and tureens holding a variety of steaming vegetables. William's father took his place at one end where he busied himself brandishing a carving knife. Next to each plate was a wine glass. William's mother was pouring wine into her glass without asking whether she wanted any.

'This is my sister Fiona,' William said, as a tall, willowy girl entered the room. 'And this is Maggie.'

'Hello Maggie. I'm really pleased to meet you at last.'

'I'm pleased to meet you too,' said Maggie and then she thought that sounded a bit formal. 'William has talked about his little sister. But you're not so little,' she added. She laughed nervously, thinking she had made another social gaffe.

'No, I just kept on growing, like Topsy. I hope he said nothing that has put you off me, Call me

Fi. Everyone else does, apart from my parents and they don't count.'

Maggie was warming to her by the second.

'Unfortunately Bob, our elder brother, couldn't make it today. He's on call,' put in William. 'He works really long hours as a GP.'

William's father was passing down plates, which bore generous slices of venison. Maggie had never tasted it before and hoped that she liked it.

'Help yourself to vegetables, Margaret, or they'll get cold. Fiona, perhaps you would pass the gravy boat and the Cumberland sauce.'

This was a very different experience to mealtimes at the cottage, where the meat and vegetables were served straight onto the plates, and what on earth was Cumberland sauce? Maggie put a small portion of everything on her plate and picked up her knife and fork. She was about to start eating when something intuitive told her to wait until everyone else had served themselves. Then she realised they had all put a napkin on their laps and hers was still on the table. She quickly put down her knife and fork and laid the napkin across her knees. Her appetite had completely left her.

'So where do your people live?' William's mother asked, when the food and accompaniments had been passed round and everyone had served themselves.

'I live at Clayton Manor,' said Maggie, having a tentative bite of the venison. She thought it might be off. It had a very strong taste.

'Oh, that will be the Barclay's place. We know them slightly. So are you a Barclay?'

William's mother was looking at her for the first time with interest.

'No,' said Maggie, wishing the deep pile carpet would swallow her up. She longed to be outside, walking through the park with William, where she wasn't about to be the subject of an inquisition and would be found wanting.

'No,' she said, holding her head high. 'My father is the head gardener of Clayton Manor and we live in a cottage in the grounds.'

There was an uncomfortable silence, apart from the sound of chewing and the loud tick of a large grandfather clock. Maggie drank some wine.

'Oh, how absolutely lovely!' cried Fiona into the void. 'It sounds like Hansel and Gretel's cottage. So romantic. Did you play in those enormous grounds when you were a child? I bet you did.'

'Sometimes, although we weren't really allowed.'

'And how many of you live in this, er, cottage?' William's mother was cutting her venison into neat pieces.

Maggie took another drink of wine. She didn't much like it but she was feeling much more relaxed.

'Well at the moment, there's my mum and dad, Auntie Ruby and my younger sister, Gina. My elder sister, Caroline, and her husband are staying there temporarily until they move into a new house.' Maggie wasn't a snob but she could just imagine their reaction if she had said 'council house'.

'My goodness, it must be an enormous cottage,' William's mother persisted.

'Actually, it's not. I've been staying at my grandparents' house to help look after my grandad who has just died. I'm planning to stay there for the time being to give the others some space.'

'I see.'

Maggie waited for her to say something about being sorry her grandfather had died but nothing was forthcoming. She picked up the wine glass to drain it but put it down again when she realised it was already empty and she was feeling a little bit drunk. She needed to stop before she started slurring her words and make a complete fool of herself.

William's father was staring at her.

'I understand that you met William at the solicitor's office where he is articled. Are you studying law yourself?' He gave her a piercing look.

'Er, no. I left there. I'm training to be a travel agent now.'

'A travel agent?' It sounded as though William's mother had spat out the words in disgust. Maggie could swear that she could see her nose turning up in distaste. It obviously wasn't an acceptable career. Again Fiona came to her rescue.

'That sounds really exciting, Maggie. Do you get to travel yourself to try out new resorts and hotels and the like?'

'Yes, I hope to.' Maggie now felt she was back on safe ground. 'I really love it. Our motto is that we're selling dreams. People come in and we can put together dream holidays for them.'

'Hardly a worthwhile profession,' said William's father.

Maggie felt that both of his parents were attempting to either test or belittle her. She took a deep breath. It helped to know that both William and Fiona were on her side. Who the hell did his parents think they were? A sudden flash of anger, and, undoubtedly, a surfeit of alcohol, made her bold. She had had quite enough of their attempts to intimidate her.

'Well, I'm afraid I would have to disagree with you.' she surprised herself by saying. 'The world is opening up and people are looking beyond the British seaside holiday. They want to experience new horizons, new cultures, new food. We tailor-make holidays, honeymoon packages and safaris. People work hard and deserve a holiday to rest and relax. I think it's very worthwhile and I find it very interesting. I'm proud to be making a career of something so ground-breaking.' Maggie sat back, pink in the face, her meal forgotten. She might as well go and get her coat now.

'Well said!' cried Fiona, clapping her hands. 'Mum and Dad haven't yet woken to the fact that it's the sixties and anything's possible.'

'And I think you've grilled Maggie enough,' said William. 'She must be thinking she's at a job interview. Maggie is doing something she loves, which is an accolade in itself. I wish I found my job half as interesting.'

'Yes, well, if you think I've been a bit intrusive then I apologise. It is an opportunity to get to know Margaret and it's hard to do that without asking questions.'

'Well I appreciate that you're taking an

interest in me,' said Maggie, 'but I wish you would call me Maggie. My parents only call me Margaret when I'm in trouble.' She smiled to try to defuse the awkwardness.

'Of course, Maggie it is.' said William's mother, beginning to clear the dishes.

'Let me help you,' said Maggie, jumping up. She felt she had perhaps gone too far and was now eager to make amends.

As she followed her into the kitchen she heard his father say, 'I like a filly with a kick in her gallop. She knows how to stand up for herself.'

William's mother took the pineapple upside down cake and a jug of cream out of the refrigerator and handed them to her. 'Thank you,' she said stiffly. 'You go on ahead and I'll bring the pudding plates.'

The conversation went on to more general things after that and Maggie felt they were no longer testing her. After lunch they all wandered around the garden. Maggie was still suffering the effects of the unaccustomed alcohol and, feeling a bit unsteady, she clung to William for support. They crossed a huge well-kept lawn towards the kitchen garden.

'We grow as many of our vegetables as we can. There's nothing to beat a freshly pulled carrot,' advised his mother.

This led to a garden which appeared to contain every variety of rose imaginable. Maggie bent to savour the perfume. 'Oh this is lovely,' she breathed. 'The colours and scents are amazing.'

'Surely not up to the standard of Clayton Manor,' commented William's father.

'I wouldn't know,' said Maggie. 'We don't go

into the grounds, but I know that my father is a fantastic gardener. He knows the names of all of the plants, including the Latin ones.' She never thought she would hear herself singing her father's praises.

At the end of the lawn was a swimming pool which, she was told, was solar heated.

'It's still freezing,' said William,' but next time you come you can bring your swimming costume if you fancy a dip.'

Beyond that was a gate which led to an extensive orchard of plum, pear and apple trees.

'We get sick to death of fruit by the end of the season so we give most of it away. Much of it lies on the ground and rots,' William told her.

Maggie looked at the magnificent spread of land and thought how privileged they were, very like the Barclays. She thought that none of it made them better people, and she realised that they had been her grandmother's words. She had had the experience of working for the Barclays at the turn of the century when privileged families had their heyday. Her gran wasn't in awe of them and Maggie refused to be in awe of William's parents. They would have to take her as they found her.

As he drove her home, William reached out and took her hand.

'I'm sorry if that was a baptism of fire but I was so proud of you for standing your ground. They'll like you more for that. I promise I won't put you through that too often.'

'And I thought my parents were bad,' laughed Maggie. 'I liked Fiona very much.'

'Fiona is a good egg. No side to her. She

would have meant everything she said. She obviously took to you, too.'

'What about your brother, Bob? What's he like?'

'Always busy and preoccupied. He can be a bit overbearing and argumentative, like my mother. He's always right about everything. When he lets his hair down though, he can be quite hilarious and you won't meet anyone wittier.'

'Is he married?'

'Yes. Angela is OK. A bit mousy. Never stands up to our parents like you did.'

'Oh dear. Did I go in with both feet? I shouldn't have had that wine, never mind the sherry. I always show myself up after a thimbleful of alcohol.'

'You were impressive. They'll respect you.'

'Phew! Did I pass?'

'You've got the job. Congratulations.'

Maggie sat back in the seat and wondered what they really thought of her. Well it was too late now. It did matter to her though. She wanted William's parents to like her. Then she thought, what did William mean when he said I've got the job?

Chapter 48

Caroline wished that the baby would hurry up. She was thirty eight weeks pregnant and felt like a hippopotamus. She went to bed totally exhausted every night and it seemed that that was the cue for the baby to start kicking. She couldn't find a comfortable position to lie in and consequently also woke up exhausted.

Graham would get up as quietly as he could and creep out of the room so as not to disturb her. He would eat a bowl of cereal or some toast and then leave for work. Alf always rose early and if Graham had an early start, the pair of them would sit at the kitchen table in silence. Alf wasn't used to having his early morning ritual disturbed and, after a brief nod, behaved as though Graham wasn't there.

Auntie Ruby rose at seven and made breakfast for her and Gina, who leaped out of bed at seven thirty, leaving herself the minimum amount of time to wash, dress, eat and catch her train to school. Theresa didn't surface until after nine and sat down to a breakfast that Ruby always had ready and waiting for her. Caroline timed hers so that Theresa had finished hers by the time she came down. She could barely stand being around her during the day but the mornings were the worst. Theresa always woke up grumpy and took it out on whoever was nearest.

'There's an official-looking letter for you,' she said one morning as Caroline waddled into the kitchen.

'Thanks,' Caroline turned it over. It was stamped, 'Surrey County Council.'

She sank down on to a chair, catching her breath. Could it be? She ripped it open, her heart racing, and scanned the contents.

'We've got a council house on Beech Road. Number 34. It was allocated to someone else but they've turned it down, It's ours if we want it.'

'There must be something wrong with it if the other people turned it down,' said Theresa, quickly taking the wind out of her sails.

'I don't care. It'll be better than being cramped here. And we don't have to live there forever. It's a stepping stone.

'Well that's gratitude for you after we took you in. Maggie even moved out so you and Graham would have a roof over your heads.'

'Of course we're grateful and we realise that you all made a sacrifice for us but we need our own space with a baby on the way. It'll be better for all of us. I can't wait to tell Graham. We could go round and have a look at it if he gets home before dark.'

Graham arrived home just after seven and he barely had time to digest his tea before Caroline was insisting that they went to look at the house. He had brought a sleek Bentley home for the night, which purred incongruously through the councul estate to Beech Road. Number 34 was at the end of a block of four. It had one of the new open plan front gardens which was just a tract of bare land with a path up to the front door. They walked round it and noticed it was brand new and had a decent sized back garden.

Some of the houses were already occupied and looked well kept.

'So, what do you think, Caroline? I think it will do very well. Lots of space, and freedom from your parents, if you don't mind my saying.'

'Well you know how I feel about that. To be honest, it's not where I imagined I would live but I think it will do very well for now. I just hope the neighbours are decent. I don't want my child growing up in a rough neighbourhood.'

If Graham noticed that she said 'my child' he didn't comment.

'As long as you're happy, darling, it'll do for me. It's got that little parade of shops at the end of the road and it's not far from the bus route. It's not what I wanted for my princess but I think it's the best we can do for the present.'

'And perhaps if we watch our pennies we can save a bit towards buying our own house one day,' Caroline said pensively.

'I'm sure we will,' replied Graham, somewhat unconvincingly. Caroline deserved the best but he had no idea how they would ever afford their own house on his salary, even with the generous tips that sometimes came his way.

Chapter 49

Maggie knew that she couldn't put off William meeting her parents any longer. She couldn't face inviting him round for a meal like he had done with his own parents, so she decided they would just drop in on them, otherwise everyone would get in a flap. They had had a lovely Saturday out at Chessington Zoo, where they had visited every animal house, before moving on to the funfair.

'I haven't had so much fun for ages,' exclaimed William, wiping the grease from the onions off his chin with a handkerchief. 'That big dipper was more terrifying than I remember.'

'I had my eyes shut all the time. I'm never sure whether they're safe. I preferred the ghost train. You can get your thrills without feeling you might be in actual danger. I felt a bit sick after the waltzer, though. All that whizzing round. Just as well we had the beer and hot dog afterwards and not before.'

'Look, the dodgems. Fancy a go on them?'

'Only if we can then go on the carousel.'

'Oh, go on then. Then I'm going to win you a huge teddy bear on the shooting range.'

'Don't you dare!' she said, dragging him away.

Exhausted and exhilirated they sauntered back to her gran's house.

'Do you want to pop in and meet my family on the way?'

She hoped it sounded casual and not as though she had been rehearsing what she was going to say all the way home.

He looked at his watch.

'It's nearly 9.30, isn't it a bit late to call in unannounced?'

'No. It'll be OK.'

She did actually think it was a bit late but she couldn't face going through all the apprehension another time. She might as well just get it over with.

'Well alright. If you're sure.'

He thought he probably didn't look his best after the day they'd had but she seemed determined.

They went in the back way, into the kitchen, where Ruby was mopping the floor. She had put the chairs up on the table.

'Hello Auntie Ruby. This is William.'

Ruby leaned on the broom.

'Well you're a sight for sore eyes, Maggie. If I'd known you were coming I'd have baked a cake. And I'm very pleased to meet you at last, William.'

'And me, you.' He held out his hand. 'I've heard a lot about you, Auntie Ruby. Can I call you that?'

'That'll do nicely, since it's my name.' She opened the door to the living room and poked her head through.

'Stand by your beds. Maggie's here and she's brought her young man in to meet us at last.'

With surprising speed, Theresa swung her plump legs off the sofa and patted her perm.

'Come in and let me have a look at you. I'm Maggie's mother, and this is my husband, Alfred.'

I knew it, Maggie thought. I knew she'd put on her pseudo-posh voice. Oh why can't you be yourself? It was oh, so embarrassing.

Alf said a gruff, 'Hello William.' without getting out of his chair.

Theresa, still in character, continued talking. The floodgates had opened and the words whooshed out.

'We've heard so much about you.' She patted the sofa, recently vacated by her feet, 'Come and sit down next to me. Ruby, will you put the kettle on?'

'What did your last slave die of?' asked Ruby, good-naturedly. They heard the kettle being filled. 'That's my housekeeper,' explained Theresa, her accent slipping slightly. 'A treasure. I don't know what I'd do without her.'

'She's a bit more than that,' put in Maggie, but her words were lost in the relentless onslaught.

'So Maggie says you're training to be a solicitor. That's a good job. You young people have a lot more opportunities than we did at your age, don't they Alfred?'

The corners of Alf's mouth turned up slightly at the unaccustomed use of his full name.

'I don't suppose it was handed to him on a plate.'

After a few minutes Auntie Ruby came in with a tray bearing cups of tea and a plate of biscuits. 'I didn't know if you took sugar so I've brought the bowl and there are some garibaldis if you're peckish.'

'No sugar, thanks but I'm partial to a garibaldi.'

Theresa said, 'Not for me thanks, my doctor

said I need to watch my weight. I have heart problems, although I'm not one to complain. Maggie, do you want to go upstairs and tell Gina and and Caroline and Graham that you've brought William in to meet us?'

'Yes, OK. I won't be a minute.' Maggie looked at William and her mother, wondering what embarrassing thing she would say next. This was worse than she thought.

She ran upstairs as fast as she could to summon her sisters and Graham. Gina said, 'Oh goody, at last!' and Caroline said, 'Give me a minute.'

Gina came into the room and shook William's hand.

'I'm Gina, so happy to meet you.'

'And I'm happy to meet you, too. You and Maggie seem close.'

'Maggie's the best,' replied Gina, looking round the room to find somewhere to sit.

'I don't enjoy good health,' interjected Theresa, trying to regain centre stage, 'but I do have three lovely daughters, all different. They're a credit to me. Maggie is kind, funny and very capable, Gina has the brains and Caroline has the beauty; she reminds me very much of myself at her age.'

The beautiful Caroline appeared fifteen minutes later with Graham in tow. She had changed into a dress, had put on a lot of makeup and had combed and lacquered her hair. Her smile turned to alarm when she saw William. She paled under the panstick and bright lipstick.

'Hello,' she stammered, holding out a trembling hand.

'Hello Caroline,' he replied, trying to keep his voice even.

Maggie eyed them suspiciously. 'Have you two met before?' she asked, a slight tremor in her voice.

'Er, yes,' said Caroline. 'I was a bit upset once and this stranger talked to me and took me to a cafe for a cup of tea and a piece of cake. He was very kind but never told me his name. He listened to me and made me feel a lot better. I've never forgotten it.'

'What were you upset about?' asked Graham.

'I can't remember now.' Caroline convinced no one. 'Anyway, it doesn't matter, all I remember is that William was very kind to me.'

'You must remember what it was you were upset about,' persisted Graham, coming over to put his arm round her. 'Couldn't you have talked to me?'

There was an uncomfortable silence. Even Theresa had nothing to say.

William smiled at Caroline.

'It's not really my place to say it but if you really can't remember, I think it was that you had just discovered you were pregnant and, er, didn't know whether Graham would be pleased or not as I think you thought you couldn't afford a baby at the time. I found you sitting on a bench looking upset. It was something and nothing. We all have our moments when we blow things out of proportion. Oh and congratulations to you both, by the way.'

Caroline had been biting her lip, but now her face had relaxed and she smiled gratefully at William.

'I still don't know why you couldn't talk to me,' said Graham looking and sounding aggrieved.

'Or me,' said Theresa. 'I'm you're mother after all.'

'It's sometimes easier to talk to a complete stranger,' said William smoothly. 'I can't believe you're Maggie's sister. Such a coincidence.'

'So where have you two been tonight?' asked Caroline, successfully changing the subject.

On the way back to her grandmother's house Maggie said, 'Well now you've met my strange family. I hope it wasn't too awful.'

'Of course not. I can hardly judge them. Mine were pretty challenging. I can see what you mean about your mother being wrapped up in herself.'

'What a coincidencc that you met Caroline when she was so upset about the baby. It sounded as though you were really kind to her. I can't imagine her being like that. She's always so self-contained. I don't think she has ever shown a weak side to anyone before, but what do I know? She and I have never been close.'

She had dropped his hand and then suddenly felt very lonely.

'Well, we all have our moments, I suppose.'

Maggie felt sure that William hadn't told the whole story and she felt upset that his loyalties seemed to lie with her sister. When they arrived at her grandmother's house she gave him a brief peck on the mouth and hurried in, her eyes prickling with tears.

Mary was sitting in her chair knitting a yellow baby cardigan.

'Hello Maggie, did you have a good time at the zoo?'

'We had a wonderful time. It was such fun.'

It seemed a long time ago now.

'Something has happened. I can always tell. Do you want to talk about it?'

Maggie was about to say that nothing was the matter and then changed her mind. In the short time that she had been living with Mary they had become very close. She knew that she could tell her anything. Mary would listen and perhaps comment. She was wise and never judgemental like her mother, wiser then anyone else Maggie knew.

So she told her about introducing William to their family and the strange coincidence of William and Caroline having met before.

'It could be just what it seems,' said Mary, putting down her knitting.

'It could be, but I could tell that Caroline was very embarrassed. You know her, rarely flustered. It also seemed odd that she couldn't remember what she had been upset about and William supplied the answer, almost as though he was saving her from having to tell the truth, or coming out with a lie. Or perhaps I'm completely wrong and that was what happened.'

There was a silence. Maggie sat trying to decide whether to go further.

'Gran. I'm going to tell you something. I have already confided in Auntie Ruby but no-one else.' She paused and took a deep breath.

'Before Caroline told us she was pregnant I saw her in a pub in Wimbledon. She didn't see me and I left straight away.'

The clock on the mantlepiece ticked away

the seconds as Maggie summoned the courage to continue.

'She was with another man, and they looked very intimate.'

Mary looked her in the eye.

'And you suspect that the baby might not be Graham's and that was why she was so upset.'

'I think she might have told William, thinking he was a stranger she would never meet again.'

'Oh dear God. I can see why you're in a state.'

'Should I have it out with William? I didn't think we had any secrets that we kept from each other.'

'Well, it wasn't anything to do with you at the time so there was no reason to tell you. He didn't know you were her sister.'

'No, I know. But should I have it out with him now?'

'No, Maggie. This is something that is far better left alone. You don't know the facts and you might be wrong. You could upset a number of people. I know you're a stickler for the truth, but some things are better left unsaid.'

'I was really short with William afterwards. How am I going to explain that to him?'

'You're not. If he asks, you could say you were tired after the lovely day out you had. I think you need to let it drop now. Thank you for telling me. It will stop here. Don't worry about it. None of this is your fault and I must say I admire William for not breaking Caroline's confidence. Next time you see him, just ignore what happened tonight. Caroline wouldn't be the first person to pass off someone else's baby as their husband's.'

She paused, remembering that Caroline wasn't Alf's daughter, but at least Alf had gone into it with his eyes open.

'I'm not saying it's right but not everything in this life is black and white.'

She resumed her knitting.

'Thanks Gran. You're probably right. I just think it's would be so wrong if poor Graham had to bring up someone else's child without knowing it. But, of course ,the child could be his. In which case, why would Caroline have been so upset that she had to confide in a stranger?' She yawned. 'It's been a long day. I think I'll go to bed.'

'Goodnight, love. Things will look better in the morning.'

Chapter 50

Maggie went to the cottage after work to pick up some vegetables that Alf had promised to give to Mary.

The back door was open but it was deathly quiet.

'Hellooo. Anyone at home?'

The kitchen was tidy and the living room empty. It was unusual for everyone to be out at the same time.

'Hellooo,' she called again, climbing the stairs.

'Is that you, Maggie?' A faint voice from Caroline's room.

The door was open and she went in. Caroline was hunched up on the bed, her face was pale and contorted with pain.

'Thank God you're here!' she gasped. 'The baby's coming.'

Maggie noticed that the carpet was soaking wet.

'Oh no! Isn't it a bit early? Where is everyone?'

'Taking stuff to the new house. I didn't go as my back was aching. I didn't realise I was in labour. Baby not due until next week.' She was panting.

'Right. I'll phone an ambulance.'

'Yes. Yes. Aagh!' Caroline arched her back. Her forehead was wet.

'I'll have to leave you for two minutes but I'll be back in a jiffy. Try to stay calm. I'll phone for an ambulance.

'The phones not working!' Caroline screamed. The men are coming to fix it tomorrow!"

'Oh God, no. I'll be quick as I can.'

Maggie ran out of the cottage, through the woods and on to the main road where there was a phone box. Someone was in it. She rapped on the window.

'I need to use the phone!'

The woman inside shrugged and turned her back on her.

Maggie wrenched open the door. 'Look. I need an ambulance. My sister is in labour. I'll just be a minute.'

The woman looked as though she was trying to make up her mind whether it was a genuine emergency.

'I need that phone now!' Maggie shouted.

The woman flinched as though Maggie was about to hit her and wordlessly thrust the phone at her.

'Thank you.' said Maggie dialling 999 with trembling fingers.' Does this convince you?'

The woman stammered that she was sorry and hurried away. Maggie hastily explained the situation to the ambulance service and gave directions to the cottage. She ran back hoping her instructions had been clear to them as it wasn't an easy place to find. She took the stairs two at a time. She could hear Caroline groaning and panting.

'The ambulance is on its way. What can I do

to help? Do I fetch towels and boil water?'

'Fetch my suitcase from the top of the wardrobe,' Caroline gasped. 'It has everything I need for the hospital. Then write a note to tell everyone what's happened if they're not back in time. Will you come to the hospital with me?'

'If you want me to. Do you want some water or anything?'

'Please. Maggie, thanks. I need you. I'm so scared.'

'You've got me.' Maggie squeezed her sister's hand. 'You'll soon have a lovely baby and all this will be over. I'll get the water.'

She held it to Caroline's lips and rubbed her back as another contraction contorted her body. Caroline screamed, 'Nobody told me it would be this bad. Can you see if the ambulance has arrived?'

Maggie went to the window. 'No, not yet. Should we be timing these contractions?'

'Yes, they feel about every five minutes. Oh where's that ambulance?'

Maggie went to the bathroom for a wet flannel and wiped her sister's forehead.

Caroline clutched Maggie's hand as another contraction rippled through her body.

'I don't know what I'd've done if you hadn't arrived.'

'Don't think about that. I'm here now.'

'Oh God! I think it's coming. I want to push.'

Maggie didn't know much about childbirth and had no idea whether Caroline was supposed to push or not. She felt a rising sense of panic at the thought that there was just her and Caroline and she might have to deliver the baby. They were too far away from any other house to shout for help. She thought of running up to the Manor but she couldn't leave her sister now.

'Look and see if it's coming. Please.'

Caroline remembered her manners, even at a time like this. Maggie rushed to the window. Again, 'No, not yet.'

'No, you idiot, the baby, see if it's coming.' Caroline hauled up her skirt.

'Oh! Right!' Maggie gently eased off Caroline's knickers, embarrassed at this intimacy. She could see something glistening.

'Oh I think I can see the baby's head!'

She wiped Caroline's forehead again with the flannel. Her sister's face was now bright red with the effort of straining. She looked again.

'The head's coming out! You're doing really well. Grip my hand. That's right. Squeeze as hard as you want.'

Caroline gave an almighty scream and pushed with all her strength. The baby slithered out and lay motionless on the bed.

'What do I do? What do I do? I don't know if it's breathing. What happens with this cord'? Maggie was sobbing with fear.

There was a ring on the doorbell, followed by the most welcome voice in the world.

'Ambulance!'

'Up here,' Maggie shouted. 'Quick! The baby's here and there's something wrong.'

There was the sound of heavy steps on the stairs and two ambulance men rushed into the room.

One picked up the baby and examined it.

He opened his bag, brought out some rubber tubing and began sucking fluid out of the baby's lungs.. Seconds ticked by and there was no sign of life. Caroline screamed, 'What's happened? Why isn't it making any noise?'

There was a little cough followed by a sharp cry.

'You have a lovely baby girl,' the first man said as he tied and cut the cord. Wrapping her in a towel, he placed her in Caroline's arms.

'Thank God you arrived in time to save the baby,' Maggie said, wiping away her tears. 'I didn't know what to do. What took you so long to get here?'

'We couldn't find the place. You're a bit isolated out here. We took a wrong turn. Anyway, luckily no harm done. You did a good job, both of you.'

The second ambulance man had helped to deliver the placenta and was checking Caroline over.

'There's a little tear which needs a stitch, but otherwise you seem OK. We'll take you to the hospital now. You coming?' He looked at Maggie.

'Yes, of course. She's my sister.'

Chapter 51

'I could murder a cup of tea. Someone put the kettle on.' Theresa threw her handbag on the table and sank into a chair.

'It's a lovely little house,' said Ruby, lighting the gas. 'How nice to have everything all spanking new. No one in it before you to mess it up with horrible wallpaper and holes in the wall where they've hung pictures. And I love those new through lounges. Plenty of room to swing a cat although why anyone would want to I don't know. Seems cruel to me.'

'That garden needs sorting,' said Alf, lighting a cigarette. 'I suppose I could give them a hand. I don't suppose Graham knows much about starting from scratch. Where is he, by the way?'

'He's gone up to see if Caroline has woken from her nap.' Ruby set the cups and saucers on the table.

'She does nothing but nap these days. She'll have to buck her ideas up when she's got a baby to look after twenty four hours a day. Good God, what's happened?' Theresa clutched her heart as they heard Graham pounding down the stairs. 'What's up?'

'She's gone! There's blood on the bed and she's gone!'

'She'll be having the baby. It wasn't due till next week. I hope she's not in labour, wandering around trying to get help,' said Theresa. 'Oh dear me, supposing she is?'

'Oh why did I leave her? What shall I do? I'll go and look for her. I've looked in the other rooms and now I'll look outside. What if you're right and she went for help and collapsed somewhere?'

'Go and phone the hospital. If she's not here the chances are she's probably there. What's this?' Theresa picked up a scrap of paper that she had just noticed on the table.

'But how did she get there if no one was here? The phone's a quarter of a mile away. What was I thinking, leaving her on her own?'

'Wait! This is Maggie's writing. She was here. Caroline's had a little girl! She's gone to the hospital with her. Well that was quick for a first baby. I was in labour for days with her.'

'A daughter!' Graham sank into a chair. 'Does it say if they're alright? Maggie must have gone to call an ambulance.' Graham had gone white.

'No. I've read out what it said. It doesn't say she's not alright. Graham, women have babies all the time. They'll be fine. Just get yourself to the hospital. Alf'll drive you, won't you Alf?'

'As soon as I've had my tea.'

Alf put his coat on again. When they'd gone Theresa said, 'I'll just put my feet up if you don't mind. This stress isn't good for me.'

'Especially now you're a grandma. Does that make me a great aunt?'

'Not if you aren't related. I expect she'll call you Auntie Ruby like everyone else.'

'I love babies. I wonder what they'll call it?

'Something posh, knowing Caroline. She won't go for a Susan or a Judy like everyone else.'

'Well, we'll soon find out. I'll nip up and see what I can do with their room. It sounds like the bed's a mess. I'll put it all in to soak with a bit of bleach.'

'I don't know what I'd do without you. All this excitement's made me hungry. Could you pass me a Waggon Wheel before you go up?'

An hour later Ruby sat down and picked up Woman's Weekly from the magazine rack, which she always referred to as 'my woman's book.' Instead of reading it she kept getting up and looking out of the window.

'Ruby, can't you relax for a minute? You're making me jumpy.'

'I can't relax until we know what happened.'

'Well you sitting down reading won't change anything. Listen, someone's coming.'

Graham and Alf came in, Graham sporting a wide smile.

'Caroline's a bit sore but she's fine and my daughter is absolutely beautiful. It seems that Maggie actually delivered her because the ambulance men couldn't find the cottage. The baby wasn't breathing and they arrived just in time to save her. It was touch and go, apparently. I wish I'd been here.'

'Graham, you didn't know she'd be born early. There's no point beating yourself up now the horse has bolted. Who does she look like?' Ruby was flushed with excitement.

'Hard to tell. All babies look the same, except ours is prettier. Maggie was at the hospital. She said she'd been really scared having to help deliver her. The ambulance men had to suck stuff out of the baby's lungs. She would have died if they'd been a minute later.'

'Thank God they did then. What was Maggie doing here?' asked Theresa.

'She came to collect some veg that Dad had promised Gran.'

'Well that was lucky. If she hadn't then the baby would have died before it had even lived.' Ruby took a large comforting gulp of tea.

'So Caroline's Ok? Kangaroo Ruby said it looked like a pig had been slaughtered in the bedroom.' Theresa turned up her nose even though she hadn't actually seen it.

'She was very tired. The baby's not in a cot next to her like the other babies on the ward. They had to take her away and put her in an incubator in the special unit. I went to see her but Caroline hasn't seen her since she was delivered. I think the baby's got to be watched closely for twenty four hours. Looks so helpless, the poor little thing but the doctor said she'll be alright.'

'Caroline must be dying to see her little daughter. Can't they take her in a wheelchair to see her or something?' asked Theresa.

'Well, to be honest, Caroline didn't seem that interested. When I was describing the baby she turned over and started crying.'

'New mums sometimes get like that,' said Theresa. 'It's called the baby blues. Some of them cry for days and don't know why they're crying. She'll be alright in a day or two, I expect. We'll go and see her tomorrow, Alf, and see how she is. I'm looking forward to meeting our new granddaughter. She should be back on the ward by then.'

'I'll have to work for a couple of hours but we can go late morning. You know, Maggie's had a time of it lately. In a matter of weeks she's had to deal with a death and a birth in the family. Not everyone could have done that.' Alf said, shaking a cigarette from a rather bent packet.

'Yes she's made of strong stuff, that girl. She reminds me of myself when I was younger, before I had all my complaints.'

'I'll finish moving the rest of our stuff over to our new house this weekend and get it all shipshape, then when they come home we can move in. I'll hire a van.'

'I'll give you a hand,' said Alf.

'And me,' added Ruby.

'I can't lift anything, but perhaps Maggie and William would like to help,' said Theresa.

'It might cheer Caroline up,' said Ruby, 'to come home with a nice new baby to a nice new house with everything in place.'

'I wouldn't bank on it,' said Graham with a wry smile. 'Wherever you put anything, it'll be in the wrong place.'

'Well you can't please everybody half of the time, or is it you can't please half the people all of the time?' asked Ruby, settling herself down once again with her woman's book.

Chapter 52

The doorbell rang and Mary hurried to answer it before it disturbed Maggie. William was standing on the doorstep looking flustered.

'Oh, hello, William. Was Maggie expecting you? She never said. She's upstairs having a little nap. She didn't get much sleep last night. Do you want to come in and have a seat?'

'Not if it's inconvenient. I phoned her at work and they said she hadn't been in today so I was a bit worried. Is she ill?'

'No, fit as a flea. Just tired. I'll go and tell her you're here. Come on in.'

He followed her into the sitting room and sank down on the nearest chair.

'Look, don't disturb her on my account.' He stood up again.

'She'll never forgive me if I don't tell her you're here. You sit right down again.'

They smiled at each other. 'You're very persuasive,' he said.

'I also know Maggie.'

She disappeared upstairs. Five minutes later Maggie came, in running her fingers through her tangled hair.

'Hello, I didn't expect you this evening.'

'I was worried about you when you weren't at work when I phoned.' He looked at her quizzically.

'It's a long story. Shall we go for a walk and

I'll tell you everything?'

They were sitting on a bench, watching the ducks on a pond.

'Well I never. So you delivered your own niece! That must have been very frightening.'

'It was. I hadn't a clue what to do and then the baby wasn't breathing. I really panicked. If the ambulance man hadn't arrived then and saved her it would have been tragic. I stayed late with Caroline at the hospital and then I went to the cottage to tell everyone what happened. When I finally got back here I tossed and turned half the night. I kept reliving it. You know, the baby so nearly dying. I kept beating myself up, wondering if I had given the ambulance men the wrong directions or something. I was really tired so I took the day off but I couldn't sleep then. Too wound up. Then I decided to have an early night. I'm glad you came round, although I'm not much company I'm afraid.'

He put his arm round her and she put her head on his shoulder.

'You're always good company. Caroline's lucky to have you for a sister. I'm lucky to have you for a girlfriend. I could be luckier though.'

She looked at him, alarmed. 'How?'

'If you were my wife.'

She looked at him, dumbstruck. She was befuddled. Had she heard him right?

'But if you don't want to..'

Her heart was hammering away. She was tired; she was hallucinating.

'I thought you just proposed to me,' she stammered, 'but I could have been wrong. I'm exhausted. I think my mind's playing tricks on me.'

'Right.' He stood up now. 'I want you to concentrate. Stay awake and watch me carefully.'

He got down on one knee and took her hand.

'Margaret Mary Langham, will you marry me?'

She blinked back the tears that were seeping from her eyes.

'Oh yes please! So much has happened, and now this. But can you ask me again tomorrow when I'm fully awake?'

'Do you think you might still say yes?'

'I think it very likely.' She smiled. 'Are you sure you want to marry a girl who lives in a small rented cottage with a family who are completely bonkers and who hasn't got a worthwhile job?'

'You little minx. I'm nothing like my parents.'

'Thank God for that, and hopefully I'm nothing like mine.'

He smirked.' Girls turn into their mothers, eventually. It's a well known fact.'

She put her hands on her hips. 'So how do you explain that my mother is not a bit like my gran?'

'Apologies, Your Honour. Statement withdrawn. Case dismissed.'

That's enough of the legal banter. It's time to kiss your fiancee.'

They walked back to the cottage, hand in hand. Maggie's tiredness had dissipated and she wanted to run and tell everyone in the whole world that she was going to marry William, but she couldn't steal the limelight from Caroline. She would leave it a week or two before she told the rest of her family. But she couldn't wait to tell Mary.

Chapter 53

'I've brought baby in to meet her mummy. She's all checked over and she's in perfect health. Now it's time she spent some time with you. I think she's ready for a feed.'

Caroline had been asleep and was feeling groggy as she watched the nurse wheel in a cot. She turned over and stared at her daughter.

'Shall I pick her up for you?'

Without waiting for an answer, the nurse plumped up the pillows and helped Caroline raise herself into a sitting position. She placed the baby in her arms.

'Support baby's head like so. Now let's try a bit of breast feeding. That's right, now cuddle her close. Undo the buttons on your nightie.'

Caroline awkwardly held the bundle and fumbled with her buttons. She wasn't at all comfortable with any of this. The baby started to cry and Caroline looked at the gaping, gummy mouth. She wanted to hand her back to the nurse and go back to sleep, but she knew she had no option but to comply. She thought she should feel a bond with the baby, but she didn't. She put it to her breast where it snuffled and sought her swollen nipple.

'That's right, now try to relax. This should be enjoyable for both of you.'

Enjoyable? What was she talking about? The baby was pulling at her. It hurt. She gritted her teeth and imagined herself in a deckchair on the beach soaking up the sun. Suck suck. She tried not to wince at the pain.

'That's right. You're both nice and relaxed. Now a few minutes on the other breast. Well done.'

Eventually the baby was sated and was closing her eyes.

'I'll take her and change her then put her back in her cot. Watch how I do it. Next time she cries, you need to do this by yourself, including changing the baby's nappy.'

The nurse deftly changed her and swaddled her in a thin shawl.

'She needs to be wrapped up like this to begin with. It'll make her feel secure. Now try to have a little nap because you're on your own from now on. But if you feel like a little cuddle, take her out of her cot any time, but don't fall asleep with her in your arms or you might suffocate her. Do you have a name for her yet?'

Caroline had already turned over and had drifted off into an exhausted sleep.

The next time she woke there was a tall man at her bedside. It must be the doctor doing his rounds.

'Hello Caroline. How are you?'

She blinked and sat up, running her hand through her hair.

'David! How did you know I was here?'

'I thought you must be due about now. I have contacts at Clayton Hospital. I asked them to let me know when you were admitted. I hear your sister delivered her at home.' He lowered his voice. 'Let me have a look at my daughter. May I pick her up?'

'Of course.'

'What have you called her?'

'Nothing. I haven't decided.'

'Oh she's beautiful. I've got a daughter,' he whispered. 'Does Graham still think she's his?'

'He has no reason not to and that's the way it'll have to stay if you don't want to be with me.' She started to sob and then found she couldn't stop.

He looked around the room quickly, afraid that someone would hear.

'Caroline, it isn't that I don't want to be with you. If things had been different, we would be together. I'm sorry I got you into this mess but look what we've got.'

He bent and pressed his lips on to his tiny daughter's head. 'And, as I said, I'll give you a generous allowance. Do we still have an arrangement that you do a bit of typing for me, or you can pretend to Graham that you're doing some typing, and tell him that I'm paying you a wage?'

'I can't think of another way you can pay me without him finding out.'

She searched for a handkerchief in the drawer of the bedside cabinet and dabbed her eyes.

'You could open your own bank account.'

'I suppose so. Let me think about it. I can't think of anything at the moment.'

The baby started crying. David tried to soothe her without success.

'She wants her mummy.'

He smiled at her and Caroline could feel her heart pound. She wished she didn't still love him. She wished she felt something for his baby. She wished it would all just go away. She unbuttoned her nightie and the baby sucked greedily.

'So will you want to see her? Have access to her?'

'I want to more than anything, but I daren't risk it. Not as things stand at home.'

Hardly five minutes after he had left, Graham appeared on the ward behind a huge bouquet of flowers. They must have passed each other in the corridor.

'How are my two beautiful girls?' he asked, laying the flowers on the bedside table. His face shone with happiness.

Caroline looked around the ward to see if anyone was staring at her. Did they guess that the first visitor was the father of her child and the second one her husband? She was being paranoic. David could have been her brother or some other close relation. She couldn't spend her life feeling guilty. She forced a smile.

'I'm still a bit sore with the stitches and I'm not finding feeding easy. It hurts. The baby's fine though.'

'Have you been crying? What's wrong?'

'Ignore me. It's just the baby blues. Childbirth plays havoc with the hormones, apparently.'

'As long as you're OK. You know, we should give her a name,' he said. 'She can't be 'the baby' forever. Any thoughts?'

'I've just read a book where the heroine was called Madeleine. Such a pretty name. What do you think?'

'Yes that is pretty. Shall we call her that for a day or two and see how it sounds?'

The baby had stopped feeding and appeared to be staring up at him with wide, unfocused blue eyes. He held out his arms and took her, cuddling her close.

'Hello Madeleine. What do you think of your name? Do you think you'd like it?' He held her mouth to his ear.

'She says she approves. My Madeleine. I think I love you to the moon and back already.'

Chapter 54   Two Years later

'Do try to sit still, Madeleine. Look, Auntie Maggie and Uncle William are coming back down the aisle now. Look at Auntie Maggie's pretty dress.'

Madeleine tried to climb on to Caroline's lap to gain a better view. Caroline pushed her off.

'You know you can't sit on Mummy's lap. There's a baby in Mummy's tummy. Your little brother or sister won't like being squashed.'

Madeleine escaped from her grasp and ran into the aisle to wave at her aunt.

'Graham, fetch her back. She's such an unruly little madam.'

Maggie bent down to ruffle her niece's auburn hair, just as Graham swept her up and carried her back to their pew. Madeleine responded with a piercing scream.

'Want see Auntie Mag.'

Graham took the wriggling, wailing body out of the church.

Maggie and William continued their slow walk down the aisle and Maggie smiled understandingly at her sister. Caroline smiled back, but the smile didn't reach her eyes. She had to acknowledge that Maggie looked stunning. Her long chestnut hair hung about her face in ringlets and she wore a dress which, though simple, was obviously haute couture. A ringlet of pearls in her hair anchored a lace veil, under which she could see matching pearl drop earrings. William looked handsome and successful in a grey morning suit. They looked like a pair from the pages of The Tatler. The guests on the bridegroom's side looked very well-to-do, the women in their silk dresses, pillbox hats and designer accessories. The Langham side looked smart enough, but there was no disguising the fact that they were the poor relations. How had Maggie managed to bag a looker like William from a moneyed family? They had already bought a house on Coombes Road, which was the posh end of town. Caroline couldn't see how she and Graham were ever going to move out of 34 Beech Road. The neighbours were rough and the front gardens were becoming unkempt. The area had gone down in the two years that she and Graham had lived there. They managed to make ends meet with Graham's driving job and David's contribution but she would never live in Coombes Road. Things would get even tighter when the new baby was born in a month's time. Her chest felt leaden. She was trapped forever.

    The rows were emptying and she listlessly followed the guests outside and looked for Graham. She saw him wandering amongst the gravestones, hand in hand with Madeleine. She was looking up at him and laughing as he threw sycamore helicopters into the air. Together, they were watching them spin and twirl to the ground.

    The three of them climbed into a sleek black limousine which was to take them to the prestigious hotel on the outskirts of town.

    'This is a busman's holiday for me,' joked Graham, but his comment fell on stony ground.

'Maggie was very lucky that William's parents offered to pay for the wedding,' he added, oblivious to her sour mood.

'She was lucky. But that won't be the whole story.'

'What do you mean? Am I missing something?'

'Well, the bride's parents usually pay for the wedding. Imagine if they'd had the wedding that our parents could afford. A few sandwiches, some veal and ham pie in the front parlour and a crate of beer. That wouldn't have gone down well with Lord and Lady Matthews. What would her ladyship's friends at the golf club think if that was the wedding of their precious son?'

Graham knew that Caroline was eaten up with jealousy. He had learned over the years that his best bet was to keep silent.

Theresa and Alf were ensconced on the top table. Theresa's generous curves were straining the seams of her turquoise crimplene two piece, teamed with a matching feathered hat, as she held court. Caroline cringed at the badly executed posh accent, which was now in full force. She saw Alf, uncomfortable in his suit, looking proudly at his daughter, slim as a reed in her tastefully understated wedding outfit. Caroline's teeth clenched as she thought about the generous wedding present from William's parents. They had given them the deposit on the house in Coombes Road. Maggie and William had been buying furniture and kitchen goods from Bentalls and it was all ready for them to move into when they returned from their honeymoon in the

South of France. The latter had been facilitated by Capital Holidays, where Maggie was now a senior travel agent. As far as Caroline could see, everything fell into Maggie's lap with no effort at all on her part. Caroline swore that she would never visit her at the house. She wasn't going to have that thrown in her face.

The speeches had started and William's brother, Bob, who was the best man, was complimenting William on his choice of wife. Maggie, blushing prettily, was the centre of attention. It was stiflingly hot. Suddenly, it was all too much. Caroline heaved herself from her seat and went out into the autumn sunshine, She sat down on the nearest bench, her breathing fast and shallow, which made her light headed. She put her head in her hands and sobbed, hot, choking tears catching her throat. She cried for the life that Maggie had, a cruel contrast to her own. If David had married her she could have had that for herself. She sat up, closed her eyes and tried to calm herself by dreaming of the perfect life that had slipped through her fingers.

A shadow blotted out the sun on her eyelids.

'Are you alright, love. You look as though you've been crying.'

Graham was kneeling beside her, Madeleine pulling at her dress.

'I wasn't feeling well,' she said, her voice drenched with misery.

'They're cutting the cake. Do you want to come back in now? Come on, take my arm.'

'Cake!' shouted Madeleine. 'Come, Mummy.'

Caroline followed them back into the

reception. She knew that she should feel happy for her sister, but Maggie's happiness made her own miserable life seem even more miserable. They went back into the hotel and, with a sigh, Caroline slumped into her seat.

Maggie and William were poised in front of the three tier cake, their joined hands on the ornate beribboned knife, They were staring adoringly at each other as cameras flashed and the guests applauded. Then more champagne and photographs.

'Don't they look a handsome couple?' Graham was beaming.

'I suppose so. I don't think Maggie was quite what William' family had in mind for their son.'

'Oh Maggie would fit in anywhere. She's very adaptable, your sister.'

'Perhaps you should have snapped her up then.' she replied sweetly.

'Oh I don't think she would have looked twice at me.' Graham clamped his mouth shut before he dug himself in any deeper. Whenever he opened it he seemed to say the wrong thing. Pieces of wedding cake had been delivered to the table so he picked it up and ate it without further comment. Caroline turned hers over with a look of distaste and returned it to the plate. The other guests on the table were talking animatedly to each other. Graham turned his back on her and engaged his neighbour in conversation while Caroline stared stonily at her plate. She wished it was over.

'I don't think I want to stay for the evening do,' she said, interrupting his conversation. 'It's all too much for me at the moment.'

'How far gone are you?' asked the woman next to Graham. 'I'm Maureen by the way.'

'Eight months,' she said, 'the baby's due on the twenty second of next month.'

'The last month's the worst,' Maureen said sympathetically. 'You just want to get it over, especially in this heat.' She looked across at the top table. 'Who's that awful woman in the turquoise who's holding court in a loud voice on the top table? That cut glass accent must be put on.'

'No idea,' said Caroline before Graham had a chance to tell her it was her mother.

The tables were cleared away and the band started preparing for the evening dance. Maggie was in the ladies, repairing her makeup and patting her hair into place, when Auntie Ruby appeared.

'Well that all went well,' said Auntie Ruby, pulling a permed curl over her forehead. 'We were all proud of you. What a posh do. Every expense spared, I'll be bound.'

Maggie looked around to make sure they were alone.

'I would have been quite happy with a small do with none of this fuss but William's mum wasn't having any of it. She had to put on a big show, but I can hardly complain as they paid for everything. I haven't seen Caroline and Graham for a bit. Is she alright?'

'She went half an hour ago. Said she was feeling tired.'

'It was probably asking too much to expect her to say goodbye.'

'Between you and me I think she turned into

the green eyed monster. She was sitting scowling all the way through the ceremony and the reception.'

Ruby stopped abruptly as the door opened.

'Oh there you are, Maggie.' Mary looked very neat in a navy costume and matching feathered hat. She had kept her trim figure and her lined face was still beautiful.

'Maggie, let me look at you. You're a dream, and as for that handsome husband of yours; you make a lovely couple. I've prayed for this day. I just know you'll both be very happy.'

Maggie bent to give her a hug. 'Thanks Gran. You're not looking so bad yourself.'

'Oh get away with you. A smart costume and a dab of lipstick work wonders. I'm looking forward to you and William having the first dance. You know,' her voice dropped to a whisper. 'I got cornered by William's mother. I thought she was quite a pleasant woman until she started probing about "Maggie's people". She wanted to know where I lived and who I knew. It was like the Spanish inquisition. I was dying to tell her that I'd been a scullery maid and her grandfather a footman. Can you imagine the sneer on her face? By the way I think your mother has had a drop too much. Her voice is getting higher and louder by the minute. Your poor father is looking as though he wishes the ground would swallow up the pair of them. He looks like a fish out of water, you know what he's like. Mind you, his speech was quite amusing. He can rise to the occasion when necessary.'

Ruby nodded. 'I'll nip out and see if I can persuade Theresa to have some strong coffee, or something. She'll wear herself out and then have one of her turns.'

'I'd better come with you,' said Mary.

'Aim not nebriated.' Theresa was shaking her head in an exaggerated fashion.

'No of course not,' said Ruby, 'but you need to come and have a little rest.'

She and Mary each took an arm and helped her into the back bar. Ruby asked a waiter to bring some coffee.

'Coffee? Aid lake another ickle dickle Drambuie. Snot every day your daughter marries mars and clunny. No thash not right. Class and money.'

'Bring her a large coffee, please,' said Mary. 'If you don't sober up, Ruby and I will have to take you home before you completely spoil your daughter's wedding.'

Theresa was about to protest when she saw the look on her mother's face. Mary was tolerant up to a point, after which she brooked no argument.

'If you don't want to think about your daughter, Girl, then think how you're going to feel when you've sobered up and realise that you've made a complete fool of yourself in front of Maggie's new in-laws.'

The waiter came in with a pot of coffee. but Theresa had fallen asleep in the chair, her mouth open and her breathing stentorious.

'I'll sit with her,' said Mary, 'You go and enjoy yourself.'

Chapter 55

Caroline was pushing the pram round the park. Louisa was sitting up, her wide eyes taking everything in, while Madeleine chattered nineteen to the dozen.

'Look Mummy, the ducks have got little babies. Can we give them some bread? Look, Louisa, look at the fluffy babies. They're called ducklings.'

Caroline sat down on a bench next to the pond and pulled a paper bag of stale bread from the pram.

'Up, up.' Louisa struggled to get out of the pram.

'Come on then, let's get you out of there.'

She lifted out her younger daughter and set her on the ground. 'Now hold my hand and we'll feed the ducks.' She gave a piece of bread to each of them. 'No, Louisa, not all at once, you give them little bits like this.'

'Like this,' repeated Madeleine, tearing a small piece off her own and throwing it into the pond. She adored teaching her little sister.

'Mummy, there's a man over there and he's staring at us.'

Caroline looked up and paled. David was there with his son, who was sailing a remote controlled boat on the other side of the pond. Michael had been four when she had seen him all those years ago in his front garden. He must be, what, eight or nine now? Even from a distance she could see a resemblance to Madeleine.

David suddenly caught sight of her and raised a hand in recognition.

'Who is he, Mummy?'

Oh how she longed to tell her that the man was her father.

'He's a doctor,' she stammered. 'I knew him when I used to work at the hospital.'

'Look! His boy has a lovely boat. I wish I could have a go. Ooh, look it's coming over here.'

David and the boy came towards them.

'I like your boat,' said Madeleine. 'I wish I had one like that. Did it cost a lot of money? I expect we can't afford it. Mummy nearly always says that.'

'Michael, would you let Madeleine have a go?' David asked. He paled. Her name had slipped out. Caroline frowned and shook her head.

Madeleine jumped up and down. 'He knows my name! That's funny, isn't it?'

'Oh I met someone who told me that your mummy had a lovely daughter called Madeleine, I thought it a pretty name so I remembered it.'

Michael was crouching on the ground, explaining to his half sister how the remote control worked. Their two heads were close together. You couldn't see where one auburn head ended and the other began. Caroline took Louise's hand and sat down on the bench. David sat beside her.

'How are you?' You're looking well.'

'OK, I suppose. I have my hands full with these two as you can see. Life just goes on, doesn't it? Money's short but we scrape by with your contribution.'

He sent her £10 every month through the post, always enclosed in a single sheet of paper that said, 'Payment for the typing, with thanks, Dr David Harris.' He never made it personal. She had told Graham that she sometimes did a bit of typing for him during the day when the children had their nap.

There was an awkward silence. They watched the two children playing with the boat.

'Michael seems very patient with Madeleine, who can be bossy at times.'

David couldn't take his eyes off his daughter.

'He's probably glad to be showing off his knowledge. He's very proud of that boat and loves explaining how it works.'

Louisa tried to wriggle off her lap so Caroline took a tube of smarties from her bag in the pram.

'Now don't eat them all at once or you'll be sick.'

She took the top off and poured three into Louisa's outstretched hand.

'How are you?' she asked him.

'I don't know whether you heard, but Fiona died six months ago,' he replied. 'It's difficult being on my own with Michael. I have a nanny cum housekeeper who's very good. Michael was very upset at losing his mother and has become very quiet and introverted. I've cut down my hours so I can spend more time with him.'

'Oh, I'm so sorry, I didn't know she'd died,' Caroline said, 'I don't have any contact with anyone from the hospital these days. It must be very hard for you.'

'It is, but you have no choice but to deal with it, you know. I've known for a long time that she was going to die, but it doesn't make it any easier.' He took a deep breath. 'And what about you?'

'Oh, you know. I keep going for the children's sake. I live in an awful house on an awful estate. Oh I'm sorry. My problems are nothing compared with yours.'

'And Graham?' he persisted. How are things with him? Any better?'

'He's OK. Like you, I try to make the best of things. When you've got children they occupy most of your life. I don't have time to dwell on whether I'm happy or not.'

There was a long pause. She emptied some more Smarties into Louisa's sticky hands.

'He's a good husband and father. I should be grateful. I am grateful.'

She felt that he was looking straight into her soul when he said,

'But you don't love him.'

It was a statement, not a question.

What was the point of pretending things were fine?

'No,' she said. She wanted to say that he, David, was the only man she had ever really loved but the words stuck in her throat. He had said that he would never leave his sick wife. But now? Her heart was beating faster as she met his gaze. She wondered if there was any chance that their relationship could be rekindled. The hope flowered and then died. She had two children now. It was too late.

He took her hand and she shivered at his touch. She looked up quickly to see if Madeleine was watching but she and Michael seemed totally absorbed in guiding the small boat amongst the reeds.

After a while, Madeleine came over.

'Michael's my new friend. He let me have a go of his boat. He said he and his dad come here nearly every Saturday. Please Mummy can we come here every Saturday?'

Chapter 56

'But what will I do all day? My job gives me an identity and I love it. Don't get me wrong. I love this house, and the garden is a dream, but I need something more to occupy myself.'

'You don't need to work,' William had said. 'I earn good money, more than enough to support us both. Look, darling, I know you love your job and we agreed that you would continue with it after we were married, but now that you've been promoted to deputy manager you're expected to go abroad at the drop of a hat. With the long hours that I work we don't see enough of each other and when we do we're both tired. Couldn't you just do some charity work to keep yourself occupied?'

Charity work? He'd be suggesting she joined the golf club next and then she would have changed into his mother. Or she could stop at home and do nothing and change into her own mother. Deep down though, she knew he was right. She couldn't have it all. She had to choose William. It didn't stop her yearning to travel and explore other cultures.

Then she found she didn't actually have any choice. She was pregnant. When she told William, he swept her off her feet and hugged her.

'Life just couldn't get any better,' he said.

She carried on working until the baby bulge was obvious. William had hired a cleaner and a gardener so she had little to do. She knew she was lucky and she also knew that Caroline would give her eye teeth to swap places with her. She loved William and she wanted to be a good wife, and if that meant complying, then she would do it.

On her last day at Capital Holidays the staff threw a leaving party for her. Mr Wilson was still the boss, but Jill had left to marry Peter, and Stella had ditched the awful Tony and had moved to Head Office in London. The inseparable pair had finally separated. Two girls had replaced them and Maggie had been the one to train both of them. She had done well for herself in the three years since she had started and she was liked by everyone.

One of the girls, Carol, had made a rather lop-sided cake and Mr Wilson had arranged for some savouries to be delivered from a local bakery. The other girl, Lesley, had brought in some cheap bubbly. Maggie was tearful as she gave a little goodbye speech; she was really going to miss them all. Mr Wilson told her she'd be welcome to come back after the baby was born, but Maggie knew she wouldn't. She would concentrate on looking after William and the baby. How she had silently mocked poor Heather, whose only aspiration had been to be a good wife and mother. She had bumped into her once or twice over the years; she now had two children and was happy as a pig in muck. She had just worked as a fill in until she got married. Maggie worked because she had enjoyed the challenge and wanted a career.

She threw herself into getting things ready for the baby. A painter and decorator had been brought in to decorate the nursery. It now had sunny yellow walls and she had stuck alphabet transfers around them. A Noah's Ark mobile hung over the cot. There was a nappy-changing area on a chest of drawers, which was brimming with white fluffy nappies and tiny baby clothes in white and lemon. She often went into the room during the day to stare into the empty cot and imagine their baby lying there, gurgling. She had put work behind her now and was counting the days until she could hold the baby in her arms. They had discussed names and had decided on James if it was a boy and Helen for a girl.

Auntie Ruby had never shared her cooking skills with her, or maybe Maggie hadn't been interested. Theresa cooked everything out of cans and packets, often burning them, so she had no role model there. She had learned a few tips from Mary, who favoured plain, wholesome food, but she now felt she needed to augment her repertoire. She bought some cookery books and spent the long days when William was at work, trying new recipes. William was encouraging and entirely honest about what he felt worked and what didn't. By the time the baby was almost due, she had honed her culinary skills to a stage where she felt confident enough to try them out on Caroline and Graham. The meal went well, the visit did not.

They complimented her on the food, which was a recipe from her Elizabeth David cookbook, but Caroline could barely suppress her jealousy of the house. She remained tight lipped when Maggie and William showed them around. Graham was garrulous, probably in an attempt to fill the silences, but at times the conversation wore a bit thin. Maggie was eager to pick up a hint or two from Caroline about child rearing, which she later regretted. It seemed that Caroline didn't enjoy motherhood and her enthusiastic questions received unenthusiatic answers.

'So when did Madeleine and Louisa start sleeping right through the night?' was met with, 'They often don't even now. It's just too trying.'

And, 'Did you start weaning her at about three months? They say it leaves them more satisfied.' was answered with, 'Louisa's two years old now. I really can't remember. Is there wine in this beef stew? It tastes bitter.'

It's not the only thing that's bitter, thought Maggie. She would never understand her sister. It wasn't just the house that appeared to annoy Caroline. She acted oddly with William as well. She didn't address one comment to him during the course of the evening. In fact she barely acknowledged his presence. It reinforced Maggie's suspicion that William knew about Caroline's affair with David and it really annoyed her that he wouldn't discuss it with her. She was his wife after all. They should be able to discuss anything.

After they left, William put his arm around his wife and said,

'That was a wonderful meal darling. The beef bourgignon, or stew, as Caroline insisted on calling it, was perfect and I loved the lemon meringue pie. Was there something wrong with your sister? She barely said a word the whole evening. although Graham was good company.'

'Oh, she's clearly jealous.' Maggie started to stack the dishes. 'My sister has always had illusions of grandeur. I don't think she can bear the fact that we live in this lovely house while she and Graham have a council house. You can bet your bottom dollar that we'll never be invited there.'

She wanted to add something about Caroline acting oddly with William but she was just so tired. Maybe she would broach the subject tomorrow. There was something going on that made her feel really uneasy.

'Well, that's hardly our fault. Leave those till the morning, love. You're eight and a half months pregnant and you look worn out. I'm not sure all that effort was worth it. She was certainly not eager to impart any child rearing tips. I don't think you'd want to take any advice from her, anyway. She doesn't seem to get much joy out of anything, her house, motherhood and possibly, not even Graham. It's a pity she feels jealous. I really like Graham. What you see is what you get with him. I think she should consider herself lucky that she married someone who clearly adores her. She doesn't seem that adorable to me.'

'Not like me.'

She put her arms round him and lay her head on his shoulder.

'No, nothing like you. You're definitely adorable. And this little one will be adorable too.' He stroked her stomach.

'It can't fail to be. Look at the parents.' She caught hold of his hand and kissed it.

'Mm I wonder if it'll be a boy or a girl.'

'As long as it's one or the other,' she replied with a tired smile. 'He or she has stopped kicking. I think it's time we went to sleep as well.'

The following morning, Maggie heaved

herself out of bed and started tidying up the kitchen. She felt leaden and had mild cramps in her stomach that she was trying to ignore. William appeared five minutes later, yawning.

'Go and sit down, love. You look a bit pale this morning. I'll put some bread in the toaster and then make a start on these dishes. What's the matter?'

'I'm probably panicking but I haven't felt the baby move. It must be a day or two now. I feel something's not quite right.' She started to cry.

He sat down beside her and stroked her stomach.

'It's probably your hormones playing havoc. Are you alright in there, James or Helen? Didn't the antenatal nurse say that babies didn't move much just before the birth? There's not much room to manoeuvre now. I suppose. Don't worry, everything will be fine. You've looked after yourself and been as fit as a fiddle all during the pregnancy.'

'I suppose so. I'm so looking forward to this baby. I suppose it's natural to worry.'

Chapter 58

Maggie was glad it was Saturday and William was at home with her. She felt unwell all day.

'I expect you did too much yesterday. You lie on the sofa and I'll make you some tea.'

For once she didn't protest that she had too much to do.

In the early hours of the next morning the cramps got worse. She shook him awake.

'I think I'm in labour,' she said excitedly.

'Are you sure? I thought you weren't due for two weeks.'

'I'm not, but I think we'd better go to the hospital.'

William was suddenly wide awake. He collected her bag, ready packed with all the things she would need for herself and the baby, and helped her out into the car. He drove fast to the hospital. There was barely any traffic. She was taken straight to the maternity ward. William kissed her before he was ushered out into the corridor to wait. He leafed through some dog-eared magazines but was unable to concentrate. Another man, who was sharing his vigil on the otherwise deserted corridor, introduced himself as Gary and they chatted for a few minutes and then fell into silence. Then he tried to doze, which proved impossible on the hard chair. After several hours, a nurse came out and he stood up expectantly, but she walked straight past him towards Gary.

'You have a lovely bouncing boy, Mr Taylor. Would you like to go in and see your wife and meet your new son?'

William slumped back down. It was the longest night of his life. Occasionally a nurse or doctor would stride past the end of the corridor. Every time he looked at his watch only a few minutes had passed. Eventually, as dawn was beginning to cast a grey light along the empty corridor, a doctor emerged from the maternity suite.

Maggie was lying with her face away from him. He sat down on the seat beside the bed and took her hand, pressing it to his lips. His voice was a croak, barely audible.

'Oh darling, I'm so, so sorry.'

She looked at him, her eyes wet with tears.

'They don't know why. He'd been dead for days. I knew it.' Her throat was hot and tight. The pain in her chest was so constricting she could barely speak.

William wiped away his own tears.'

'I know,' he managed. 'Are you alright?'

'All that pain, then nothing at the end of it. Why couldn't he have stayed alive? Just a few more days.'

A baby in a cot on wheels trundled by outside the room. Then minutes of painful silence

A nurse put her head round the door,

'Do you need anything, Mrs Matthews?'

She shook her head.

William said, 'Are we able to see our baby? To say goodbye? What do you think, darling?'

She looked at him bleakly, then nodded.
'Can we?'
'Of course, if you feel up to it.'

She returned a few minutes later, carrying a bundle in a shawl and placed him gently in Maggie's arms.

'He's perfect.' Her voice came out as a sob, 'He just looks as though he's asleep. He's beautiful.' She kissed the top of James' head.

William sat next to Maggie on the bed and put his arms round her.

'Our son is indeed beautiful.'

They gazed at their son for the first and last time.

Chapter 59

'Who's David?' The question came out of nowhere as they were eating their tea after the children had been put to bed.

Caroline tried to stop her hand from trembling as she poured Graham a second cup of tea.

'What do you mean, "Who's David?"'

'When I went up to kiss the girls goodnight Madeleine said someone called David had bought her an ice cream in the park.'

'Oh that David! He's a doctor who used to work at the hospital. You know, the one I sometimes do a bit of typing for. We bumped into him and his son, Michael, in the park. Madeleine's taken quite a shine to Michael. He's apparently her new friend. He's actually a bit older than her, about four years, I think, but they seem to like playing with his remote controlled boat together. He's an only child. I think he actually likes our precocious child's company.' She knew she was babbling.

'Oh. Any more of that nice ham? Did you get it from that new butcher's?'

She relaxed. Guilt had made her expect an inquisition. They had 'bumped into each other' in the park four times now. She had to be careful as Madeleine's eagle eyes missed nothing, She knew she was playing with fire. If Graham noticed her new hairdo or the fact that she was wearing makeup, he said nothing. Her daughter, however, didn't miss a trick. She would say,

'Mummy, that's a nice dress. Are we going anywhere special?' Or 'You smell nice, Mummy.'

The more often they met, the more she wanted him and the more she became irritated with Graham, who felt he could do nothing right. She was constantly critical. Their sex life, never good to begin with, dwindled to nothing. Graham started coming home later, saying he was working longer hours, and smelling of drink. Caroline found she didn't care and felt relieved that she had the house to herself.

Into this misery came the news of Maggie's stillbirth. Ruby went to see Caroline the day after it happened.

'Poor Maggie can barely speak, she's that upset. She feels it's something she did or didn't do when she was expecting, but I think it's just nature. It wasn't meant to be.'

'Poor Maggie,' agreed Caroline. 'It just shows you can't be too complacent. We all thought she had everything.'

After Ruby left, she drew her children towards her and held them tightly. They're not always easy, but they're healthy and they're mine. I've got something precious that Maggie hasn't.

She visited Maggie in hospital the next day, having taken the children to the cottage for Ruby to look after. They had moved Maggie to a gynaecological ward so she didn't have to be among mothers with babies. She was pale and listless as she thanked Caroline for the flowers. Caroline was at a loss to know what to say to her.

'I'm really sorry. Having two healthy

children myself, I can't begin to imagine what you must be feeling.'

Maggie wiped her eyes and swallowed.

'You're so lucky, Caroline, having your two beautiful girls.'

And for the first time in her life, Caroline felt that she was lucky.

William appeared a few hours later, almost hidden behind a huge bouquet of red roses.

'How are you, love?

'Lovely flowers, thank you. I'll ask a nurse to put them in a vase.' She tried to fight back the tears. Her voice was wretched.

'Oh, William, I feel as though a part of me, us, has been torn out and thrown away. Will we ever get over it?' She gulped, her voice now hoarse. 'And then I get visits and crass comments from my family.'

She told him what Caroline had said.

'I'm sure she didn't mean it like that,' he said.

'I suspect she knew exactly what she was was saying. And my dear mother, who came in earlier with Dad, said, "Well, you're young, you could always have another one." It was like James had been completely dismissed, as though he was a puppy or something who could easily be replaced.'

Maggie could no longer hold back the tears. He lay on the bed and held her tightly in his arms, his tears mingling with hers.

'It's difficult for everyone. People can't always find the right thing to say. Our boy can never be replaced.'

Chapter 60

Caroline did genuinely feel sorry for Maggie and William, but she wasn't going to be made to feel guilty that she had two beautiful, healthy children. However, this feeling of superiority was short lived. A few days later, she was sorting clothes, ready for washing, when she extracted a handkerchief from the pocket of Graham's shirt. She looked closer at what she thought was a smear of blood and realised it was lipstick. It was a deep ruby red colour, not a colour she ever used. Maybe it was his mother's or sister's, but to her knowledge, he hadn't seem them for a few weeks. The handkerchief also had a faint whiff of perfume, again not one that she wore. She sat down on a chair, her heart pounding. Surely he couldn't be seeing another woman. Not Graham. He adored her. Then she recalled the rows, the nights when he came in later and later from work. He had stopped even trying to persuade her to have sex. It had been months and months. He no longer called her 'darling' or tried to please her with little gifts of flowers or chocolates. He always seemed preoccupied. She didn't know what to do now that the shoe was possibly on the other foot.

When he finally arrived home, just before ten, she looked at him as another woman might. He was good looking and had crinkles round his eyes from smiling, which gave his face character. He was tall and lean. She hadn't really looked at him properly in ages and she suddenly realised that other women would find him attractive.

'Would you like anything to eat, or a snack? I thought we could sit by the fire, turn the TV off and have a chat.'

'No thanks,' he said. 'I'm tired. I think I'll turn in now.'

Ten minutes later, listening to make sure there was no sound from upstairs, she went into the hall and, with trembling fingers, searched through the pockets of his coat. Her hand located a screwed up piece of paper which she flattened out on the hall table. It was a restaurant bill for a meal for two, including a beer and a gin and tonic. She screwed it up again and thrust it back into the pocket. She was aware of a huge, suffocating lump in her chest.

Caroline lay awake beside her husband, unable to sleep. Did this definitely mean he was having an affair? It had never occurred to her that she might have pushed him over the edge. She had treated him like a dog who would always give her unconditional love, however badly she behaved, She felt a rising panic. What if he left her and the girls?

She decided not to let him know what she had discovered. She would be a better wife. She still wanted David, more than anything, but she realised there was no guarantee that they would be together. She didn't want to end up with nothing, a sad woman trying to raise two children on her own.

She was up before him, preparing a cooked breakfast.

'Bacon on a weekday?' he said. 'What are we celebrating?'

'You work such long hours. I thought you deserved a decent start to the day.'

He looked a bit mystified but wasn't going to look a gift horse in the mouth.

'I thought we could ask Auntie Ruby to babysit tonight and perhaps go to a restaurant. We haven't been out on our own for ages.' She smiled at him across the table.

'Well, that's a nice idea but I don't know what time I'll be home. You know what odd hours I work. It all depends who I take where and when. It's not a nine to five job, as you know.'

Caroline thought his voice sounded a bit sharp. Up to now it was she who had always called the shots. Now she felt as though she was pleading with him. Only last week she'd read an article in Woman. 'Is Your Husband Having An Affair?' The tell tale signs included a lack of interest in sex, often late home from work, paying more attention to his appearance. Was he doing that? Well, he had to wear a smart uniform as a chauffeur so that didn't really count. Lipstick on collars, unfamiliar perfume. She looked at him and felt dizzy. There were enough signs for her to be convinced that her fears weren't unfounded. Should she confront him?

'Right, I'm off. Have a nice day.' He kissed the children and gave her a brief peck on the cheek.

'Bye Daddy.'

'Bye Dada.' Louisa toddled over to him and tried to grab the bottom of his coat.

'Bye darling, Daddy's got to go. Be good for Mummy, both of you.'

Surely he wouldn't leave his children?

The door slammed and she sank on to a chair.

'Why are you sad, Mummy?' Madeleine was looking up into her face. 'Is it cos Daddy's gone to work?'

'Yes, that's it. Now, what shall we do today?'

'Let's go to the park,' said Madeleine, jumping up and down.

'Par par.' echoed Louisa, trying to jump up and down too. Caroline caught her as she was about to topple over.

Chapter 61

By the time Maggie came home from hospital, William had packed all the baby things away and stowed them in the attic, including the cot and pram. The alphabet frieze was the only clue that the sunny yellow room had been prepared for a baby. It was a week before she ventured into the room. She slowly started peeling off the frieze, letter by letter. The weight of sadness made her steps slow and heavy, like those of an old woman. She sighed. The room needed another function, perhaps as a laundry or sewing room. She didn't dare consider the possibility that they might have another child. She imagined nine months spent worrying that she would give birth to another lifeless baby.

She decided there was only one way out of her misery.

'I want to go back to work,' she said.

William didn't really want her to; he wanted to be able to support his wife. That's what husbands did; but he was a sensitive man who realised that it would be the best therapy for her. She was choosing to resume doing the job she loved rather than sit around the house mourning their loss. It just took one phone call to Mr Wilson and she started back in the office as soon as she felt strong enough to cope.

At first the staff didn't know what to say to her; they didn't know whether she wanted to talk about it or not. Then it was too late to say anything anyway and so the easiest way was to ignore it. Mr Wilson stammered a few words about hoping she felt better and the girls looked uncomfortable.

She threw herself into her work, coming up with new ideas for the office. She suggested having a day where potential customers were offered snacks from different countries, like Morocco or Spain, and arranged for these to be specially made by the local baker. She set up a record player to play music from diverse cultures softly in the background. Sometimes she procured national costumes for the staff to dress up in. Business boomed due to her energy and enthusiasm.

She didn't forget about James but she learned to live with the pain. It became part of her life, part of her. She didn't go abroad for work anymore and instead, she and William started to go abroad themselves. Sometimes she felt a pang when she saw other families with babies, but she tried to count her blessings. They had a lovely house and car, were comfortably off and had the freedom to go out and enjoy themselves. She and William never discussed having another baby. It was the one thing they found they just couldn't talk about.

On the few occasions when she and Caroline met up, which was invariably at their parents' house, Maggie always made a fuss of Madeleine and Louisa, but Caroline was no longer smug about her motherhood. She now envied Maggie's freedom to have an interesting job, exotic holidays and meals at smart restaurants, and it made her even more bitter. She couldn't help comparing it with her own humdrum life, spending day in day out in a house she hated, trying to keep two demanding children amused, with barely two halfpennies to rub together. She was jealous of Maggie and William's close relationship. They had suffered a cruel blow which seemed to have made them even stronger. She didn't consider that Maggie might be suffering from crippling pain and fear of repeating her devastating experience.

She had her two children, but she was no longer sure about her husband.

Chapter 62

Things came to a head three months later. Caroline had given up trying to regain the upper hand with Graham. It became clear he wasn't interested in her any more. He was an attentive father, but she knew something in him had died. He had become more and more withdrawn, until she could ignore it no longer.

'Have I done something to upset you?' she finally asked, her voice trembling.

'No,' he said.

'Then what's the matter? You barely speak to me these days. I'm at home all day with the children and I look forward to your company in the evening, Then you come in late and go straight to bed. It's no life for me.'

He wouldn't look at her. Instead he pretended to look out of the window, at the garden which he had never bothered to maintain after Alf did the preliminary work for them. He took to interest in that or in the house these days.

'It's no life for me either,' he ventured. 'You don't love me. You haven't for years, if ever. You've never thought me good enough for you. I can't be what you want me to be. What's the point of it anymore?'

She couldn't believe what she was hearing. Her brain was in a turmoil. Graham had always adored her. She used to be able to wrap him round her finger. How did he know that she didn't love him. Did he know about her relationship with David? She didn't want to have this conversation. Words would be said that could never be retracted.

She started to cry. In desperation, she sobbed,

'I do love you, of course I do. Why do you think I don't? And you are good enough for me. What can I do to convince you?'

He looked bleak. 'It's too late.'

'What do you mean, it's too late?' She was terrified now.

He still couldn't look at her. Quietly, he said, 'I've met someone else.'

She felt sick. Her head was spinning. She clutched the back of the chair.

'Someone else? Who?'

'She's called Maureen. She works in the office. I love her. She loves me.'

'Have you been having an affair with her?' Her voice was a whisper.

'Yes.'

'How long?'

'A few months. We didn't mean it to happen, but she makes me happy. She loves me for who I am. You could never do that.'

'And I don't make you happy?' She sank on to the chair. She couldn't believe she was having this conversation.

'We've never made each other happy.'

'Could we try?' Tears were running down her face, her eyes burned. She was pleading now. 'What about the children? What about them? They don't deserve this.'

'No, they don't but they're never going to be happy in this marriage. I'll see them as often as I can. But I deserve happiness.'

'So do I. How can I be happy on my own with two children?' She could hear the whine in her voice.

'You weren't happy with me. What difference does it make?'

'Well, as long as you're happy, that's alright then.' Her voice had become sharp. Bile rose in her throat. Why hadn't she tried a bit harder before it was too late? Her head had been filled with stupid dreams about David and now she had nothing.

'Please don't.'

'I'm sorry. We'll talk about it tomorrow,' he said. 'I'm exhausted. I'll sleep on the settee.'

She paced around the bedroom for half of the night. Her head spun. She wanted to throw a brick at this Maureen's head. She would contact David and lay her cards on the table. What did she have to lose?

Chapter 62

When Maggie discovered she was pregnant again, she didn't know how to feel. The longing for a child was there but this was tempered by the fear that something would happen to the baby again. She stopped work straight away, ate healthily, rested and exercised in the right proportions. She didn't buy anything new for the baby and didn't even bring the baby things down from the attic, or clear the potential nursery of her sewing things and ironing board. William said she was being pessimistic, but she said she was just trying to protect herself. He would hug her and say there was no reason why they wouldn't have a lovely, healthy baby this time. It wasn't in her nature to look on the dark side of life, but this was so important to her. She was sure her mother-in-law had blamed her in some way for the loss of James. Her own mother had almost dismissed it by saying that was how nature behaved sometimes. It wasn't that uncommon.

They went round to the cottage for Sunday lunch, which had become a monthly get-together for the whole family.

Auntie Ruby was setting the table and Maggie noticed that the extension leaves hadn't been pulled out.

'Aren't Caroline, Graham and the kids coming? I haven't seen them for ages,' she said, gratefully sinking into the nearest chair. She was eight months pregnant and it would be the last time they'd all be together for some time.

'You obviously haven't heard,' said Gina, taking the seat next to her.

'Haven't heard what?'

Gina looked at her mother. 'Can I tell them?'

'Someone has to,' said her mother, tutting at the roast potatoes which were slightly burnt. 'You can't turn your back for five minutes.' The smoke made her cough and the steam had fogged up her glasses.

'Take these from me Georgina, I can't see a thing. We can scrape the burned bits off. They'll be alright.'

'Someone tell me what I haven't heard,' persisted Maggie.

'Well.' said Gina, full of her own importance. 'Graham has another woman and he's leaving Caroline and the kids.'

'What? You're joking! I thought Graham worshipped the ground she walked on.'

'Who knows what goes on behind closed doors?' asked Auntie Ruby darkly. 'When love flies out of the window then another woman flies in.'

'Couldn't have put it better myself,' said Gina. 'To be honest, I don't know how he stuck her this long.'

'She's always been a bit of a cold fish, in my opinion. Treats him like dirt sometimes,' added Auntie Ruby.

'I've told her time and time again,' said Theresa sagely, 'that a real man won't put up with being spoken to the way she does sometimes. She's just gone and pushed him too far,'

'That's as maybe,' said Alf, stubbing out his cigarette, and taking the chair at the head of the table. 'But a man's duty is to support his wife and children. He can't just go swanning off like that because another woman catches his eye.'

'It's always the quiet ones,' said Auntie Ruby, serving the vegetables, which had been at their best about half an hour before and were now boiled to a pulp. 'And I always thought he was a parazone of virtue.'

Gina shared a look with Maggie. 'Did you see him as a parazone of virtue, Maggie?'

'Always,' said Maggie, 'but seriously, how is she going to cope with two kids on her own, especially financially?'

'Graham's going to give her money every week,' said Theresa.' Come and sit down and eat this while it's hot.' She had already started on hers. 'We managed on next to nothing. She'll have to stop buying all those convenience foods; they're expensive for a start.'

'Yes, but they're so convenient,' commented Auntie Ruby.

'She might qualify for benefits,' said Alf. 'That'll bring her down a peg or two.'

'So where's Graham going to live?' William asked.

'His fancy piece lives somewhere in London, Tooting I think. She's got her own flat. It seems he's been going there after work for you know what.'

'Mum, if you mean sex why don't you just come out and and say it?' said Gina.

'Not at the dinner table,' said Auntie Ruby.

'Any more runner beans anyone?'

On the way home Maggie said, 'Well that was a bit of a bombshell,'

'Yes, wasn't it?' said William, appearing to give his driving his full concentration.

'You know, I've never said this before, but I've always suspected that Madeleine might not be Graham's.'

When William didn't comment, she said, 'I saw her with a man in a pub in Wimbledon just before we found out she was pregnant.'

'It could have been anyone, a colleague, her boss.'

'Not the way they were behaving. They looked very intimate.'

'Did you tell her what you saw?'

'Of course not.'

She waited for him to tell her about his meeting with Caroline around that time, when she was sure Caroline had confided in him.

'If she needs a good solicitor, I would do it for nothing. You might want to tell her,' was all he said.

Chapter 63

She took the children to the park while Graham moved out. She couldn't bear to watch him pack his possessions. It was so final. They hadn't told the children. She couldn't find the words. She had asked him to do it, after all he was the one leaving, but he had refused. She told him what a coward he was. He said he would come and spend some time with the girls every week and he would give her as much money as he could afford.

In the weeks before he left she had taken enormous trouble over her appearance, had cooked his favourite meals and had been as pleasant as she knew how. But he had made up his mind. There was nothing she could do to stop this nightmare happening.

'Where's Daddy?' Madeleine had asked when they returned to the house, which already felt hollow and empty.

'He's had to work up north for a few days,' she had replied. She needed time to find the right words.

Before he arrived to take them out the following weekend, she knew she couldn't leave it any longer. She sat them down with a biscuit and a glass of lemonade, a rare treat for them.

'I've got something very sad to tell you both.'
They looked at her, wide eyed.

'Daddy has decided he doesn't want to live with us anymore.'

Oh no, that wasn't right but she couldn't help laying the blame on him.

'Doesn't he love us anymore?' asked Madeleine, starting to cry. 'I'll be a good girl all the time.'

She couldn't let them think it was their fault, however much she wanted to.

'He loves you both a lot.' But not enough to stay with us, she thought bitterly.

'He just doesn't love me any more.' She could feel the catch in her voice.

'Were you horrid to him?' asked Madeleine.

'I don't think so,' she said. 'Sometimes Daddies and Mummies just stop loving each other.'

'But this is his house. Where's he going to live?'

'I don't know. You'll have to ask him when you see him again.'

'I hate him! I don't want to see him if he's leaving us.'

Louisa started crying even though she didn't understand much of what was going on.

'He still loves you and he'll come and take you both out every week, starting tomorrow.'

'I'm not going!' screamed Madeleine.

'And me not go,' said Louisa, stamping her foot.

'We'll see,' said Caroline, wiping away her own tears. 'We've all got to be very, very brave.'

When Graham arrived the following day, the

girls were dressed ready, but they didn't fly to the door when they heard the knocker.

He looked different somehow. His clothes, though casual, were flattering. His hair was cut in a more modern style. Could this woman have changed him already?

'Hello Caroline.' His voice was jaunty. 'Hello you two. Are you ready to go, girls?'

They remained silent.

'We'll have a lovely day. Look, the sun's shining.'

'Why don't you want to be our daddy any more?' Madeleine was pointing at him accusingly.

'I'll always be your daddy and I'll always love you. Come on, are you all ready?'

'No. I'm staying here with Mummy.'

'Well, alright, if you really want to. Do you want to go to the zoo, Louisa? There'll be monkeys and lions and tigers and there's a funfair with lots of exciting rides.'

'Yes!' shouted Louisa, jumping off her chair. 'See monkeys.'

Caroline handed Louisa her little bag and put her coat on. As she and Graham reached the door Madeleine said,

'I'll come. I'll help you look after Louisa.'

Caroline handed her her bag and closed the door after them. How children were easily persuaded. So much for loyalty.

After they had left, she went across to the phone box and, with trembling hands, she dialled David's number.

She changed into a dress which flattered her

figure and she curled her hair. Her hand shook as she patted face powder on to her nose and applied lipstick. She assessed herself in the hall mirror. She didn't look too bad. She searched through the bathroom cabinet and found perfume in a spray bottle. She sprayed some on her wrists and neck and then tried to wash it off again. She didn't want to look as if she had tried too hard. She looked at her watch then tidied away the children's toys and plumped up the cushions. She looked at the clock. Four minutes had passed since she last looked.

     She sat by the window, watching for him.

     When he rang the doorbell she appraised herself again in the mirror, patted her hair and opened the door. She was trembling as she stood aside.

     'Thanks for coming.' She led him into the living room.

     'So, what's this about? Why did you have to see me so urgently? Has something happened? Are you alright?' He was pacing up and down.

     'Please sit down, David. I just wanted to talk to you while the girls are out with Graham. Can I make you a cup of tea?'

     He looked at his watch. 'No. No thank you. I haven't much time, I'm afraid.'

     She sat in the chair opposite him and took a deep breath.

     'Graham and I have separated and we're getting divorced.' She blurted it out before she lost her nerve.

     'What? Can I ask why? Did he find out about Madeleine?'

     'Possibly,' she said. 'I don't know. We are

just so different. We've nothing in common. I couldn't stay with him, after what you and I had. I was living a lie.'

She knew she was rewriting the truth. She also wanted him to take some blame for it. There was no way she was going to tell him that Graham had chosen another woman over her.

'I've tried to make it work over the years, but I'm lying to myself.'

'Well, this is a bit of a shock. How are the children?'

'Angry at the moment. Graham has taken them to the zoo.'

'And what about you?'

'I'm relieved. Our relationship wasn't going anywhere. It's better this way. I feel bad about what it might do to the girls at the moment but it wouldn't be good for them in the long run.'

'Are you sure you've made the right decision? It will be hard bringing up two children on your own. Is he supporting them?'

'Yes, we haven't worked out the details, but with the money you give me for Madeleine I'm just going to have to make ends meet. The rent is cheap on this house, awful though it is, but it's still a big chunk out of my income.'

He got up.

'Look, I need to go away and think about it. If you need anything, you know where I am. I think you're very brave, you know. Few women would have had the strength to do what you did. I really admire your spirit.'

She watched him walk down the street, tall,

upright and confident. There had been no hug or kiss. If she had thought he would fall into her arms at the news, she was very disappointed. She hoped, more than anything, that he would want to rekindle their relationship, but he hadn't given her a single ounce of encouragement.

Graham returned with the girls a few hours later.

'Mummy, it was such fun. We saw giraffes and zebras and polar bears.'

'And monkeys,' said Louisa. 'Funny monkeys.'

'And we went in the reptile house and saw big snakes and turtles. And when we had seen all the animals we had rides on the funfair and I went on the banana slide and then we went on the carousel and I rode on an elephant.'

'And I rode a horsey with Daddy,' added Louisa.

'It was the best day. Can we go every week, Daddy?'

'No, 'said Graham. You'd soon get fed up with it and I can't afford it. We'll think of something else to do next week.'

He had completely won them over, as Caroline knew he would.

Chapter 64

Maggie cried with relief when she gave birth to a perfect, healthy, baby boy.

'I told you the chances were it wouldn't happen again,' said William, gazing adoringly at his brand new son.

'So, are we settled on Daniel? Do you think he looks like a Daniel?'

'Definitely. Daniel James Matthews. Welcome to the world.'

'Welcome to our world.' Maggie smiled, taking William's hand. 'It seems such a responsibility, shaping a new human being.'

'You'll be a great mother,' he said.

'I'll certainly do my best.'

Later, Theresa, Alf and Gina appeared, bringing grapes and chocolates. By the way her mother and Gina were picking at them they wouldn't last the visit.

'Aren't you clever, having the first boy in the family?' said Gina. 'We won't know what to do with him.'

'We had John for seven years, don't forget,' said Theresa. 'He was only four when we took him out of Dr Barnado's and gave him a lovely home with us.'

'And only eleven when you sent him back,' said Gina, looking accusingly at her mother. 'I wonder what he's doing now? I hope he's been adopted by someone who loves him.'

'Gina, this isn't the time to rake up the past,' admonished her father. 'What's done is done. Your mother's health was at risk.'

'So what are you going to call him?' asked her mother, successfully changing the subject. 'I always thought Terence was a good name. Then he'd be named after me.'

'William and I have decided on Daniel James.'

'A good strong name,' said Alf.

'Yes, it's a good name,' agreed Theresa. 'If you don't like Terence.'

'Will you call him Daniel or Dan?' asked Gina.

'We'll see how it goes. It's hard to know at the moment. Where's Auntie Ruby? I thought she'd be eager to meet Daniel.'

'You know Ruby,' said Theresa, 'she doesn't think she's proper family and she didn't think you'd want too many visitors straight away. She coming with your gran tomorrow. Are you in here for a week?'

'Yes, I don't know why. I want to get home as soon as possible. It's so hard to get any sleep. Things happen all night long, babies crying, nurses talking, women wanting pain killers. Being in hospital is definitely bad for your health. The food's appalling.'

'Why? What sort of things do you have?' asked Theresa. Food was her favourite subject.

'Well today, I had porridge for breakfast, cauliflower cheese for lunch, and fish and mashed potatoes tonight. Everything was white. I'm not joking. Nothing had any colour.'

'So if people ask you about the food, you can say, 'Oh it's all white,' Gina quipped.

'Oh you are a wit, Gina.' Maggie yawned. 'Well, it's lovely seeing you all but I need to catch up on my sleep now before his lordship wakes up wanting attention. Childbirth is exhausting.'

At that precise moment, the bell rang to signal the end of visiting time. She looked at Daniel, who was sleeping like a little angel. As she lay there, she thought about John, whom their parents had fostered. He had been sent back to Dr Barnado's when he was eleven because he had been stealing from Theresa's purse. He was a lonely little boy who had wanted the money to buy sweets to try and make friends at school. They never gave him a second chance. No one wanted him. Then she thought about her grandmother, who's daughter had been snatched from her for adoption by the cruel nuns in Ireland. She felt the tears trickle down her face as she looked at her precious, newborn son. How could any parent bear to give up their child?

Daniel woke up and started to cry. She gently lifted him from the cot and held him close. She felt an all-enveloping love, unlike anything she had ever felt before.

Chapter 65

David called round a few days after their last meeting. Caroline hadn't been expecting him and she wished that she had put on some makeup and a flattering dress. She followed him into the living room, trying to pat her hair into some sort of order and straightening her shapeless jumper. Her heart was pounding painfully. This could seal her fate. He would either tell her he was no longer interested in her or he'd tell her that he wanted her to be in his life. David wasn't one to prevaricate. She felt sick with apprehension.

'How are you?' he asked. She thought he sounded rather formal.

'I'm coping,' she said, putting on a brave smile.

'Where are the girls?'

'They're playing in the garden. They wanted to play with the children next door but I had to say no. They're a bit rough. I was just getting on with some housework while I had a minute. This is why I'm dressed like this.' She pointed to her well worn skirt and jumper. 'Can I get you something to drink?'

'No thank you. I'm back at the hospital in an hour. I've been thinking about your predicament and I've come up with what might be a solution for both of us.'

She held her breath. This didn't sound very romantic.

'I've had a woman coming in to look after Michael when I'm at the hospital and to do to a bit of cleaning and cooking. She's finding it a bit too much as she has her own family to look after.'

Caroline could feel her heart sinking. He's going to offer me a job.

'You were saying that it's hard for you to find the money to pay the rent and you hate living here, anyway. Michael and I are rattling around in that big house in Wimbledon.' He took a deep breath before ploughing on. 'So I was thinking you and the girls might want to come and live there. You'd be around for Michael, and maybe you could do a bit of cooking and keep the house clean and tidy.' He looked around. 'You seem to be quite house proud.'

'So,' she stammered, 'you'd want me to be a sort of nanny-cum-housekeeper. Is that right?'

He reddened. 'Yes, I suppose so. You'd then have no rent to pay and I'd pay for the food and household expenses.'

She sat down heavily. His housekeeper and nanny.

'So, would we have any sort of relationship or would we be purely employer and employee?' Her voice was thin and cold. It wasn't meant to be like this.

He sighed. 'Caroline, I'm afraid I can't be seen to be living with another woman so soon after my wife's death, particularly a man in my position. But it would be perfectly acceptable to have a housekeeper. You and the girls would have your own quarters.'

She wanted to ask if she would be sharing

his bed. He hadn't really answered her question. She fell silent. Housekeeper. It sounded on a par with Auntie Ruby. On the plus side she would be living in a wonderful house in the smartest part of Wimbledon. She wouldn't have to worry about the girls mixing with the rough children on this housing estate, where the crime rate was rising by the minute. And she would see David every day. With any luck their relationship would become something more, especially once she was divorced from Graham.

David looked at his watch. 'It's a lot to think about. Do you want some time to mull it over?'

'No,' she said decisively. 'It's a good solution, thank you. The other plus for you of course is that you would be living with your daughter.'

He looked uncomfortable. 'Yes, of course, but no one must know that.'

They had agreed that it might as well go ahead as soon as possible. After he had left she called the children in and sat them down.

'I have some wonderful news for you. We're going to move to a lovely big house. And you'll never guess who lives there, Madeleine.'

'Who? Is it Daddy?' Madeleine stared at her wide-eyed and expectant.

'Your friend, Michael.'

'Michael? How smashing! And David?'

'And David.'

'Play with boat,' added Louisa, entering into the spirit of excitement.

'That's right.

'Where's Michael's mummy?' asked Madeleine.

'She's gone to heaven. It's very sad that Michael has no mummy. David wants me to look after Michael while he's at work at the hospital and also look after the house. He wants us all to live there.'

'Wow! When can we see it? Will you be his mummy? As well as ours?'

'We're going to look at it on Saturday and then we'll probably move in as soon as we can get everything sorted. No I won't be his mummy, but I'll look after him. You and Louisa will have to be very good girls for David and be nice to Michael.'

'Course we will. What'll happen to all these things?' asked Madeleine, pointing round the room.

'David's got a big dry cellar where we can store them in case we ever need them.'

'But aren't we staying there forever?' Madeleine asked, her forehead wrinkled.

'I hope so. But we need to see if it works out for us all.'

'What about Daddy? Will he be living there?'

'No. You know we talked about this. Daddy wants to live with another lady now.'

'Will we still see him? Will he know where to find us?'

'Of course he will. I'll tell him and he can still come and take you out.'

'Yippee!' shouted Madeleine. 'Come on, Louisa, let's start sorting out our toys. Oh, Mummy I was so sad when Daddy left, but this is an adventure. We'll be ever so good, won't we Louisa?'

'Good girl,' said Louisa, running upstairs.

Caroline heaved a sigh of relief as she

looked round the room. She'd be so glad to leave. She wondered what Graham would have to say when he saw where they were living. She put on her Marigolds. There was so much to do.

Her next door neighbour leaned over the fence.

'You having a clearout?'

'Yes,' she replied. 'We're moving to Wimbledon.'

'Oo you lucky cow.' She removed the cigarette from her lower lip and threw it on the ground, stubbing it out with her foot. Narrowing her eyes, she added, 'I haven't seen hide nor hair of your Graham lately. Is he alright?'

'Oh, yes,' she replied, vaguely. 'We've both got so much to organise at the moment. Excuse me, I need to get on.'

Just two weeks later, David arranged for a removal firm to transport their belongings. Caroline took the children to her parents' cottage and set about cleaning the house. She looked round the empty rooms and felt no regrets for what she considered had never been a home. She locked the door for the last time and returned the keys to the council offices. She had no idea what the future would hold but she knew she would pull out all the stops to win David over.

Chapter 66

'So,' Theresa said, stretching out her plump legs on the sofa. 'Are you telling us the whole story here? Graham moves out to live with his bit of fluff and five minutes later you're moving in with this doctor.'

'Mum, not in front of the children.' Caroline sat down neatly in her father's armchair.

'Come on girls, let's see if we can find you a nice biscuit in the kitchen. I think we've got some chocolate bonbons. Mummy and Granny need to have a chat in private.'

'Thanks, Auntie Ruby. That's very kind of you. I appreciate it.' Caroline's smile didn't reach her eyes.

Ruby took a girl in each hand and firmly shut the kitchen door behind them.

'So?'

'It's not like that.'

'What's it like then?'

'It's a live-in job. David, Dr Harris, lost his wife six months ago and he needed someone to look after his son and his house while he's at the hospital. I knew him when I worked there.'

'So how come he seeks you out for the job? You left years ago.'

'Oh, I've been doing a bit of typing for him since then. We needed the extra money and I could work from home. We got talking and that was that. It suited both of us.'

'Well, it sounds like you landed rather conveniently on your feet. What about the girls? What do they think?'

Theresa lit a cigarette and coughed. Caroline coughed as well, wafting the smoke away from her face.

'I wish you wouldn't smoke those filthy things. They pollute the air and they'll kill you.'

'I need some pleasure in life. There's little else.'

'Well it's your life I suppose. The girls are really excited about living in a big house. I think it will be good for everybody.'

'And this Dr Harris, what's he like? I take it he's got plenty of money. How old is he?'

'Oh he's very nice, about thirty.'

'Well, it sounds a bit too good to be true to me. I have to say I've never imagined you working as a housekeeper or nanny, let alone both.'

'No, me neither, but what choice have I got? I could stay in that horrible house on that horrible estate on my own, scraping along with no money, or I could take this job with someone I know. No rent to pay and he buys all the food. There wasn't really much to think about.'

'Well, good luck to you, that's all I can say. Are you sure he's not going to want anything else from you? You're not bad looking.'

'Mum! It's not like that. He's just lost his wife.'

'All the more reason to be on your guard.'

'We'll have our own quarters to live in. I don't suppose we'll see much of him, really. He's a busy man.'

'Can we come in now?' The door was flung open and the girls rushed into the room.

'Yes. We'd better get you home.'

'Yippee! Home to Wimbledon! Is David coming to collect us in his big car?'

'Shouldn't you be calling him Dr. Harris?' Theresa waved her cigarette at them and scowled.

'No,' said Madeleine. 'He's Mummy's friend. We've been meeting him and Michael in the park for ages. He sometimes holds Mummy's hand. Michael's my best friend. He shows me how to drive his remote controlled boat.'

'Does he now? said Theresa, knowingly.

'That's enough, Madeleine. Come on. Let's get you home. We've got a bus to catch. Say goodbye to Granny and Auntie Ruby.'

After they'd gone, Theresa said to Ruby,

'I smell a rat. It's all just a bit too convenient, but I suppose she's big enough to look after herself. On the bright side, it might come in useful her living with a doctor, especially for me with all my ailments. He'd have a field day. Are there any of those bourbons left?'

'When one door opens, another one always shuts,' said Auntie Ruby, fetching the biscuit tin.

Chapter 67 Two Years later

Maggie couldn't remember the first time she suspected something was wrong. When Daniel was referred by the doctor to the audiology clinic and they learned that he was profoundly deaf, she was devastated, but not surprised.

'He's so placid,' she would tell William before the diagnosis that was to change their lives. 'I was hoovering outside his bedroom door and he slept right through it.'

She also noticed that when they spoke to him he watched their faces intently and tried to imitate their mouth movements. But he didn't speak. By the time he was two, she had to admit that she was worried.

'According to all the baby books, he should at least be saying single words by now. Caroline said that her girls were using complete phrases before they were two,' she had said. 'Supposing he's, you know, subnormal?'

'Oh, there's plenty of time,' William had replied. 'I'm sure babies develop at different rates. I remember reading an article in The Times that said that boys are notoriously slower than girls to learn to talk. I think it's a bit early to worry that there's something wrong with him.'

But she knew.

When they had returned home from the audiology clinic she had sobbed and sobbed.

'We'll get through this, darling. Daniel's deaf, not stupid. He's a bright little boy.' William had put his arms round her and held her close.

'The audiologist will fit him with hearing aids and we'll have lots of advice about teaching him to talk.'

'But he may never talk,' she said. 'When you have a baby you imagine him growing up, going to school, university, getting a job, getting married, having children. Daniel may never have any of these things. His life will be a struggle. Our lives will be a struggle. How will we cope? He said Daniel might have to go to a residential school and learn sign language. How will we communicate with him?'

'We'll learn sign language as well.'

Maggie was pacing round the room, rearranging ornaments and straightening cushions.

'Yes, but what about everyone else? I don't suppose they'll want to learn sign language. They won't be able to talk to him and he won't be able to talk to them. What kind of life will he have, cut off from everyone? He won't be able to hear music, watch the TV, or anything.'

'Maggie, sit down and look at me. You're in shock. This isn't like you. You're usually so positive and optimistic. You can cope with just about everything life throws at you. You'll get through this. We'll get through this. He's still our gorgeous little boy.'

She knew he was right, but the shock and disappointment at that moment had destroyed all of her reason. It was one thing suspecting something was wrong. There's always a chance that you're mistaken, but to have it confirmed was totally life changing.

'I feel such a failure. So far, I've had a stillbirth and a profoundly deaf little boy. Caroline has two perfect little girls. It just doesn't seem fair.'

Maggie knew she would have swapped all the material things that she and William had for just one perfect child. For the first time in her life, she actually envied her sister.

Daniel was fitted with hearing aids which he tried to pull out. The audiologist advised her to start by inserting the aids for just a short time and play games with him. She learned to distract him while she gently put them in his ears. She would read simple books to him, pointing to the pictures and making sure he could see her lips. She sang to him and clapped out rhythms.

The specialist teacher, a lovely, matronly lady called Ann, explained what Daniel might hear through his hearing aids. It wasn't the same as what a hearing person would hear and he would need a lot of time to make sense of the meaningless sounds. As the months passed, Maggie spent her time working with Daniel and reading every bit of literature about deafness that she could lay her hands on. There were days when she became so frustrated by his lack of progress that she wanted to scream. William would come home to find her exhausted and tearful.

'I've decided I'm going to go to classes to learn sign language. I don't feel I'm getting anywhere with him. This just isn't working,' she sobbed.

'We were told it's going to be a very slow, frustrating process,' he said, lifting Daniel in the air, which made him chuckle with joy. 'Are you sure this is the right step? Won't he be cut off from the hearing world?'

'Oh I don't know,' she sighed. 'There's so much controversy about it. I thought we should try to do both. If he doesn't learn to talk then he's got no way of communicating. How's he going to learn anything? On the other hand, sign language is a language in itself. It's really hard to use both at the same time.'

'I'm not sure what you mean.'

'Well,' she picked up Daniel's teddy bear. 'I can tell him it's a teddy and I can sign "teddy".' She showed him the sign for teddy.' But if you want to say, "Where's teddy?" in sign language you say, "Teddy, where?" It's all the wrong way round.

'That seems totally confusing. Why can't it just be the same? What does Ann say?'

'She says it's a language in its own right which is different to spoken language. He would need to learn to be bilingual. Oh William, I'm just going round in circles. Why does it have to be so hard?'

'It seems a bit ridiculous to me. You're the one who needs to decide as you're with him all day. My gut reaction is to go with both, like you say. How will we learn sign language? Are there classes we could go to?'

Maggie hugged him. 'So will you come with me if I can find a class? You're so busy at work and often exhausted when you come home.'

He kissed her. 'We're in this together, you, me and our lovely boy. Of course I'll come with you.'

Maggie found a class on Wednesday nights

and Auntie Ruby agreed to babysit.

It was hard going but gradually they learned to sign and finger spell which they practised on each other, making a game of it. After only a few weeks Daniel was communicating simple things to them. It seemed to be so much easier for him to learn signs. He could tell them when his nappy was wet or if he wanted a drink or a biscuit. He soon knew Mummy, Daddy and teddy. Their repertoire grew. Alongside this, they encouraged him to watch their lips. One day, when he was nearly three, he quite clearly said, 'Mummy.' It was the sweetest sound she had ever heard. She no longer wanted to go back to Capital Holidays. Her work now was to enable Daniel to communicate.

'We need to teach our parents some basic signs,' she told William.

This of course was easier said than done. Both sets of parents had to be won over and it was tough going. William's mother was concerned about the stigma of having a deaf child in her family and made it obvious she thought it was Maggie's fault. His father just ignored the problem and acted as though Daniel could hear like everyone else, especially if he shouted.

Theresa's reaction was, 'Well it didn't come from our side of the family.'

Alf responded with, 'It's no one's fault, there's absolutely no point blaming anybody. We all just have to make the best of it.'

Gina loved playing with her nephew and quickly picked up some sign language, deciding that she wanted to be a teacher of deaf children. Auntie

Ruby was more than willing to try, but invariably got mixed up, just as she did with spoken language.

'Ooh I was trying to tell Daniel my name in the sign language but I think I've just told him I've done a number two.'

Theresa, like William's mother, couldn't get her head round sign language and fruitlessly tried to talk to him in a loud, exaggerated voice. When Daniel screamed and had a temper tantrum she gave up, and slowly and reluctantly began to learn a few signs which at least received some response.

Progress was agonisingly slow, but every small step was a major victory. Maggie and William hedged their bets and gave equal time to teaching Daniel sign language and developing his speech and listening skills. The specialist teacher visited them weekly at home, worked with him for the short time he could concentrate and left them exercises to do with him in the intervening period. He was the centre of Maggie's universe. His speech, when it came, was flat and toneless and not everyone could understand him. But she persevered. She alone understood everything he said and found herself in the role of interpreter.

When Daniel was three, she found she was pregnant again. The doctor reassured her that it was unlikely that she would have another deaf child. By this time she didn't really mind. Whatever she and William had to face, they would deal with it together. Being Daniel's mum brought huge challenges, but like many difficult things in life, it brought the biggest rewards.

Chapter 68

When Caroline started being sick in the mornings and her breasts began to feel sore she had mixed feelings about it. She had searched David's face for signs of joy when she had told him the news. Instead, he had stared at her, his face expressionless, causing her stomach to knot.

'Haven't you been taking the pill?' he asked, in a voice that implied she had done it deliberately.

'Of course I have. I've never missed. I've been thinking about it and I remembered that about two months ago I had an upset stomach and spent two days vomiting. Might that have brought the pills back up?'

'Possibly,' he said.

'Aren't you a tiny bit pleased at the prospect of being a father again?'

'I would have preferred it to have happened within wedlock. I have my reputation to think about. We'll talk about it tonight. I have a busy day today.'

He left for the hospital without kissing her goodbye, his forehead furrowed and his face bleak.

Caroline had suspected that he would never have got round to asking her to marry him, even though she and Graham were now divorced. This could change everything, although she had a niggling fear that he would suggest an abortion. She spent the day pacing up and down, knowing that this would be a turning point in their relationship. She had a bath, carefully applied her makeup and chose her most flattering dress. She cooked fillet steak and lemon chiffon pie and had been going to open a bottle of wine, but decided against it. That would be jumping the gun. She had absolutely no idea which way this evening would go and felt sick with worry.

When he arrived home, his face gave her no clue that things would be alright. He didn't comment on the effort she had made with her appearance or on the meal she had cooked. It had turned out surprisingly well considering how distracted she had been, but the succulent steak felt like cotton wool in her mouth. She wanted to talk about the pregnancy but she knew she couldn't rush him. She felt nauseous and breathless with anticipation.

He finally put down his knife and fork and looked at her steadily. Then,

'Well, we'd better make an honest woman of you. It will need to be as soon as possible before you begin to show, and I'll arrange for you to attend an antenatal clinic. It can't be at Clayton Hospital.'

It was hardly the romantic proposal that she had hoped for, but at least it was a proposal of sorts. She let out the breath she didn't know she'd been holding.

The following day she started to make plans for a simple wedding. She was disappointed to learn that they couldn't get married in a Catholic church, as she was divorced. Although she was no longer a practising Catholic she couldn't bring herself to try a different church. In the end she obtained a special licence for a week's time at Clayton Registry Office.

The next few days were lost in a whirlwind of shopping and wedding arrangements. She bought a pale pink dress and jacket and ordered a simple bouquet. David left all of the arrangements to her.

She was also disappointed that they weren't to have a honeymoon. When she had mentioned that she longed to go to Paris, David had replied,

'I really can't spare the time. I'm so busy at the hospital at the moment. Besides, you could hardly call it a honeymoon when we've been living in the same house for two years.'

She would never know whether it had been stress, or whether it would have happened anyway, but two days before the wedding, she started having stomach cramps. She staggered to the toilet to find that she was bleeding copiously. She dragged herself across the floor to to phone for an ambulance but never made it. The clump of cells that should have been their baby, was expelled on to the kitchen floor. She lay there, sobbing and clutching her stomach, laying her clammy head on the cold tiles. When the worst of the pain had passed, Caroline cleaned herself up and slowly mopped the floor, flushing the clotted lump down the toilet. She rammed her soiled clothing and bloodstained towels at the bottom of the rubbish bin outside. That done, she crawled into bed where she wept until exhaustion overtook her, setting the alarm for two hours before David was due to return.

'You look a bit peaky,' David said when he arrived home.

'I think I'm just a bit tired with the wedding preparations,' she had replied.

'Yes, you need to rest if you can, the first

trimester can be very draining,' he said.

None of her family had been invited to the wedding.

'Well it's quite obvious you're ashamed of us,' Theresa had snapped. 'Though why you should be I can't imagine.'

'It's not that, Mum,' she had replied defensively. 'We just don't want any fuss. We both wanted a quiet wedding. We haven't invited David's parents either so there's no need to get upset.'

This wasn't true. David had been to see his parents on his own to explain about Caroline's pregnancy and the hasty wedding. He didn't relay to Caroline the bitter conversation he'd had to endure. They accused Caroline of engineering the whole thing. She was a gold digger from a council house and he could have done much better than marry his housekeeper, particularly one with two children in tow.

He told Caroline that they were unable to attend the wedding at such short notice. But she knew what they thought of her.

'Why don't you tell them that Madeleine is their grandchild? ' she had asked, her voice sharp. 'It doesn't seem fair that they'll never know that she's actually their own flesh and blood. And what about Madeleine? Don't you think she has a right to know that you're her father and they are her grandparents? I just don't understand why it has to be such a secret.'

'Caroline,' he had said with a sigh, as though explaining to a child, 'There are several reasons. One is that they would think it very odd that we were just telling them now when Madeleine is eight years old. Can you imagine how upset they'd be?Secondly, they are very straight-laced and they adored Fiona. How do you think it would look if they learned that I had been having an affair when she was so sick?'

'I suppose so,' she had said, although she didn't agree with him. He was saving his own skin rather than doing what she thought would be the right thing. She had long ago realised that he wasn't the man she had thought him to be, but then again, she was harbouring her own dreadful secret. When she whittled about it all, lying sleepless in the big bed, she tried to concentrate on the positive aspects of her life. She had swapped a porter for a doctor, a council house for an elegant Victorian house in a good area, and living on a shoestring to being comfortably off. That had to be enough.

Two weeks later, when his wedding ring was firmly on her finger, she told him that she had just lost their child.

Chapter 69

Graham saw Madeleine and Louisa regularly at first, but this gradually became more sporadic. He pleaded pressure of work but she gleaned from the children that he and Maureen were engaged and that they were busy preparing for the wedding. After her marriage to David, Caroline had insisted that Graham stop paying maintenance for the girls. She had told him that there was no need, financially, but in fact she harboured a deep-seated guilt for the many years he had supported a child who wasn't his.

She settled comfortably into the role of being a doctor's wife and living in an elegant house with tasteful furniture and décor, and sumptuous deep pile carpets. She even had her own cleaner. The fly in the ointment was Michael.

'You're not my mother, you can't tell me what to do. You can't ever replace her.'

He was often sullen and resentful. She was relieved when he was finally sent off to a minor public school and she only had to deal with him in the holidays, which she dreaded. When she had originally agreed to be David's housekeeper it had been a means to an end for her. After their marriage, that was how Michael continued to treat her. When he came home after the first term, with a friend in tow, he had even introduced her as his father's housekeeper, all the while smiling slyly at her. When she told David about this, he promised to have a word with his son, but she suspected that he hadn't. Michael knew that he had the upper hand and she had given up thinking she would ever win him over. When David wasn't around, he sneered at the meals she cooked and either ignored his stepsisters or played cruel tricks on them. Madeleine had stopped hero-worshipping him a long time ago.

'He's so mean, Mummy. I left my best doll in the living room and when I went to get it it was all broken. I know it wasn't Louisa because we were playing outside when it happened. When I told him I knew it was him he just laughed and said girls and dolls were silly.'

'And he stole a sausage off my plate when I wasn't looking,' added Louisa.' I hate him. I wish he never came back from that school.'

Caroline had tried to talk to him herself but gave up when she realised it was a waste of time. He was so superior towards her, egged on, she suspected, by David's parents.

'Michael, would you mind picking your clothes up from your bedroom floor?' was met with, 'You did that when you were Dad's housekeeper. What's changed?'

In the end it was easier to ignore him and hope he would eventually come round, although mealtimes were a nightmare. Michael would commandeer his father's attention and behave as though the rest of them weren't there. It was even worse if David was absent. He would sit at the far end of the table with his head bent over his plate. If the food wasn't to his liking he would push it aside and, without a word, go into the kitchen and make himself a sandwich or cheese and biscuits, leaving the extra mess for her to clear up. His silent actions were more cutting than if he had thrown the food on the floor.

Every time he came home for the holidays, she and the girls counted the days until he returned to school. She no longer turned to David for advice. He made it clear that it was something she needed to sort out herself.

One evening, Caroline decided to try a recipe from one of Fiona's many cookery books. As she chopped the onions and vegetables and prepared the chicken, she thought back over her relationship with David. His career had gone from strength to strength and he had become the youngest consultant in the hospital's history. The long hours at the hospital, coupled with the research papers that he was writing, the meetings and the afternoons networking on the golf course, meant that he was able to spend less and less time with her and the children.

At first she had been so happy that she had finally got what she had wanted after waiting so long. But as time went on, and his career took off, she recognised that cracks had already begun to appear in their relationship. Even when he did spend time with them, he was tired, distracted and often short tempered. She often felt lonely and even began to suspect that he was bored with her. Staying at home looking after the children, wasn't stimulating and she had never been able to easily make friends. The books she chose to read and the television programmes she watched, didn't interest him so she had nothing to talk about. She knew that she fell short intellectually.

From time to time he was asked to attend social functions connected with the hospital. At the beginning of their marriage she had been delighted to accompany him. She could now always afford a new dress or earrings and a visit to a beauty parlour and hairdresser, which made her feel like royalty. Then slowly he stopped inviting her to accompany him.

'Oh it's all medical stuff. You'd be bored to tears. We'll go to the theatre next week, instead,'

When this happened more and more she came to the inevitable conclusion that he was ashamed of her, not for the way she looked, but her conversation. Or lack of it. She was often struck dumb by the wit and intellect of his associates, and found herself smiling inanely until her jaw ached, as the chatter went back and forth over her head. She often felt invisible, even in her own home, and sometimes even found herself looking back with fondness at her marriage to Graham, who for many years had clearly adored her.

Gradually, her appreciation of her status, and the luxuries that David's salary could provide, began to diminish. Even the beautiful house, where for years she had yearned to live, started to feel like a prison.

After Maggie's misfortunes, Caroline had felt that her own life was infinitely better than her sister's. Caroline had everything she wanted, a husband with status, an impressive house in a good area, a comfortable income and two beautiful, healthy children. Now she saw how Maggie had embraced Daniel's disability and actually seemed to be enjoying the challenges. It was apparent that Daniel had brought her and William immense joy and it seemed to have brought them even closer together. And now they were expecting another baby which would no doubt be perfect. Maggie always fell on her feet: and no matter what Caroline did, something always seemed to go wrong.

She felt so miserable and distracted as she prepared the meal, that the coq au vin went completely wrong. She had desperately wanted to please David, to put him in a good mood, and had thought that she could match up to Fiona's standards by using a recipe from her cookbook. He was very particular about the quality of his meals and she knew that if she served this one it would put him in a foul temper.

She made macaroni cheese for the girls and then rang hers and David's favourite restaurant to book a table.

'I thought we'd eat out tonight,' she said, when he arrived home, looking absolutely worn out. 'Mrs Parsons next door is going to babysit.'

'Oh I just wanted a quiet night in,' he sighed. 'I've had a long, difficult day.'

'I'm sorry. I haven't cooked anything, David. I'm stuck in with the children all day and every day.' She was aware of the whine in her voice, 'I thought it would be quite nice to have a change of scene.' She hadn't dared tell him about the spoiled meal. She knew her culinary skills fell far short of those of his late wife, as did most things.

He was hungry and hunger always made him bad tempered.

'You might have asked me.' He turned away. 'Oh very well. I'll go and get changed.'

They drove in silence. She had put on a smart dress and had taken trouble with her hair and makeup. She had been looking forward to a night out.

The waiter knew them and treated the doctor and his wife with deference.

'I recommend the lobster,' he said. 'It's chef's speciality.'

'Yes, I'd like that,' she said, giving him her most dazzling smile.

'Same for me,' said David, not even glancing at the menu.

It was as though he just wanted to get the whole thing over with.

'So how was your day? she asked.

'The last thing I want to talk about is work,' he snapped.

She waited for him to ask how her day had been but he remained silent. She was racking her brains to find a subject that would interest him when she caught sight of Graham at a table over the other side of he room. She studied him. She thought he had grown more handsome as he had got older. She hadn't really noticed this when she saw him briefly when he came to collect the children.

She looked at the woman he was with, Maureen she supposed. She was young and, although not particularly pretty, was attractive in a girl-next-door sort of way. He said something and she threw back her head and laughed. Then she said something to him and he listened intently. Caroline remembered that had been one of the things that had attracted her to him When she had talked to him, he had given her his full attention, as though everything she had said had been important. Graham was looking at Maureen as he had once looked at her. She suddenly felt as though she wanted to cry. David was staring into space, tight-lipped, his fingers drumming an impatient tattoo on the table.

'That's Graham over there,' she said, trying to keep her voice light. 'That woman is his fiancee. Don't they look as though they're having a good time?'

David didn't even look across to see whom she was talking about. She might as well have spoken to the cruet. He looked at his watch.

'I wish they'd hurry up with that damn lobster,' he said. 'I've got better things to do than sit here all night waiting to be fed.'

Chapter 70

Mary maintained she didn't want any fuss, but Maggie had been at her most persuasive.

'Gran, you're the matriarch of this family. None of us would be here today if you hadn't been swept off your feet by the handsome George.'

Mary's faded blue eyes still had their Irish twinkle.

'I'll agree to a birthday party, but only as an excuse to get the whole family together. We seem to have grown so large these days. It will be a rare treat to see you all under one roof. So, you've booked the private function room at The Bluebell, you say? And who's going to foot the bill?'

'Me and Caroline, of course.'

'And has she agreed to this extravagance?'

'Oh yes. You know her. She wouldn't pass over a chance to get all dressed up like a dog's dinner with that handsome husband of hers on her arm.'

'Handsome he might be, but give me your William any time. David seems to get more dour every time I see him. You know, I sometimes wonder if Caroline's as happy as she makes out.'

'What makes you say that?'

'Oh, she doesn't confide in me but I can just tell. She works hard to keep up the image of the wife who has it all. And that Michael is a handful. The few times I've seen him he's quite rude to her. I can't take to him at all.'

'You're right there. I know the girls don't like him much. I once heard him taking off Daniel's voice. I could have clocked him one. Instead, I explained to him, in the most patronising way I could, that Daniel is profoundly deaf, as well he knew, and we were very very proud of the progress he has made with his speech. I told him he should know better, having a doctor as a father.'

'What did he say?'

'Oh that he was only having a bit of fun. Full of blustery bravado. No I don't envy Caroline having him as a stepson.'

'You've got nothing at all to envy her for. Look at you. You hit the jackpot with William, and Daniel is the loveliest little boy. He'll go far, deafness or no deafness, you mark my words. You and William are doing a brilliant job with him. And as for baby Lucy, she's just about the cutest little mite I've ever seen. I've never known such a happy baby.'

'Well I wouldn't disagree with a single thing you've just said! So, Gran, back to the party. You and I are going clothes shopping to Bentalls. Never mind Caroline, you're going to be the belle of the ball.

Chapter 71

'Auntie Ruby, will you just sit down and enjoy yourself?'

Maggie took the empty plate out of her hand and set it back on the table. There are waitresses to do that.'

'Well I just thought I'd help by stacking them, Maggie. You know I can't sit still. I've got bees in my bonnet.'

Maggie laughed. 'Look Mum's sitting on the chair that I did up for Gran with all the artificial roses on. I wanted it to look like a throne.'

'You know Mary doesn't like being the centre of attention, even on her eighty fifth birthday.'

'It's the perfect place for Mum to hold court. She's putting on that posh accent again which doesn't fool anybody. Where's Dad? He's nowhere to be seen as usual.'

'My guess he's outside having a fag.'

Ruby picked up a serviette from the floor and folded it.

'When the doctor ordered your mother to stop smoking, he promised he'd stop as well, but I know damn well he never has.'

'Sneaky old bugger. How do you know?'

'He goes for long walks and comes back smelling like a chimney. And I can smell it on his clothes when I put them in the wash; and that cigarette burn in his best cardigan wasn't put there by moths.'

'Well how come she doesn't know?'

'Doesn't want to know, perhaps. I'm sure I don't know. I'm not a voyeur. Look at David and William deep in conversation over there. They seem to get on well.'

Maggie smiled as she studied her husband.

'Two professional men. They've got more in common with each other than with the rest of the family. Certainly more than me and Caroline.'

'Yes, you weren't sisters made in heaven. Caroline's not a bad sort really. Graham was never good enough for her in her eyes. And maybe David's a bit too good to be true.'

'What makes you say that?'

'Can't put my finger on it. There's something about him I don't trust. I've heard rumours he has an eye for the ladies.'

'Oh dear. Let's hope they aren't true. You know, I was always quite fond of Graham.'

'Me too. He's married now, to that girl, Maureen, who works in the taxi office. I can't keep up with it all.'

'What are you too gossiping about?' Gina's walk was unsteady.

'The usual, Caroline, David, Graham. Gina, you're slurring your words. How much have you had to drink?

'Not nearly enough, Maggie.'

'That dress is very short. I can almost see your knickers.'

'Oh Maggie, you're so starchy these days. Everyone at college is wearing mini dresses and skirts. You should bring yours up an inch or two, you've got smashing legs.'

'Talking about starchy, our big sister is on her own in the corner. Shall we go and talk to her?

'If we must.'

'I'll go and see if your mother wants anything.'

Auntie Ruby quickly stacked the last few plates.

'Just take her another full plate. Pile it up with jumbo sausage rolls. That'll please her.'

Luckily, Auntie Ruby didn't hear as she was already scurrying towards the throne.

Maggie put her arm through Gina's.

'You've got a sharp tongue in that mouth of yours, Gina Langley. You're going to make a formidable teacher.'

'Our mother brings out the worst in me.'

'And me, as I know to my cost.'

'Will you ever forgive Dad, beating you up that time?'

'I probably have. But I'll never forget. Any love I might have had for him died that day. It was also the day I realised I could stand up for myself. I was the stronger person. Anyway, we're getting maudlin. Let's have another drink.'

They moved towards the bar.

'OK. Watch this.' Gina put on her teacher voice.

'Madeleine, Louisa, stop running round. You'll send people's plates and drinks flying.'

The two girls smiled sheepishly.

'Yes Auntie Gina.'

'I'm impressed.' Maggie nodded approvingly, taking two glasses of wine and handing one to her.

As the girls disappeared into the throng, they heard, 'No Auntie Gina, Three bags full, Auntie Gina.'

'Little scamps. You might have to work on your school discipline.'

'I know. I may have a bit to go yet.'

'Well, Caroline,' Maggie said with a smile, 'it looks like our husbands have plenty to talk about.'

'And the girls seem to be enjoying the party. I've just attempted to curb their high spirits. They're like Tigger on speed,' added Gina, sitting on the vacant chair beside her sister. Are you OK?'

'I'm fine,' replied Caroline. 'Just not really in the mood for small talk.'

'Well you don't look fine,' said Gina. 'Are you sure there isn't anything wrong?'

'Why should there be?' Caroline's voice was sharp.

'Mummy.' The little voice was confident and clear.

Maggie looked down at Daniel, who had clasped her hand.

'What's the matter?' She signed automatically now.

'More cake.' He said the words and signed at the same time.

'Please.' she prompted.

'Please.'

'Of course, my darling. We'll go and get you some.'

'I'll go with him,' said Gina quickly, already glad of an excuse to escape. She took his hand.

'Come on Daniel, let's see what's left. I would like some more too. It's delicious.'

'Thanks, Gina. Your signing is coming on in leaps and bounds,' said Maggie.

'I know it's none of my business,' began Maggie, emboldened by alcohol, 'but I noticed that you and David have hardly spoken this evening. Have you two had a row? You can always talk to me you know. If you want to.'

'No. You're right. It isn't any of your business.'

Maggie studied her sister and saw tears in her eyes. She waited.

Caroline was in a turmoil. She wanted Maggie to think that everything was perfect in her life, It would be so easy to pretend. If she told Maggie, or anyone, the truth, she would have to face it herself. Status and money had come at a huge cost. When she searched David's eyes these days, she couldn't find any love there. Perhaps she never had.

She had once thought that she had everything, but she now knew she had nothing of any value. Her life was empty. She looked uncertainly at her sister.

'Maggie. Can you come round sometime tomorrow? We could have a chat.'

Maggie smiled. 'That would be lovely.'

Printed in Great Britain
by Amazon